THE
BONE ROOM

JAMES VITARIUS

Knowing sorrow well, I learn to succor the distressed.

-Virgil

CHAPTER ONE

Dr. Ezekiel "Zeke" Oswald was sure that the bone was broken.

The doctor, who hated loose ends, didn't trust the Emergency Room physician who'd read the hip x-ray of his newest patient. So even though he'd found that her left foot was grotesquely and unnaturally turned outward, an obvious sign that her hip was fractured, Zeke was on his way to look at the x-ray with his own eyes. Another clue: her chart from the nursing home, or "skilled nursing facility" as it was euphemistically called, had a hastily scribbled note; *"fall OOB."* Fall out of bed.

She was a typical patient to go with a so far typical night shift for the doctor at Saint Twigleighct, pronounced like the word "twilight," a small hospital in Albany, New York. Zeke knew that nursing home patients were usually frail and demented to the point where they were not able to make their needs known or to speak out against neglect. Zeke was thorough at his job, but he was also making sure his newest patient didn't fall through the cracks. He didn't want anyone to feel like they were reduced to a few letters scribbled on a hospital chart. Zeke was also concerned as to *why* she fell. There was no mention of a cause to her accident on the chart. Was she delirious from an infection which caused her to be confused? Nursing home patients seemed to be coming in with a lot of bacterial infections lately.

Tall, with a wiry build, Zeke was dressed in his usual blue surgical scrubs. He avoided wearing a white coat and stuck to blue or burgundy to avoid drawing attention to his unnaturally pale skin. Walking down the institutional green corridor, Zeke wondered how long it would take for the hospital to enter the digital age of medical care so he could read x-rays on a computer and not have to track down the plastic films. Financially strapped, the hospital was slow to upgrade anything, especially things that made their doctors' lives easier but didn't help their bottom line.

The hospital's chief of staff Dr. Newby had warned Zeke of the hospital's shortcomings during his interview two months before.

"You know, working at Saint Twigleighct might be a big culture shock for you, especially with you coming from your last position at, Johns Hopkins, is it? We don't exactly have the, um, modern facilities you might be used to," Newby had started off the interview.

Zeke had smiled politely in response. But he could sense that the smile never made it from his mouth to his dark eyes. He wasn't trying to be coy, he just couldn't come up with a reply that wouldn't sound condescending.

"And you understand you'll only be working the night shift?"

"Yes, I'm more of a night owl, so that doesn't bother me." At least it hadn't since he left John's Hopkins twenty years ago...

"I see." Newby had a hopeful, almost supplicating look. "Well, we could certainly use a doctor of your caliber around here. We had a recent..." he let out a small cough... "mortality when a trainee gave a dialysis patient an overdose of potassium. He had called the patient's attending doctor but the attending hung up on him, screaming not to bother him in the middle of the night with such a...stupid question. The patient died and I don't have to tell you it caused a big mess, so we figured we'd hire someone experienced to stay in the hospital overnight. But we didn't expect someone with your credentials."

In fact, the hospital administrators had been so impressed and desperate for qualified help that Newby offered Zeke the job right then and there, overlooking the fact that Zeke's most recent references were twenty years old.

And Zeke had accepted the job on the spot because it was exactly what he was looking for: shiftwork only during the night hours, caring for patients temporarily then passing them to someone else, in a place that was far away from his last place of employment. He needed a change in scenery after the FBI had started poking around, getting close to exposing Zeke's involvement in a black market blood bank at the hospital in Montana. He had wanted out of this foolish entanglement anyway, but the Russian gangsters weren't pleased and had made it clear to Zeke he risked bodily harm if he left the business. Impossible to get a job as a doctor using an alias, Zeke hoped his former associates wouldn't track him down to Albany. He was willing to put up with things like tracking down x-rays as long as he could make a clean break to a job where he could leave after his shift and only have to return for the next one.

Which was why, shortly before 3:00 AM on that August night, Zeke didn't mind walking to the bone room, the smug nickname for the orthopedic radiology suite, the place where medical images of the human skeleton were examined for disease.

As he approached the door to the suite, Zeke thought he smelled blood.

He tried opening the door but it wedged against something inside. The contact made a thump and Zeke pushed harder, meeting resistance that felt like there was a sandbag on the other side of the door. He crinkled his nose as the air wafted out of the room, intensifying the musky odor which now also had a sweet note, like candy coating on an apple. The smell brought a wave of mixed feelings. At the same time he felt exhilarated and afraid.

Zeke managed to slide through the door, his heart pounding and his breathing rapid. He wasn't sure where his sense of foreboding was coming from. He patted the wall until he found the light switch which turned on a small lamp on the workstation at the opposite side of the room. In the dim light of the lamp, saw an indistinct form on the floor. The area around it looked like the site of an oil spill. His uncertainty turned to horror as he flipped another switch, revealing a corpse in the glaring artificial light. A crimson puddle of blood had seeped to the point where it met Zeke's hospital clogs.

Zeke felt frozen in place as he gaped at the body. The sight of the corpse's face, with its wide, dead eyes, grimace, and pallor of the skin against the body's tan hospital scrubs, startled him although he had seen a dead body many times before. The body's trunk was arched back ward and twisted, and the chin was extended, exposing a long cut from one side of the jaw line to the other. The muscle and cartilage protruded from the incision as if the neck had exploded.

Zeke's emergency training took over. Moving quickly, he attempted to feel for a pulse in the neck with his fingertips. Zeke grunted in disgust as a severed artery popped out of the gash like a piece of rotten pasta in an alley dumpster. He thought to call the emergency team to the scene, but when he moved his hand to search out a femoral artery pulse in the leg, he realized the skin was cold to the touch. The corpse had been dead for several hours.

"I can't believe this," Zeke said through closed teeth. He had expected a quiet existence in this job. After nearly getting killed or arrested at his last job, now he had this to deal with. He brought his hand down his face and shook his head in disbelief.

"I could really use a drink right now," he muttered, before reaching for the phone to call the hospital security team.

CHAPTER TWO

Detective Selinda Bruchart craned her head through the doorway into the orthopedic radiology suite which was now officially a crime scene complete with yellow police tape. "Do we know who smeared this blood?" she asked. When she arrived at the hospital just before dawn, the detective, just shy of thirty years old, felt as if she had just caught the biggest case of her two year career.

"It wasn't one of us," a uniformed officer announced gruffly. Selinda was used to disrespectful responses to her questions. She was a high-ranking young woman in a male-dominated profession. Her good looks didn't exactly help the situation. She was tall with a shapely athletic build and wore her thick black hair long. She'd often been told that her eyes, a striking shade of violet, were her most attractive feature.

"It was the doc who found him."

"And where is he now?"

"We were taking his statement when he said he had to go back to emergency. He said we could meet him there later. His name's..." the officer looked through his notes... "Oswald."

"Hmm. What do we know so far?" Selinda asked, kneeling over the body to begin her survey.

"The vic is a thirty-seven year old nurse named Caleb Fisher. He worked in intensive care. He's been an employee here for about fifteen years. He clocked in his usual time about 7:00 PM last night."

Taking in these initial details, Selinda began to think about what more she could learn about the gruesome murder by examining the scene. The victim appeared to be short, stocky, and younger than described by the officer. There was no sign of a struggle in the room, so the victim had either been incapacitated first or had been taken by surprise. The position of the body and the blood pool pattern suggested that this ill-fated nurse had died face down and been turned over afterwards. Perhaps the doctor who discovered the body had moved him. Selinda made a mental note to ask him whether this were true when she tracked him down.

The decedent's right hand was positioned up near his throat. He was right handed, using his dominant hand to try to stop the bleeding. There were no defensive wounds that Selinda could see. Probably caught by surprise, she thought again. The desk and the chair in front of the workstation were spattered with blood. The blood droplets were elongated, indicating that the body had been in motion as or right after the carotid artery was opened and the blood pulsed out through his fingers on his neck.

The wound, a very clean incision, must have severed the right carotid artery. "Death by exsanguination," Selinda muttered to herself as she absentmindedly stroked her own neck. A picture was beginning to form in her trained mind: Nurse Fisher entered the room, the perpetrator surprised him from behind, covered Fisher's mouth with his left hand to silence him and force his victim's head to turn leftward to expose the neck and quickly slit his throat with something very sharp. The perp was probably right handed as well, most would slash with their dominant hand. The killer, if acting alone, was probably a large person, able to overpower his victim in case of a struggle.

Typical of a case like this, there were many more questions than answers at this stage. Was the killer already in the room, ready to spring, or was he following the victim? What was the murder weapon? Why was an intensive care nurse in a radiology reading room at night?

Early in the analysis of a case, Selinda relished the intellectual challenge of being presented with a single scene and attempting to discover the actions leading up to it, along with motivations of the participants. And she was good at this part of investigation; she had so impressed her instructors with her analytical work at the police academy in Schenectady that they had suggested she try for the FBI. She applied and was accepted, but in the end she decided the return to her hometown Albany to join the same force her on which her father, Lieutenant Nicholas Bruchart, had served as a homicide detective until his untimely death at the hands of murder suspect. Even though he had been gone from her life since she was eight years old, on some level Selinda still craved his approval, and joining the Albany PD was a way for her to feel closer to her father's memory and try to get that approval. Selinda used her father's Glock as her service pistol, hoping someday to put it good use and apprehend lots of the types that took her father's life. It wasn't on the list of approved guns, but because she was Nick's kid, the powers that be looked away.

Promoted quickly to detective in the coveted homicide division, there were those who grumbled that she scaled the ranks because her father's legacy and not her qualifications, and Selinda wasn't sure they were wrong. While she was bright and able to analyze a crime scene, she often fell short in the investigation after that. Maybe this would be the case where she could prove herself to her peers and to her father's memory.

Her mother, on the other hand, made it clear to Selinda that she did not approve of Selinda's choice of career, and reminded her often during their daily phone calls.

Just then, her cell phone rang with her mom's ringtone. *Not now, mom, I'm at a crime scene. I'll call you later* Selinda thought as she silenced the ringer..

Selinda cleared her throat and her mind and said, "Anything else, gentlemen, before I go question the doc?"

"Yeah, he looked nervous." The officer said, shaking his body to mimic nervousness.

"Just look for the guy in the white coat who looks like he's just seen a ghost," another laughed.

Did the doctor have something to do with this crime? Selinda asked herself as she left the bone room on her way to the emergency department to find Dr. Oswald.

Selinda walked down the same corridor Zeke had earlier, but by now it was filled with people and hospital equipment. Doctors and staff arriving at work, patients being transported in wheelchairs and stretchers. The hospital intercoms were crackling, buzzing and calling doctors to phone extensions. She almost ran into a fast-moving man in a suit and tie as she rounded the hallway corner.

Selinda recognized the person she nearly collided with as Duane Rogers, a former classmate of hers in high school. She heard he had become a doctor, but hadn't seen him since Homecoming Day the year after they graduated. As she had done at Homecoming, Selinda intended to walk past him without acknowledgement. His face registered familiarity, and when he was a few feet past him he called her name.

"Selinda?"

She turned around. "Yes?"

"I thought that was you. Nice to see you. Duane Rogers." He extended his hand.

She squinted at his hand, then took it. "Oh, yeah, I remember you. Albany High, right?" she said, unsuccessfully attempting a tone that suggested she was just realizing the fact. She tilted her head to the right and turned her eyes up towards his and wondered *why did I just do that?* "So, you're a doctor here?"

"Yes. Pulmonology." He raised the ID tag that hung around his neck. "Lung doctor."

I know what a pulmonologist is Selinda thought, holding back a sigh. Before he could ask what she was doing in the hospital, Selinda said, "Let me ask you a question. Do you know a doctor who works here, a Dr. Oswald?"

"The new hospitalist? Not real well. He keeps to himself."

"What's a hospitalist?"

"It's a relatively new breed of doctors that just work the inpatient units. No office practice. They were created when physicians like me, who were working more and profiting less, started to cut back on our hours when we were on call for hospitalized patients. We found that we could make more if we spent more time with patients in our offices than traveling to and rounding on them when they were hospitalized. Hospitalists take care of my patients when they're inpatients. The job of hospitalist also rose out of the fact that hospital resident's hours were scaled back by their accreditation organization. Resident physicians are also inexperienced, so to pick up the slack hospitals decided to hire experienced, internists that were looking for shiftwork to stay in the hospital to take care of patients the residents couldn't and to provide supervision."

"Actually," he said, grinning in an attempt to be charming, "when they work at night, like Oswald, they're called *nocturnists.*" He lowered his tone at the end of the sentence to sound dramatic. Selinda, expressionless, thought he might raise his arms and start walking like a zombie for effect. Pleased with himself, Rogers laughed, looked down and up at the detective and asked, "So...what are *you* doing lately?"

"I'm sorry, I gotta run, we'll catch up sometime." She turned to go. "By the way, did you work last night?"

"Oh, no, I'm just coming into round on my patients. I never come in at night, that's why we have residents and Dr. Oswald."

"Oh, okay, well nice seeing you."

"Yeah, same here." As she walked past him, Selinda caught a pleasant scent in the breeze their passing bodies created. It had a clean, fresh smell to it, like laundry right out of the dryer. She found the automatic swinging doors of the rear entrance to the emergency department at the end of the hallway. The doors swung open and Selinda walked in. Any memory of the fresh scent from Selinda's interaction with Duane Rogers was suddenly replaced by the odors of urine, vomit, and a gasoline-like vapor.

Each bay she passed on her way to the front desk seemed to contain a different story of human misery. Unbeknownst to her, Selinda had entered through the critical area, where sicker patients were placed to be closer to the emergency equipment and staff. Out of the corner of her eye, Selinda saw an elderly man, emaciated and frozen, his limbs contracted and head extended as far as possible. Crossing to the next curtain a patient was grey, hyperventilating, his eyes darting at the doctors, nurses and technicians preparing to place a tube into his lungs.

"Doc! Doc! Help me!" A patient called out as the detective passed by another bay. *Do I look like a doctor?* Selinda asked herself.

"Murmy...murmy...murmy," an old woman gurgled in the next slot. The intonation repeated until Selinda was out of earshot.

Selinda passed into the main area of the Emergency Department and spotted a desk in the center. Staff was scurrying around, patients on stretchers were being pushed back and forth, and the air was buzzing with noise from people and hospital equipment. She approached the desk and sought out the obese clerk sitting behind it. Selinda moved close to the bench and excused herself but the clerk did not look up from her computer screen. Selinda stepped back and brushed her jacket away from her body to expose her badge as she shifted her weight. Still not receiving a response, the detective removed the badge from her belt and tapped it on the surface of the desk while clearing her throat.

The clerk didn't look up but asked, "Yes?"

"Who's in charge?"

Without moving her head, the woman pointed in the direction of a short, bearded man standing at the adjoining counter, writing a note. He wore khaki pants, hatched dress shirt, solid tie, and a stethoscope around his neck. "Are you the doctor in charge?" she called.

He didn't look up either. "Uh-huh," he replied, drawing out the second part as if to say, *what is it now?*

"Excuse me, I'm Detective Selinda Bruchart, Albany PD. And you are?"

Now he looked up. "Oh, sorry, I'm Dr. Breitbart, chief of the ED."

"I'm looking for Dr. Oswald, he should be expecting me."

"What's this about?"   Breitbart asked. *He doesn't know anything yet,* Selinda surmised.

"I need to speak with him," the detective said, as if politely addressing a child.

There was a pause and then the doctor turned back to the computer, his face expressionless. "He works at night," Breitbart offered.

"I know, I was told he would be here."

"Haven't seen him."

"Doctor, number six is coding!" came a call from a nurse.

"Try paging him," the Emergency doctor said over his shoulder as he dashed away.

Selinda walked through the Emergency Department, asking if anyone had seen the doctor who had discovered the grisly scene earlier that morning.

"Oh, I think he split." One of the nurses told her. "I saw him walking out the Emergency entrance. Dr. Oswald doesn't like staying in the hospital after his shift is over."

What's your hurry, Doctor? Have something to hide? She thought of trying to get more information from the ED chief but he looked busy. Selinda saw him first pumping on some patient's chest, then sticking a large needle under his ribs. Besides, she should find Dr. Oswald as soon as possible and interview him while his recollection of the discovery would be still fresh in his mind. Selinda also needed to eliminate him as a suspect. Or include him.

CHAPTER THREE

It was quiet at the 649 that night, and a warm breeze was wafting through the gravesites. The cemetery was called the 649 because of the iron gateway that marked its entrance. At the top of the gateway, the iron was shaped into the number, the cemetery's address on verdant Adamley street in Albany. Patience McMorris sat cross-legged on a stone bench, sipping from a pint bottle of peach schnapps. Her medical school textbooks were sitting next to her on the bench, but she hadn't opened them yet, and she was already thinking of going home for the night. Five feet, two inches tall and a few pounds overweight, Patience was dressed in a grey sweat suit with a zippered, hooded top and ALBANY MED written across it in bold Varsity font. As she tilted her head back to drink, her fine auburn hair fell away from her face, revealing pretty, delicate features and fair skin. This was Patience's second bottle of what would probably be three for the evening. She kept a case of the liqueur in her trunk of her blue Nissan Altima so that she wouldn't risk running out on days like today. She preferred Potter's brand. She liked the taste, but it was also the cheapest.

Patience was replaying the scene from that morning's rounds at Saint Twigleighct, where she was working on a medical team. Her interaction with Jodi, another medical student, had landed Patience another meeting with the medical school dean as if she'd been a high school student called to the principal's office. Just great. It was bad enough that after her first trip to the Dean's office earlier in the year, Dean Dickhead had assigned that creepy Dr. Oswald, the nighttime hospitalist, to babysit her. What next?

"What do you think, Patty?"

It all started when that fucking cunty bitch had asked Patience the question as the team was walking back from the patient's room. Jodi had put on a breathy, childlike voice to make herself sound innocent, and Patience had fallen for it. She hated Jodi with her expensive clothes and perfume and perfect make-up no matter what time of day or night she was in the hospital. She resented Jodi's perky, punctual nature, too. Worse—sometimes when they were standing close to each other, that perfume getting her attention, Patience had a sudden desire to kiss Jodi. Patience found this desire to be very confusing as she wasn't ordinarily attracted to women. She didn't think Jodi was gay either; if she was, why sport that huge diamond engagement ring?

"It's *Patience,*" she had whispered in reply. She didn't like being called Patty. Only her parents used that nickname and that was before they split up when she was eleven years old. Since then, she had corrected everyone who used it, including her parents, whom she still hadn't forgiven for breaking up. She'd told Jodi what she thought the diagnosis was and the reasoning behind the conclusion.

When they had arrived at the conference room, Patience had assumed her usual position in the rear of the room, leaning against the air conditioning unit. The unit made a good bench when the room was full. And as usual, as the questions were being asked, her fear of answering them before the group had prevented her from offering responses. Finally, the question came: "What do you think the diagnosis is?" Patience had been confident she had come up with the correct diagnosis, but palpitations and a lump in her throat caused her to freeze. She was paralyzed with fear, afraid that these feelings would worsen, afraid of stammering, afraid of hearing her own voice, and afraid she might offer the wrong answer. Jodi had taken advantage of the hesitation, and had answered the question with Patience's thoughts. Praising her abilities, the supervisor had asked Jodi how she came to the correct conclusion. She had answered without hesitating, using Patience's reasoning as her own.

Patience had been furious that Jodi had highjacked her answer. She'd kept quiet, however, anxious about how an outburst during rounds might be received. *Too late now, Patty,* she had thought, *they probably won't believe it was my answer, anyway.*

But after rounds were over, after Jodi had given her a snotty smile at the elevator, Patience had exploded.

"What the FUCK was that all about, *Jodi?*" Patience had raised her usually soft, raspy voice.

Jodi had looked scared of the aggression for a brief moment and then her face had gone blank. "I don't know what you're talking about, Patience." She'd turned away to break eye contact.

Patience had grabbed her arm and Jodi had shaken it off. Patience had gotten up in her face anyway. "You don't know what I'm talking about? How about stealing my answer?"

"Well, it was obvious that *you* weren't going to answer." Jodi had replied casually. *You snooze, you lose,* Patty.

"You could've..." Patience had stammered. "You could've...given me credit." Before she'd even completed the sentence Patience had realized how stupid it'd sounded. Like Jodi would have done that.

"You should have spoken up, then," Jodi had said through clenched teeth. She'd pressed the elevator button and it opened immediately with a cheery *ding.*

Patience's eyes had welled with tears of salty rage. She'd known Jodi had been right. "Fucking asshole bitch," she had muttered.

Jody must have heard the insult because her eyes had been wide as the elevator door had shut.

Later in the day Patience had gotten a call inviting her to the Dean's office the following morning. *Oh, shit, tomorrow morning* Patience reminded herself. *Fucking bitch I hope you rot. Because of you I'm now on the Dean's list. Just not the one I was expecting.* Patience took another sip to punctuate the curse. The liquor was sweet yet burned her throat and the back of her nose. She laughed. The alcohol was stifling her anger over the confrontation. It was like throwing sand on a fire.

The cemetery wasn't far from Patience's apartment building, and the gate had caught her eye shortly after she moved in three years ago at the start of her medical education. Patience had developed a penchant for cemeteries, drawn to them because she found them peaceful and soothing to visit. She enjoyed walking through, reading the headstones and imaging the family histories of the grave's occupants. She would create vignettes in her mind that marked important points in the deceased's life: a first kiss, a group hospital visit to a sick loved one, a retirement party. Out of an interest in the human body and its failings, she often played a game guessing at the cause of death, using common illnesses of the time period and age of the dead as clues.

After a few visits, Patience started to use the 649 as a quiet place to study. She usually sat on the mausoleum steps, and when the weather wasn't accommodating, she moved inside the stone edifice. She spent many hours there, especially in the first two years of medical school. Those years were filled most by class work, and Patience spent her time memorizing the details of anatomy, like the names and pathways of the twelve cranial nerves; microbiology, like which bacteria fermented lactose; histology, like the components of the five strata of skin; pharmacology, like the Vaughan Williams classification of drugs used in the treatment of abnormal heart rhythms.

Back in those days, Patience would bring a pint of schnapps along as a reward for two or three hours of studying. She would sip from it until she felt drunk and then leave for home, the buzz ensuring an easy time falling asleep. As her tolerance to the alcohol built, drinking became a daily occurrence. Now it took two to three bottles to do the job.

After such a stressful day, Patience figured that at least three bottles were on the menu that night. Yet she began to worry about how many empty bottles were accumulating. Disposing of the empty bottles of schnapps was becoming a challenge. An empty glass bottle here or there was never a problem. Patience could dispose of them with the rest of her recycling at her apartment building without raising suspicion. As the empties began pile up, however, Patience began to fear discovery, so she began to return the empty bottles to their original case. So no one could see her carrying cases of the liqueur in or out of her apartment building, she left cases in the trunk of her car. When she filled two cases of empty bottles, Patience looked over her shoulders in the deserted hours of the night and disposed of them in the dumpster of the public library. Storing and disposing of the empty schnapps bottles had become a sort of shameful preoccupation for her.

While debating whether she should open another Potter's, Patience spotted a small figure near the cemetery's east fence. As it cantered in front of a few gravestones, she realized the outline was that of a fox. It paused and turned its head towards Patience. The moonlight reflected off the fox's eyes, creating a dual flicker of light. Then it straightened its head and continued its path parallel to the fence. As the fox departed, Patience wondered, *where did you come from?* How out of place it seemed, a fox running around the middle of the city, a misfit out its natural habitat.

Gently closing her eyes, Patience raised the bottle once again to her lips. This was out of habit; she knew the bottle was drained.

"How out of place you must feel, little guy," she said aloud, softly, punctuating the statement with little sympathetic clucking sounds. The pressure of intoxication set behind her eyes, it was time to leave.

"Okay, you win. Only two bottles tonight," she said to no one in particular, now that the fox had left. Besides, better she not be too hung over later. She had her meeting with the dean in five hours.

CHAPTER FOUR

Selinda rapped her knuckles against the apartment door. The door's red paint felt thick and cold against the backs of her fingers. Like other techniques associated with her career, Selinda had worked on perfecting how she knocked on a potential suspect's door. The sound had to convey a certain urgency but not so much as to put anyone on the other side on the defensive. She wasn't there quite yet, and she bit her lip, fearing that she had knocked too loudly and sharply.

As she waited for a reply, Selinda noticed a buzzing noise like that of an electric razor coming from some indistinct place. A musty smell, probably coming from the hallway carpet, reminded her of the apartment building she'd occupied when she was first at the academy. It was an emotive memory, placing her in the exact emotional state of those times: anxious yet hopeful about a bright future. Selinda recalled how she had met her days back then, leaving her apartment for an early morning jog.

Selinda tilted her head to listen for sound on the other side of the door and thought of knocking a second time. She heard nothing within the nocturnist's apartment; she only heard that distant electric hum and the occasional clink of dishes.

Selinda turned to go, wondering where the doctor could be at 7:20 AM on the same morning he'd discovered a corpse when she heard the latch click and the door open. *Strange how I didn't hear any footsteps coming up the door,* she thought.

He didn't speak, just stood there looking at her from the threshold as she turned back towards the door. She extended her badge to show him as she began the conversation, but Zeke didn't take his eyes off of hers to inspect it.

"Dr. Ezekiel Oswald?"

"Yes," he said softly.

"I'm Detective Selinda Bruchart of the Albany PD. I need to ask you a few questions about last night at the hospital."

Selinda returned his gaze as she returned the badge to her belt. His eyes were dark, almost black. They were kind, with a weary appearance that suggested some pain in his past. *Typical doctor's complexion,* Selinda mentally noted. *Probably doesn't spend much time in the sun.*

"May I come in?" she asked.

He hesitated, then nodded.

As she crossed the threshold, Selinda heard a low growl and a dog's bark. It was at these times she wished she had a partner to provide immediate backup in the event of a vicious dog (or suspect). But that was too much of a luxury for the Albany PD.

"Do you have a dog?"

"What?" Selinda thought she detected a hint of anxiety on Zeke's face.

"I heard a dog."

Zeke seemed to relax. "Oh, I didn't hear anything. It's probably the neighbors." He walked over to a mirror and pulled down on his cheek as if he was checking his eye.

With Zeke occupied at the mirror, Selinda surveyed the apartment. It was a studio, with tall walls that looked like they were covered with many layers of paint. The floors were laminate wood and dark wood trimmed the doorways and windows. The kitchen area was partially enclosed and there was a closed door, probably leading to a bedroom. The place was sparsely furnished—no paintings or pictures on the walls, minimal furniture. There was a burgundy couch with a plain coffee table, and, against the wall, a small table that supported a personal computer. What impressed Selinda, however, was how clean the apartment was—no clutter, no dust. There were several cardboard boxes stacked in two corners. It didn't seem as if anyone was living there. *Who doesn't have a TV in their living room?*

As Selinda continued her survey, she wondered what the doctor had been doing before she arrived. He didn't look as if she interrupted his sleep. There were no cooking or food smells, the computer was off, and there were no newspapers scattered about.

In her best unassuming tone, Selinda began her the interview. "So, why did you leave the hospital in such a hurry?"

"I thought my statement to the uniformed officers was all you needed." His back was still to her.

"Hmm, I see." She didn't pursue a line of questioning. Better to move on so he couldn't anticipate the questions.

"Could you tell me in your own words how you came to discover the body?"

He sat down on the couch shifted his legs to one side, and told the story as it had happened. Selinda was silent as he gave his account, when it appeared he was done she asked, "May I ask you a few questions?"

"Of course. Sit down if you like." Zeke nodded in the direction of the chair by the computer desk. She grabbed the chair, sat down and took out a notebook. Leaning slightly forward, she began, "Did you know the victim?"

"Not well. When I leaned over the body...to attempt CPR...I noticed his ID clipped to his lab coat. He was a nurse in the MICU. The medical intensive care unit."

"So I'm guessing you wouldn't know if he had any enemies."

"No."

"Did you ever work there? In the MICU?"

"Sometimes. I don't recall any specific interactions with him."

"Did you work in the MICU last night?"

"No."

"No?"

There was an uncomfortable pause as the two looked at each other. He didn't answer. The detective stood and walked over to the window. "I wonder why an MICU nurse would be in a radiology reading room in the first place?" She turned back to face Zeke. "Any idea?"

"Not really."

"Did you move the body?"

"What?" he asked, showing some irritation.

"Did...you move...the body?" She repeated slowly, with mock patience

Zeke recovered quickly. He seemed like the stoical type to Selinda. Or maybe he was stonewalling? "No," he replied.

"I see. Why were *you* in the radiology reading room, Dr. Oswald?"

He answered as if he had anticipated the question. "A patient I was admitting had a hip x-ray taken earlier in the evening."

Selinda deliberately held a response to hear what Zeke had to say next.

Zeke continued. "Since the radiologist wouldn't read it until the next day, I wanted to see if there was a fracture."

"The name of the patient?" she queried.

"Christie." She wrote it down, slowly, deliberately, as if to say *I'll be checking on that.*

"Did you notice anything out of the ordinary at the hospital last night? Unusual occurrences, new employees, unexpected staffing changes?"

"Not that I can think of."

"Thank you, doctor. I won't take up any more of your time today. Please, if you think of anything that might be helpful to the investigation, give me a call." Selinda, said this to every interview subject in an investigation, but had never known anyone to comply with the request. She took a business card out of her pocket, waved it in the air, and placed in on the coffee table.

"I will detective." Zeke rose and accompanied her to the door. She turned to take another look at the apartment.

"Been here long?" she asked

"About nine months."

Selinda smiled professionally, opened the door and exited.

He closed the door behind her. Selinda waited a few seconds at allow Zeke to begin his next task and then rapped sharply on the door again. This quick return was a technique she learned in her investigative training. A guilty suspect would often impulsively do something incriminating immediately following the stress of an interview: call an accomplice, hide or destroy potential evidence, or simply appear suspiciously flustered when encountered the second time.

As usual, part of this approach included reserving a final request. Selinda wanted to ask for the shoes the doctor was wearing when he discovered the body to see if the blood smear left at the crime scene matched the pattern of the sole. The blood on the shoe could also be sample to see if it matched the victim, the doctor, or others.

She heard footsteps this time. The door open halfway and Zeke, standing in the space, asked if there was something else.

"Yes, sorry, I was wondering if I could take the shoes you were wearing last night for analysis. They might be helpful in piecing things together."

With very little hesitation he consented. "Sure. Wait here." He shut the door completely, yet gently.

The door opened again in a few minutes and he handed a pair of clogs across the threshold. Selinda turned them upside down. There wasn't a trace of blood on them.

Still an inexperienced detective, Selinda didn't notice that the plain black sedan was still parked across the street from the doctor's building. She didn't know the lone figure inside the car had seen her come and go. He watched her with steely eyes as she opened her car door.

As Selinda drove away, there was a hum on the seat next to the figure. The cell phone that he would destroy after he left the area was silently ringing. He picked it up and pressed a button to connect.

"Yeah, he's still in there." The figure in the car kept his voice low. "It looks like a cop just visited him. I think I saw a badge on her belt and she climbed into a shitty sedan. Very cop-like. I'll run the plates."

There was a pause as he listened. "Yes. I said *her*."

After another pause he continued. "Okay. I'll continue to track him and approach him if I get a chance."

CHAPTER FIVE

Zeke's sleep was fitful. His mind was racing from the agitation that followed the early morning discovery and his unsettling meeting with the detective. The image of the dead nurse's throat kept appearing in front of him, the artery popping out of the wound as he touched it. He swallowed each time he thought of all that blood. "They might be helpful in piecing things together," the detective had said of his clogs.

And the stress of Zeke's predicament had triggered the craving to drink. He hadn't touched a drop of alcohol since July 17, 1989, the day of his disastrous attempt at self-experimentation that changed his life forever. The cravings would still come, of course, usually in a reaction to the anxiety of a stressful situation, but Zeke knew if he resisted giving in to the temptation for a couple of hours, the craving would begin to subside. He left that evening to return the hospital confident that he wouldn't fall off the wagon.

Green signal lights pulsed against the dark sky as the bus he was taking to the hospital crossed block after block. Gazing out the window, Zeke replayed his meeting with the detective. As the one who had discovered the body the police would naturally want to question him. But didn't that also make him a suspect? *Damn that hospital* Zeke thought as the bus neared the stop across from the back end of medical center by the loading docks. If they weren't so cheap because of their financial difficulties he could have viewed the x-rays from any computer and he wouldn't have had to make the trip to the bone room. This was attention that he didn't need. Once the police started poking around it threatened to expose everything.

On the other hand, maybe this was an opportunity. He could help solve the case, which would clear any suspicion and make him feel like he was redeeming past wrongs.

I doubt it Zeke thought as he disembarked from the bus, jogged across the street and entered the hospital though the loading dock

The medical wards were the sixth, seventh and eight floors of the center's main hospital building. Zeke took the elevator to the sixth floor to the small room the hospitalists used as an office. He found the door locked. Probably the colleague he was relieving had already left and had secured the door on the way out. Turning the key and opening the door, Zeke had an expectation that the door would only partially open, hitting against a body that felt like a sandbag.

But the door opened freely and after turning on the lights he spied the sign-out sheets left for him on the desk, which contained the information the previous doctor needed to communicate to the arriving one and the names and locations of the patients Zeke was responsible for on tonight's shift. The sign-outs were organized in tables and next to the locations were brief descriptions of the reason for hospital admission and course since then. Some rows had to-do lists enumerated with check boxes to indicate what tasks needed to be fulfilled.

There were about forty entries on the papers—a routine number of souls in Dr. Oswald's care tonight. The last line was brief; "IC, ED, heart block." A location of ED meant the patient was in emergency department, waiting to be admitted the hospital. Zeke would be responsible for the admission of "heart block," which meant he would be interviewing and examining the patient, coming up with a plan of care and placing the orders to execute the plan in to the medical center's computerized ordering system.

He surveyed the sheets to see if there were any pressing issues he needed to resolve before seeing IC. There were a few blood test results he would have to interpret, mostly chemistry panels that determined levels of important salts and sugar in the blood and INRs—the measure of the blood's ability to clot, which was used to monitor the status of those on blood thinners. None of these seemed urgent, so Zeke left the office, heading to the elevators that would take him to the emergency department to meet his newest patient.

"Code blue, Code blue, eight B," the hallway speaker sounded. At the same instant, Zeke's pager went off, the two alarms agitating the previously calm evening. The elevator bell added some punctuation but instead of entering the opening door, Zeke turned and headed toward the nearest stairwell.

For Zeke, responding to a "code," the nickname for a cardiac arrest, was exciting. Knowing that he was on his way to potentially restore life gave him a thrill each time. For this usually reserved doctor, it meant a much needed adrenaline boost. In the event of a code he was forced to act, to come out of his shell. And because most codes were life and death situations, Zeke saw them as opportunity to try and cheat death.

He continued up the stairwell to the eighth floor and on to the nursing station. He didn't see any commotion in the hallway as a clue to the location of the emergency so he asked the ward clerk, "Where's the code?"

"Room 239."

Once at the room, Zeke turned sideways to squeeze past the crash cart that held the defibrillator and drawers filled with medications and supplied to support a failing heart and circulatory system. He took an extra breath in to avoid contact between the sharps container and his abdomen.

"What's the story?" Zeke asked the room as he approached the bedside through the room crowded by nurses, doctors, students and technicians. One of the nurses was over the patient, pushing down on the chest of lifeless body. *That isn't doing much,* Zeke thought as he noticed the chest was only being compressed about a quarter inch with each thrust.

"I was...making my rounds...with the other patient..." the nurse began, "when he became unresponsive..."

"I need a med student or intern to take over the chest compressions. Is a senior resident here?"

"Right here, Dr. Oswald," said a stocky man with greasy, uncombed hair and hospital scrubs that were too tight.

"Okay, good, please start bagging the patient."

The senior resident connected a blue bag to a face mask and oxygen supply, placed the mask over the patient's mouth, adjusted the head and began squeezing and releasing the bag slowly.

"Did he get anything yet?" While Zeke was speaking he was moving the crash cart closer to the gravely ill man. A respiratory therapist entered the room with supplies for intubation. Zeke grasped the handles of the defibrillator pads and moved to place them on the patient's chest.

Thinking that the doctor was going to charge the defibrillator and shock the patient, the nurse who had discovered the unresponsive patient and was now standing next to the crash cart said, in an accusatory tone, "We don't have a rhythm yet, *Doctor.*"

Zeke responded calmly. "I know. I'm getting a quick look." The defibrillator pads could be used to analyze the heart rhythm, allowing the discharge of shock without the delay of placing adhesive contacts on the body and connecting electrode wires. "Please attach the defibrillator electrodes while I do that." The nurse was quiet as she opened the drawer looking for the electrode stickers.

Zeke squinted at the defibrillator screen. "It's asystole," he remarked. Flat line. *Oh no you don't, my friend,* Zeke warned the patient silently. "Give epi."

As the nurse injected liquid epinephrine solution into a vein, the respiratory therapist used a metal blade to prop open the victim's throat and inserted a plastic tube held rigid by a thick metal wire down into the trachea. He swiftly removed the wire, attached the blue oxygen bag to end of the tube and restarted bagging. Zeke leaned over the bed and used his stethoscope to listen to the rising and falling chest.

"Breath sounds equal on both sides," he declared.

The therapist removed the bag and secured a square plastic carbon dioxide detector on the end of the endotracheal tube. The material under the clear plastic square became stained purple. The carbon dioxide level of the exhalant was high enough to cause the stain, indicating that the tube was properly placed as a conduit to the lungs and not the stomach.

"Atropine."

As he watched the nurse inject a vial of atropine, Zeke started analyzing what had made the patient's heart stop in the first place.

"May I have the chart?" The resident, relieved of his respiratory duties, ran to the nurse's station to fetch the notebook that contained the patient's admission and hospital course data. He returned to the room, opened the book and handed it to Zeke.

As he did this, he added hopefully, "The patient was admitted with viral syndrome and dehydration."

"Thanks. Check rhythm," Zeke directed as he started leafing through the pages.

The nurse looked at Zeke dismissively, as if to say that he was wasting his time looking at the chart.

"Still asystole."

"Another round of epi, please."

The patient was seventy-five years old, had a history of diabetes and congestive heart failure, and had been admitted the previous day after a fainting spell which followed a few days of vomiting and diarrhea. Upon admission he was found to suffering from dehydration due to "viral syndrome" or an unspecified viral infection. Just then, a note from the doctor who saw the patient earlier that day caught Zeke's eye. *K 3.0* was written in the last section of the note.

"Let's hang some potassium."

"Potassium?" the nurse repeated incredulously. Her expression said, *Are you* trying *to kill this patient?*

"Potassium was low this morning," Zeke explained, this time with a slight edge in his voice.

With a sigh of futility, the nurse injected a vial of potassium chloride in to a plastic bag of saline and hung the bag on a pole to drip its contents into the patient's veins. The nurse stepped back, crossed her arms, and scowled. Her expression transformed into one of embarrassed surprise, like that of someone revealed to be the victim of a practical joke, when the green line on the defibrillator monitor jumped and contracted into regular spikes.

"Check for pulse."

The medical student performing chest compressions paused and placed her fingertips over the femoral artery. "I've got a pulse," she said cheerfully.

"Check vitals." Zeke looked over at the doubting nurse, whose expression had become neutral once more. "Call the MICU for admission, status post asystolic arrest due to hypokalemia."

With the pulse and blood pressure restored, the senior resident could look after the patient until he was transferred to the intensive care unit. His detour completed, Zeke continued his trip to the emergency department. Such a simple thing. Give a small amount of potassium, save someone's life. Too much potassium and it becomes lethal. Use it on a healthy person in order to kill. It was like rage, too little or too much and someone could die.

In the emergency department, Zeke met Mr. Ira Carswell, the middle aged writer who was to be admitted with an abnormal heart rhythm. As he approached the stretcher, Zeke saw a fit-looking man with a medium build and a head of thick salt and pepper hair. A red, black and white collection of wires connected Mr. Carswell's chest to a monitor mounted on the wall above his head. The monitor was displaying the heart rate, erratically blinking numerals: 48-42-37-50. The electrocardiogram image on the monitor showed irregularly occurring waves, the small, round initial wave distancing itself from the second larger spike until a spike was dropped and the process repeated itself.

Zeke looked from the monitor to the man's anxious face. Smiling professionally, Zeke extended his hand.

"Mr. Carswell, I'm Dr. Oswald. The internist who will be admitting you to the hospital."

"Hi," he said as he took Zeke's hand and shook it hesitantly.

"So what brought you into the hospital tonight?" Zeke began.

"I had a physical examination for my employer and they said my pulse was 'low.'" Carswell made quotation marks in the air with his fingers. "They even called an ambulance, much to my profound embarrassment. I feel fine. No dizziness, fainting, chest pain, shortness of breath," he listed rapidly.

He answered these questions before, Zeke mused. He had more.

"Any palpitations?"

"No."

"Trouble breathing at night or while lying flat?"

"No."

Zeke asked about heart disease, asthma, diabetes, high blood pressure, high cholesterol, to which the answers were all negative.

"Anyone in your family have heart disease at a young age?"

"My mother had quadruple bypass surgery two weeks ago. She's eighty-four."

"How old was she when she first came down with heart trouble?"

"This was the first time, unless you count the times she was left heartbroken by my father."

Zeke laughed politely, not too enthusiastically in case the comment wasn't meant to be amusing. "Any one in your family die suddenly at a young age?"

"No."

"And you live in an apartment in Albany?"

"Yes but I travel a lot to Manhattan, I'm a writer for the *New York Times.*"

"You live alone?"

"Yes, and I smoke cigarettes and drink scotch, I have thought of stopping in the past and choose not to," Carswell expanded, anticipating upcoming questions with a slightly defensive tone.

A scotch drinking writer, huh? "How often do you drink, every day?" The patient nodded. "How many drinks per day?'

"Six or seven."

Mr. Carswell's new doctor grunted but tried not to sound judgmental. "I need to examine you, okay?"

"Do I have to stay in the hospital?"

"Yes, you're being admitted to monitor your heartbeat."

While Carswell considered that, Zeke examined his hands, neck, felt his pulse in his wrists and neck, listened to his heart sounds and lungs and checked his legs for swelling.

"What do think doctor, am I terminal?" The scotch drinking writer was joking but had an anxious look on his face. Zeke looked at the heart rhythm monitor again-no change in heart rate. Looking calmly into his patient's eyes, Zeke reassured, "You're in good hands, Mr. Carswell."

But to begin to truly answer his question Zeke had to review Mr. Carswell's electrocardiogram. The heart rate was forty-six beats per minute and the rhythm was irregular, which suggested a more benign process in this case. Every few beats a spike would disappear.

"Wenckebach," Zeke said softly to himself.

"What?" Carswell asked.

"Oh, I was talking to myself. Wenckebach. The type of abnormal heart rhythm you have is called Wenckebach."

"Sounds awful. What is the name's origin? Is it eponymous?"

"Exactly," Zeke began to explain. "Wenckebach was a Dutch scientist specializing in cardiac anatomy. He was first to describe a type of abnormally slow heart rhythm at the turn of the twentieth century." He gently shook the electrocardiogram. "*Your* type of abnormal heart rhythm."

Maybe it was too much information, but Zeke knew that one of the ways people dealt with anxiety was through intellectualization, which distracted them from their anxious feelings. He also knew that a more common sense approach was through simple reassurance. "It's not considered a dangerous type." He paused to allow Carswell to process the statement. Then, more practically, he added "You'll be headed upstairs soon to our monitored cardiac ward and I will be here all night in case there are any problems."

"Okay," Carswell said with a sigh.

Zeke patted his knee. In closing, he said professionally, "Nice meeting you."

"Please don't take offense, but I hope not to see you soon."

Zeke chuckled as he turned to leave Carswell's bedside. He had heard that one before.

Leaving the room Zeke couldn't help but think about the days when he was a "six or seven a day" drinker.

CHAPTER SIX

1989

Bloodshot. It was the best way to describe Dr. Zeke Oswald when he awakened on that warm July morning. His mouth was dry, so the first thing he did after getting off the threadbare couch where he'd fallen asleep the previous night was to stagger into the bathroom of his plain studio apartment. After cupping some tap water in his mouth to rinse it, he looked at himself in the mirror. His eyes were red, his face puffy, and he looked ten years older than his age of twenty-five. But it went deeper than his face. Heavy drinking every day for the past six years had taken its toll on Zeke both physically and spiritually. Never mind his blood, his soul was shot too.

Even with his addiction, Zeke had managed to become a successful resident doctor and postdoctoral fellow at Johns Hopkins where he was enrolled in an educational program that trained him to become a physician scientist. He divided his time between caring for patients and working in molecular biology lab, specializing in addiction medicine research.

Zeke was at a point in his training spending almost all of his time on the research end. With little patient care duties, moonlighting some weekends, his time was more flexible and his drinking increased with the flexibility. Two six packs of beer and a quart of vodka most nights. But not last night, because he had a big day in the lab, he limited himself to just enough to get to sleep: a six-pack of beer. While he had no hangover his eyes felt layered in fine gravel, the left side of his face was congested, and breathing deeply felt like having the business end of a large needle positioned near his chest. The indoor air was caustic to his lungs. Urinating relieved the pressure in his bladder, and the steam from the shower cleared his head to an extent. After washing his hair and body, Zeke turned up the temperature of the water and ran it on the back of his neck, and as the muscles loosened with the heat he considered the work for the day. It had been eight days since he fed mice DNA fragments encased in liposomes, microscopic bubbles made of fat particles, and the first thing Zeke needed to check and record when he arrived at the lab was the mice's consumption of alcohol and compare it to the group of mice fed liposomes only. If there was a significant difference in alcohol consumption, Zeke planned on making another supply of the liposomal complexes for other experiments. Also on the schedule was a task to determine if the mice were producing messenger RNA and protein from the genetic material fed to them in the liposomes. To do this he needed to take blood samples from the tail veins of the mice to test for RNA and protein.

Zeke brushed his hair, brushed his teeth twice, and applied Visine to his eyes. Needing a cup of coffee, he dressed quickly in blue jeans and a black Hard Rock Café-Albuquerque t-shirt and burst out into hot morning air. The studio was located on the Hopkins Campus, a short walk from the lab in Rush Hall. As usual for his walk to the lab, he stopped at a street vendor to breakfast with coffee and a buttered roll.

Standing in line at the vendors truck (he wouldn't have to say anything besides thanks when his turn came, the vendor knew his usual order and would prepare it when he spotted him), Zeke's mind began to wander like a breeze in the humid air. He shuddered as he remembered the overdose incident that took place a few weeks ago. If Zeke was beginning to wonder the incident was a sign he had hit rock bottom.

A car passed the vending cart, pumping hip hop music in the July air. Zeke scowled as he asked himself how it had come to this.

The answer, as with most behavioral questions, was part temperament and part environment. His problems with alcohol abuse had started when he arrived at Arizona State. He was always on the shy side, socially awkward, preferring the company of books over others, but in his first year he started to develop problems with anxiety. Zeke started to experience a generalized nervous mood, making it difficult to concentrate while studying. His circle of friends would attend parties most weekends. Zeke's drinking career began with these gatherings, out of peer pressure and the need to self-medicate. Binge drinking was encouraged by this lifestyle, and the damage inflicted on his REM sleep from intoxications worsened his mood and well-being, and he gradually became addicted.

And the regrets began to pile up like accidents on a rain-slick freeway. He stubbornly refused to forgive himself for the missed opportunities and difficulties in personal relationships, and intoxication was his escape, his way of putting off dealing with his troubles. He functioned well for many years, however, maintaining a perfect grade point average, easily getting into medical school, and landing a coveted residency.

But that all changed when he nearly killed a child.

He had already drunk half a bottle of vodka when the phone call came.

"Zeke Oswald? This is Mike the peds resident on call. Where are you? I'm calling to sign out."

Shit! "Uh, I'm just coming into the hospital now. Anything urgent?"

"No."

"Just leave the sign-out in the on-call room."

"Okay."

Zeke had forgotten he had a moonlighting shift that night, covering the pediatric ward so the on call pediatrician could focus on new patients.

Should I have just told him I was sick and couldn't make it?

Yeah, and then never get another shift again. Besides, he only had a couple of shots, he could do this no problem. Also it didn't sound like it was all that busy. He would probably sleep most of the night.

Zeke had rushed to the hospital, happy to confirm that it was going to be a slow night. After checking out the sign-out sheet, he had stretched out on the on call cot and fallen asleep.

He had awakened at the sound of his pager. Groggily, he had reached for the phone and dialed the ward.

"Dr. Oswald. You paged?"

"Yes doctor, the gentamicin order on patient Hill expired. The next dose is due right away. I can't give it until it is renewed."

Not wanting to move, Zeke had asked, "Can I give you a verbal order?"

"We don't usually do that in the neonatal unit. You promise you'll come soon to write it?"

"Yes, yes," he had answered dismissively. "500 milligrams q eight."

Before falling back asleep, Zeke had said aloud, "I should really go and write that order…"

Sometime time later, there had been a loud knock on the on call room door. "Zeke, are you in there? It's Mike, the pediatric resident."

Zeke had stumbled to the door.

"Jesus, you look like shit. Anyway, the nurse in the neonatal unit called me. Did you really ask to give an infant 500 milligrams of gent?"

"I, uh…uh…"

"This is why the nurses don't take verbal orders. She heard you say 500 milligrams. The correct dose is *five* milligrams. *Nice work.*"

After letting that sink in, he had continued. "Luckily one of the other nurses saw her drawing up the dose and called me. I'll assume he heard you wrong so I won't take this any further. No more verbal orders. That baby could have died from an overdose of gentamicin."

In line for his breakfast, although Zeke's impatience began to simmer, he controlled the urge to express his frustration. The line moved slowly.

"Butter roll, large, black extra sugar?"

"Yeah, thanks." He grabbed the brown paper bag, paid the vendor and continued his path to the laboratory.

Personal trials and unpleasant memories often drive a physician to learn to care for those who are afflicted by the same, and Zeke, when considering which direction to take he found himself drawn to the field of addiction research. He set out to search for genes associated with addictive behavior. Identifying genes that are responsible for a particular characteristic, or phenotype, can involve laborious and time consuming experiments where large groups of genetically distinct mice are bred over a period of years. The DNA of the offspring is analyzed for known areas or markers of DNA that are linked to phenotypes. Large areas of genetic material are identified to narrow the search for the controlling genes. The regions are then painstakingly searched for candidate stretches of DNA that could modify or produce a characteristic.

Zeke had devised a way to possibly get around the years required to link a section of DNA to a characteristic. Instead of doing an actual breeding, Zeke had written a computer program which took DNA information from distinct mice strains and simulated a breeding, using the concept of genetic recombination, the process in which DNA is broken and reassembles in a slightly different pattern. The program was a mathematical translation of what goes on in nature and saved enormous amounts of time in predicting what areas of DNA would match with a phenotype, in Zeke's case addictive behavior.

Armed with this program, Zeke had simulated a breeding between two strains of mice: C3H/J, a strain which can easily become addicted to alcohol, and DBA/2, which resists becoming addicted. On the lab's personal computer, it took two days of continuous number crunching to produce results predicting several hundred areas of DNA that could hold the key to addictive behavior in the mice. Zeke then searched gene databases to look for genes that are known to be involved brain pathways that lead to reinforcement of a human's response to alcohol intoxication. The brain's chemical pathways most often implicated in addiction are operated by the chemicals dopamine, serotonin and gamma-aminobutyric acid. Therefore, the young researcher was thrilled to have found a gene in his results called *A2p2* that contributed to the synthesis of proteins in the brain that coupled with dopamine to produce brain responses. Excitedly Zeke thought if the gene were overproduced or mutated in a way that increased its activity it could lead to increased dopamine activity and therefore greater reinforcement behavior. On the other hand, completely blocking the gene might attenuate reinforcement, leading to less reward with the addicting substance. Even more enticing for Zeke was the possibility of *modifying* the gene's function, perhaps allowing an alcoholic to drink moderately.

He dreamed of a cure for alcohol and drug addiction.

For Zeke, the realization of such possibilities would produce a thrilling feeling of excitement that was superior to any substance-induced euphoria. The moment the realization occurred, he could feel his heart race with anticipation, a pleasurable sensation similar in some ways to fear. His head would clear of uncertainty and drudgery, replaced with razor-clear thinking and wild ambition for discovery. Like a lion waiting to his prey to appear, Zeke felt like the leader of the pack, anticipating a chase and a possible kill, to satiate his intellectual hunger. Intellectual curiosity notwithstanding, a huge scientific discovery leading to a cure for addiction would make Zeke famous and, in a way, immortalize him.

Zeke's mind was far from clear that day. He was in the unexciting phase of research, hypothesis testing, which was an exercise in delayed gratification full of tedium that could easily jeopardize success. He felt groggy, not fully awake, and the caffeine from his breakfast hadn't awakened him but did make him jittery. Anxious to see if there were differences in alcohol consumption between the treatment group and vehicle group, Zeke hurried to the animal facility. He swiped his ID card to enter the door of the brick building and walked over to the elevator, then swiped his card again to gain access.

Once outside the room that held the mice in cages, Zeke donned a paper gown and used a key on his key ring to open the door. He pushed to door open with his back, and, while standing on one foot, applied a shoe cover to the airborne foot, then stepped in the clean room with the covered foot. Lifting the other foot, nearly losing his balance, he hopped to regain his balance as he covered the opposite shoe and stepped fully inside.

As the animal colonies were located in rooms within the interior of the building, the room holding Zeke's mice was artificially lit. The fluorescent lights flickered and buzzed as he walked across the dark, grey flecked floor. The floor's surface was slightly pliable, and walking across it that day, Zeke felt an excited uncertainty like he was traveling across another world. The cages he was looking for held six mice that had been injected with liposome encased DNA fragments and six injected with empty liposomes. He was planning on taking the cages over to a vented hood for careful measurements, but as he grew close Zeke stopped abruptly, his eyes widening.

"Holy…"

The mice who had received empty liposomes had consumed a usual half of the alcohol solution.

The water bottle serving the mice treated with the gene had barely been touched.

Zeke's decision to drink the gene solution was indistinctly made, there was no internal debate, no declarative moment, and it seemed like it was always intended to turn out that way. Zeke did wonder if the goal to treat himself with gene therapy was an unconscious attempt to rid himself of his addiction. Or at least temper it.

Most of the day was spent preparing more of the gene solution, not for his own consumption but for additional mice experiments. The mice treated with the gene had stopped drinking alcohol almost completely, showing that the gene therapy had blocked the desire. Now that he had seen an effect, he would have to confirm the effect, determine how long the effect lasted, and as final proof, see if he could restore the drinking behavior by treating the mice with interfering RNA that targeted the transcription of *A2p2*. Restoring the alcoholic behavior by specifically blocking the gene used in the treatment would support the hypothesis that the gene, and not some other part of the process, was responsible for the change.

As usual, Zeke became lost in the work, losing track of time, and when he finally looked up from his bench and out the window, he saw that darkness had fallen. He also realized he was hungry—he hadn't eaten anything since the half bagel in the morning.

Your stomach's empty, a good time to take the liposomes. Zeke considered this as he picked up one of the amber vials containing the gene solution, examining it like a fine wine, twirling it to allow the solution to run up the sides of the glass.

There was little risk and much to gain. There was the potential for an uncontrolled autoimmune response, with Zeke's blood creating antibodies that could attack normal cells. But there was a chance for life without hangovers, without a significant barrier to success in his career and personal life, and a chance for...redemption. The contents of the amber vial could be the nepenthe Zeke was desperately seeking, a way to forget a life dominated by alcoholic cravings, enabling him to remember his life without them. He could start healing his soul by righting wrongs that made up the deep running currents of regret.

He removed the vial's black cap and waved the escaping scent towards his nose. Trial and error showed Zeke that the liposomes dissolved best in buffer with a small amount of ethanol, but it had to be added right before administration. If the treatment worked, it would have to include a small amount of the very thing Zeke wanted to quit.

Nothing like a little homeopathy to help the medicine go down.

He took a glass pipette, drew up some ethanol, and added a few drops to the vial. The alcohol hit the surface for the liquid, expanding and making small circular swirling patterns. Zeke made a circular motion with his hand to gently mix the alcohol in.

He sat at his desk at the end of the lab bench in case there would be any immediate disabling effects of drinking the concoction. He placed the vial on the desk in front of his computer display and, trying to appear casual, looked around the lab to be sure no one could be watching. At the time of night, the lab was usually pretty empty of people except for the odd postdoctoral fellow working mostly around the clock.

On the computer display, the screen saver restarted, beginning with dot which expanded to a large circle. The circle eventually broke to form a large dynamic spiral. This pattern repeated in multiple area of the screen like a pyrotechnics show of dahlia breaks that evolved into fractals.

As he swirled the vial again to mix the contents, a subtle odor from the small amount of ethanol reached Zeke. Head hanging low, his eyes began to well with bitter tears as the painful moments of his life took over. Was it him or the drinking? Zeke remembered from his childhood and adolescence a trouble with self-motivation—a disabling hesitation starting tasks. Readying himself to drink the solution, he felt like a great portion of his life had been wasted in inaction. In his adult life, he would often arrive home with ambitious plans, only to start soaking himself in the incapacitation of inebriation. His plans would be wasted, letting himself down, and this would fuel the feelings that he wasn't accomplishing enough.

Zeke choked on the shame he felt over his inadequacies as he raised the vial and swallowed slowly. The mixture burned slightly and left a slight sweet aftertaste, then...nothing.

His pulse quickened at the unanticipated thought that he might have had an allergic reaction to the brew. Better stay here and wait for a half hour so I could phone for help if anything happens, Zeke planned. But what to tell the EMS workers? *I'm having an anaphylactic reaction after imbibing the potion I used in a mouse experiment in a bizarre act of self-experimentation and self-destruction to rid myself of personal demons?*

The half hour passed uneventfully and he left the lab at 11:37 that night in July of 1989. Walking through the door to his apartment, Zeke was pleased to discover he didn't have the usual craving for beer and vodka. Was this like having a positive effect to a placebo or were the genes weaving themselves into Zeke's DNA and blocking the urge?

Things turned unpleasant in the middle of the night. Zeke, in a state somewhere between the reality of wakefulness and the cloudiness of a dream, began to experience the odd sensation of his eyes pivoting in their sockets and a bilateral dull headache near the angle of his jaw. It felt like his face was locked in a grotesque grimace, teeth clenching and baring. A feverish pressure was building in the imagined space behind his eyes, creating a nauseating vertiginous sensation that seemed partly physical and partly emotional, like a scream without the feeling of release. The dull jaw pain turned lancinating, localizing on the right side of his face, the suffering shooting upwards. Zeke wished for a bullet to bite, grinding the metal against his teeth.

Overcome with a wave of uncomfortable arousal that was somewhere between rage and sorrow, the wave repeated, cresting over and over in a delirious cycle that finally broke as he startled awake. Still dazed, Zeke stood and staggered into the bathroom.

Grunting, hyperventilating, he switched the light on to illuminate the blue tiled room. Fearful of what the light might reveal, Zeke shut his eyes tightly like someone who had eyes had become accommodated to darkness. He blindly felt for the sink instinctually and began to slowly open his eyes. When he caught sight of himself in the mirror, his eyes suddenly opened wide with panic as he saw that his reflection was pale and anemic, his lips white and cracked. His mouth felt dry, and a powerful thirst billowed inside his core. He jerked forward, turned the faucet and cupped some water in his hand. He fed it to himself but it tasted like vomit, acrid and bilious, and rather than swallow, Zeke gagged.

Oh, shit. The nausea rose in his body until it burned in Zeke nostrils. Darkness reached his eyes and then he blacked out.

When he was awake the following morning, Zeke rolled over to find a cool section of the pillow. This pleasant feeling against his skin eased him fully awake. After he stretched his spine by extending his legs downward, he noticed his head was clear and this would be a day without a hangover. Despite his overnight experience, Zeke felt fully rested and content, like a reassured child. There was no headache when he turned his head or his eyes, the globes felt moist and clean.

He was enjoying the thought of another night free from intoxication when he stepped into the humid morning air. Zeke was looking forward to the warmth of the sunlight on his face, but when he emerged from the shade from the maple trees outside his apartment, the skin on his cheeks began to tighten as the sun hit. He changed his facial expression to make the tightness worse as proof he was experiencing the abnormal sensation. His ears began to burn and he instinctively touched one with his index finger and thumb. This caused such intense pain that flashed appeared before him and he began to feel faint. "Shit!" he cried, falling to one knee, coughing as he tried to draw in the heavy air. The coughing sounded like deranged laughter.

Supporting himself with one hand outstretched on the pavement, the skin on his hand felt about to tear. Zeke turned his head to stand up and the light stung his eyes. He squinted and brought the back of his raw hand up to his face, using it as a shield in a defensive posture. He let out a sound like a wounded canine and scurried back indoors.

The relatively cool interior of his apartment provided some relief and Zeke regained some composure. He examined his hands, pronating and supinating his forearm to see both sides of his red and swollen extremities. With his palms upward, Zeke appeared to be begging for assistance.

What is happening to me? he thought. *What did the gene transfer do to my skin?* The idea of treating himself, which Zeke so casually accepted the previous night, now seemed like a disaster. Chastising himself, he asked, *How could I be so* fucking *stupid?*

How was he going to do his experiments today? Zeke panicked as he ventured into the bathroom to survey the damage. *Did the sunlight damage my skin? Why am I sensitive to light?*

His cheeks appeared sunburned as he examined his reflection. Zeke turned his head to expose the painful side of his neck. The skin was covered by a large blister—a second degree burn. *It had to have been the sunlight; it burned when it hit my skin.* The skin broke under the tension and blood-tinged fluid rushed out of the blister to run down his neck to collect in the triangle where the neck met the chest. Zeke shuddered from the appearance and the clammy feeling of the fluid on his neck, causing the liquid to drip down his chest. Now the skin of his whole body changed from hot and flushed to cold and clammy. In the mirror, Zeke's skin was grey.

Maybe it's not from the experiment, Zeke began to rationalize. *Maybe it's something in the air.* Was it a sudden hole in the earth's ozone layer, leading to severe damage from ultraviolet light? Or was it radiation from a power plant accident or a nuclear war attack? He rushed to a window that faced the sidewalk. Pulling the curtains back (he kept them closed during the day to keep the heat out), he jumped back as the sunlight streamed in through the glass. Zeke expected his hand to burn in the light and he readied himself for the pain, but it didn't come.

The sidewalk was sparsely populated, but students were walking along as usual for the time of day. The seemed completely normal, not rushing or showing signs of panic, and none looked like a burn victim. Were they immune from this new danger? A young woman Zeke recognized as a fellow resident turned her head to peer at him and her eyes widened with a shocked look as she hurried away.

A mark of his own poor judgment, Zeke stepped back away from the window like a fugitive caught in a spotlight. Christ, was he going to have to hide for the rest of his life? Wait, no he didn't burn when the sunlight passed through glass or in the artificial light.

Zeke skulked over to the television, thinking if there was some natural manmade disaster that unleashed skin-damaging radiation, there would be reports of it. But he could only find daytime talk shows and soap operas as he flipped through the channels. There were no reports, no emergency broadcasts of a universal health threat where people's skin was blistering in natural sunlight, or of hospitals reporting widespread viral infections, or of an epidemic thirst unquenchable by water.

The thirst Zeke had developed—a gritty feeling in his throat that radiated to his lips—was more than a desire for water, it felt more like the impulse to kiss. With the television show *Days of Our Lives* playing in the background, Zeke filled a paper cup with water from the kitchen sink. A man and woman were embracing.

"I need to be true to Jack's memory," the woman said, leaning back and looking up at the man she was embracing.

Zeke tried to drink the water but he couldn't get it down. He gagged on the gasoline-like taste. His lips were so dry the stuck to the wax coating of the paper cup and peeled part of it off as he removed the cup from his mouth. With the disappointment, the thirst intensified.

Zeke began pacing around the room, worrying, *what am I going to do? Is there treatment for this, whatever it is?* Afraid to try going outside again, Zeke decided to use the phone to try to get some answers.

"Johns Hopkins Hospital," an operator answered. *Excuse me, is the hospital ER flooded with radiation burns?* "Could you please page dermatology on call?"

"One moment," the nasal voice replied.

Would sunblock work? Zeke's mind raced as he waited. *Will this get infected?*

An impatient female voice: "Dermatology."

Zeke tried to sound professional but his voice croaked when he started to talk. He cleared his throat. "Hi, it's Zeke Oswald, who's this?"

"Dr. Greenberg. How can I help you, Dr. Oswald?" the dermatologist said quickly.

"I was wondering if I could curbside you on a patient...of mine," he said, using a term to indicate he wanted to ask an informal medical opinion.

"Sure. Wait, who is this again?"

Probably shouldn't have used your real name. Zeke wasn't very good at obfuscation. *You may have to learn how to mislead better if this turns out to be a long term thing.* "Zeke Oswald, one of the residents."

"Oh, okay, go ahead."

He stammered, he hoped not too noticeably.

"I have a...a young guy who I'm seeing as an outpatient who developed a sudden onset severe sun reaction (*after drinking a gene therapy concoction only tested on animals*). Zeke swallowed hard and his neck stung. "A second degree burn."

Her reply sounded incredulous and condescending. "Are you sure he didn't just fall asleep in the July sun on the beach or forget to use sunscreen?'

"No. It happened a few minutes after he went outside." *Just after he emerged from the safety of the shade.*

"Hmm."   Now Dr. Greenberg sounded interested. "Any medications, Accutane, NSAIDs?"

"No."

"Any new cologne, or perfumey soap or shampoo?"

"No."

"Anything else going on?"

Should I tell her he's pale and very *thirsty?* "No." *Why not tell her?*

"So no reason to think he has SLE?"

Lupus. *Maybe I have lupus.*

There was a pause as the dermatologist considered other causes.

"Do bloodwork for tyrosinemia and pellagra, if these are negative send him to see me in my office."

"Thanks," Zeke replied, but she had already disconnected.

Lupus? He thought. That was unlikely, the disease was much more common in women, the burn wasn't limited to his cheeks and nose and he had never had any arthritis-like joint pain.

Pellagra? The nutritional deficiency made famous by the Russian Gulags in the era of Stalin? Nowadays it was uncommon in the U.S. but Zeke remembered it from his medical school classes so he turned to one of his textbooks of medicine to look it up. The disease, caused by dietary lack of the vitamin niacin and the amino acid tryptophan, could cause sensitivity to sunlight, aggressive behavior, an inflammation of the tongue called glossitis, confusion and imbalance. The constellation of the main symptoms of the disease were known colloquially as the four D's: diarrhea, dementia, dermatitis, and…death. Pellagra was also characterized by some specific psychological manifestations which included unusual annoyance to bright lights, intolerance to certain odors, restlessness, and querulousness.

Pellagra is a disease well respected by medical historians because it is regarded as the first known collection of symptoms combined as a syndrome in modern medicine. It was first known as Austrian leprosy, from the book in which it was first described in the mid eighteenth century. It was later named pellagra, which in Italy meant "rough skin." Joseph Goldberger, a physician working for the U.S. surgeon general in 1915 showed that pellagra was the result of a poor diet by feeding a restricted diet to prisoners. Several years later, niacin was shown to reverse the canine version of the disease called black tongue.

Zeke's tongue wasn't black or swollen, and he wasn't guilty of eating unprocessed corn, which was a major cause of pellagra until it was discovered that corn treated with a base released tryptophan, which could be converted to niacin by the body. Zeke considered the fact that pellagra could occur in alcoholics, but mostly in one who was homeless, destitute, an outcast. Like a black-tongued dog. It wasn't a fitting description of Zeke Oswald, although he felt like one at times.

Tyrosinemia is due to the body's accumulation of tyrosine due to the inability to metabolize the amino acid. It was usually found in childhood, Zeke wondered why his consultant would suggest testing of the condition. Could adults aquire tyrosinemia? Perhaps body builders and health nuts could from taking too many amino acid supplements? Zeke didn't think tyrosinemia was the likely cause of his problems, but reading about it triggered his memory. There was another disease he recalled learning about where the buildup of substrate concentrated in the skin and caused photosensitivity. What was it?

He was trying to recall the name of the condition when the phone rang, startling him, and he assumed a posture like a dog crouching in the face of a threat.

"Hello."

"Hi Dr. Oswald? It's Leah." The lab's most senior technician. "Are you coming in today?"

How long have I been investigating this? He looked at his watch: 2:00 PM. *Boy, did I lose track of time. Why am I not hungry?*

"Yes, yes, I'm not sick or anything," Zeke replied, a little too loudly. *Why did I say that?* He forced himself into composure. "I'll be in later."

"Do you need us to do anything with your experiments in the meantime?"

How considerate, Zeke thought sardonically. In reality, the phone call wasn't an offer of help, it was designed to satisfy Leah's nosy curiosity or to check up on Zeke's whereabouts when he didn't arrive to the lab at his usual time. She was probably calling on the lab director's actual or perceived behalf to see if there were any potential productivity issues with the young physician scientist.

"No, thanks, everything's…fine."

Zeke hung up and stared at the phone for a long time.

The mixture of trepidation and self-pity Zeke was feeling eventually gave way to relative calm as he contemplated a plan. He found his medical instrument kit in his bedroom closet and checked his blood pressure. He listened to the angle of his arm as he pumped the pressure cuff up and then turned the valve open to allow the pressure to release slowly. 94/64 millimeters of mercury. He counted his pulse for one minute. Sixty-four regular beats per minute. The pressure was a bit on the low side but normal, and since he didn't have a reason to check it frequently, he had no measurements to compare it to. The heart rate was slow and reassuring to Zeke, as his pale skin could occur from severe anemia, a low red blood cell count. A severe case of rapidly developing anemia should lead to an abnormally fast heartbeat.

So Zeke didn't think he was in any immediate danger where he needed to see medical attention right away. After the threat of the sun was over, he could run some basic blood tests in his lab later that day. Hopefully this problem would be temporary and would resolve on its own and he could keep the whole experience a secret. After all wasn't the medical adage that the doctor's role was to keep the patient busy while nature resolved things?

Zeke took pause to evaluate his plan. He asked himself if this was the right thing to do. Should he seek help from an objective mind? It probably wasn't a good idea to try to act as one's own physician; there was too much potential for bias in one's judgment. He had seemed to make a mess of things so far, perhaps it was time to find a trusted soul and reach out for assistance. But who could be trusted?

Also, Zeke couldn't be certain that it was his experimentation that resulted in the problem. It could just be a coincidence, and in fact, the more he thought about it, the less Zeke thought the photosensitivity and aversion to water was caused by drinking the liposomal concoction. It was probably some allergic reaction to a clothing detergent or something with which he came in contact at the lab. He might never identify the source of the reaction, it would be best to withdraw from any suspicious contact. His skin wasn't itchy so Zeke didn't think that applying a steroid cream was necessary; still he should put something on the burn to treat it and prevent infection. He could pick up some silvadene cream on the way to the lab.

No, the more Zeke thought about it, the more convinced he was he could handle the situation without any outside help. If misguided self-experimentation were the cause, exposing this fact would probably lead to the end of his career as a doctor and a researcher. Unless he could somehow turn using relatively untested brew into a positive, like the researcher who publicly drank liquid insecticide to prove its safety to humans, he could lose his medical license if anyone were to find out he did something so reckless. Letting the truth out could also ruin his research reputation—he wouldn't be able to get a decent job or funding for that kind of scientific judgment.

Even if I wanted to tell someone, who could I? Zeke thought as he concluded there was no one he could trust with such sensitive information. This lack of someone to turn to was a product of his own tendency towards isolation. He had no close relationships, not with his family, his coworkers, nor his friends. This realization, along with the stressful events of the day, should have been enough to trigger cravings for inebriation. Zeke even thought, *a drink could settle my nerves and even out my temper in the middle of all this. But wait*, he caught himself, *this was just a conditioned response from my brain,* and in reality he felt no craving for alcohol.

For the first time in a long time he wasn't craving the burn.

After the sun went down, Zeke ventured outside again. He stepped gingerly outside his apartment door but it wasn't necessary. It was a warm evening, but he felt nothing unusual. In fact he felt recharged. And for the first time in his life, he thought he might blow off the lab that night at go out somewhere to make new friends.

Before Zeke left, he found some gauze pads to place over his neck to cover the skin involved in the burn while he walked to the pharmacy. At about eight o'clock, Zeke entered a chain pharmacy on a street corner in Baltimore, Maryland. Someone was leaving the leaving the store as Zeke entered. The man opened the door and when he noticed Zeke, stepped aside to allow him entrance. *Did his eyes widen when he looked at me?* Zeke asked himself as he passed through the thick glass doors. Fearing discovery, Zeke quickly exited the store after making his purchase, skulking through the doors.

Back at home he removed the bandage to apply the cream. The old gauze was stained brown from the discharge and had a putrid smell. The wound was moist, reddish-pink, the color of rotting salmon flesh. The dead skin that used to cover the blister was a grey and lifeless peel, looking like something intended for disposal. He pulled on the dead skin to see if he could remove it, but stopped abruptly when it began to tear at the junction between harmed and unharmed.

After redressing the burn, Zeke waited at home until 2 AM to return to the lab to reduce the chance that anyone would be working. He set out along the same path he'd tried seventeen hours before. While walking he noticed the thirst again, and realized he hadn't eaten or drunk anything all day. Probably the adrenaline was suppressing his appetite, but how long would it be before he became dehydrated?

"What happened to *you*?" the voice said. Zeke thought he was alone and should have startled at the surprise. He didn't, and he turned calmly towards Brian Westing, one of the lab's postdoctoral fellows.

"I'm fine, just a bachelor cooking mishap." *Could he lie about everything?*

"Oil or steam?"

Zeke didn't answer the question. "I'm fine. The emergency room doctor said I'll heal up in a few days." A lie designed to distract and provide an explanation for his absence during the day. Zeke was getting good at this.

Keeping odd hours was a common practice among scientists so meeting in a laboratory at two am wasn't particularly unusual for the two researchers. However, Zeke suspected that Brian would wonder why Zeke was there so late.

"I have to run some blood tests on my mice," Zeke explained. "Hope I'm not too late."

"No problem, I was just checking my cells and I'm outta here."

Soon, hoped Zeke, as he wanted to perform the tests on his own blood not the mice's and didn't want to go through the effort or risk of concealment. The postdoc was true to his word, leaving shortly.

While Zeke was waiting for Brian's departure, he tried to drink some water to stave off dehydration. Although it tasted like acid, he forced himself to drink it, gagging in between gulps. *I could use a real drink,* Zeke thought after he was done gagging, but the reality was he couldn't.

Looking over the laboratory to see if anyone was left, Zeke went through drawers, gathering supplies needed to draw blood: butterfly needles, named so because of their butterfly-shaped handles, alcohol pads, glass blood tubes, and a rubber tourniquet. He resembled a drug addict as he, staring blankly forward, turned the tourniquet around his left bicep, then tucked the ends under the loop to secure it. The burning odor of isopropyl alcohol filled his nose as he wiped the inside of his elbow as the tourniquet caused the veins to bulge. The large vein glistened for a moment as the alcohol evaporated.

Pinching the butterfly wings between his thumb and forefinger, the bevel of the needle facing upwards, Zeke drove the needle into the vein, guiding the needle until he saw a flash of blood enter the thin plastic tubing attached to the needle's other end. He pulled the end of the tourniquet to loosen it as the blood flowed through the purple rubber top of the first tube.

Holding the other glass tube steady with one hand he switched the needle tube end to a new red-topped tube. While waiting for the new tube to fill with blood, Zeke inverted the purple-topped tube a few times to mix the blood with anticoagulant. He pulled the needle out through his skin and folded a gauze pad in his arm by bending at the elbow to allow the puncture wound to stabilize. He took the second tube over to the centrifuge, slid the tube in the machine and set it spinning to force out the serum. During the spin he removed the purple top by popping it off with his thumb as if he were striking a match head. Zeke thought the blood in the tube smelled like chocolate, only with a quality that made him nauseated, like the smell of vomit would. With a pipette he drew a small amount of the unclotted blood into a capillary tube, removed the pipette and stuck one end of the tube into a soft clay block to plug the bottom.

While the cells in the unclotted blood were settling, Zeke removed some serum from the tube spun in the centrifuge and injected it into the analyzer. He pressed a button, and the machine clicked and buzzed for a few minutes, then printed a report on a narrow paper roll. Zeke tore the report from the printer and saw that the results were mostly normal: his sodium, potassium and chloride concentrations; creatinine, a measure of his kidney function. The blood sugar, measured as glucose, was slightly low: sixty-eight milligrams per deciliter. Zeke felt no symptoms of hypoglycemia like jitteriness, sweating, palpitations, and he certainly wasn't hungry.

However, when he looked over the paper to the capillary tube in the distance, he felt like his blood sugar had suddenly plummeted. Something was very wrong; he wasn't sure at first, because he couldn't really see the level of packed cells closely. The primitive area of his brain must have noticed something first to tell his body to react with shock. As he moved closer to the tube, he could clearly see what his unconscious was reacting to. The contents had settled to a low level in the tube.

The capillary tube, after settling, measures the percentage of red cells to the rest of the blood. The hematocrit, as it is called, normally occurs around forty. Zeke looked with horror at the level of his own blood, resting at about one quarter of the tube's length. *This must be some mistake,* he thought, hyperventilating, rushing over to pick up the tube and hold it against a measure. The top of his head felt like it was going to explode as he struggled to concentrate on the numbers.

Twenty-four percent. Severe anemia.

Such a sudden drop! In the absence of extensive bleeding, a rapid drop in red cell count usually meant something was destroying the corpuscles and they were decreasing to dangerous levels. Panicking, Zeke frantically drew up another sample into an empty capillary tube. He swallowed hard (the thirst was intense!) and watched the cells settle in the new sample. His eyes widened as the level slowly dropped lower and lower.

Unable to contain himself anymore, Zeke grabbed the tube threw it across the lab. It hit the wall with a *click,* but because the tube was so light it didn't break when it struck. Chanting "No, no, NO!" he found the tube on the floor and stomped, punctuating each foot strike with a "NO!" and crushed the tube, destroying the remaining cells, leaving on the floor a smashed spatter of purple blood and tiny glass shards, like a broken jar of grape preserves.

I am self-destructing! He thought with frenzied anguish. Zeke felt it was a putrefying process, a decomposition of body and soul. *What have I done to myself,* his mind shrieked. *Or did God do this to me?*

Is it leukemia?

Will I die from this?

"God wouldn't let me off that easily," he growled aloud through clenched teeth.

Zeke remained in that state a few minutes more, breathing deeply. He slowly regained composure, his head cleared of the pressure, and his thoughts became more rational. *Ok, I will figure this out and fix it. Blood cancer doesn't explain the phototoxicity, I will have to think of something that connects the two.*

If it was the gene transfer, how could a mutation of a gene responsible for conditioned responses cause anemia? Maybe I've invented a new disease? I'll be famous after all.

Scanning his memory of uncommon diseases he memorized in medical school, he recalled a condition causing anemia in which the red cells were broken, spilling their contents into the plasma, leading to an accumulation of the cell's contents in the body. The contents built up in the skin, and some on the chemicals absorbed light, raising the skin's susceptibility to sun damage. The condition was called porphyria, and Zeke remembered that those affected lost their red cells due to hemolysis, or a shearing of the cells coating. Losing the red cells caused some to have strange cravings, and some developed a strong desire to drink blood to replace the deficient red cells.

Oh my God, my...thirst. I'm not thirsting for water or alcohol any more. I want...blood!

Dr. Zeke Oswald was *bloodthirsty*.

CHAPTER SEVEN

Present Day

"Uggh."

Patience groaned plaintively as the radio alarm began, playing "6th Avenue Heartache" by The Wallflowers. She had already pressed the snooze button three times. As groggy as she was, peach flavor still lingering in her nostrils, she knew if she pressed the button one more time, the alarm wouldn't sound for another twenty-three and a half hours. She rolled out of bed, her white t-shirt pulling upwards by the motion, exposing her thigh, hip and the soft flesh of her lower back. As she stood up and stretched, her shirt fell back into place and she shuffled towards the kitchen in well-worn, terry slippers which had once been a bright hot pink.

Yawning, she grabbed a large earthenware mug from a cabinet and placed it on the counter top. Her mother had given her the mug when Patience was twelve after her parents' divorce was final. The mug, adorned with sickeningly cute Precious Moments toddlers was supposed to be a way to tell Patience *Let's have a cup of tea together and talk about our feelings* but her mother never acted upon this implied intent. Patience smirked as she popped open a can of RockStar energy drink and poured her morning caffeine fix into the mug while reading the familiar saying written on it in flowery script.

Life is just a chance...to grow a soul.

She gulped down the drink. "Fuckin' A." Patience belched as she spoke. "Let's see what the *dean* thinks about that."

She arrived three minutes late to her appointment with Dean Bertram Perkins at Albany Medical College. It was conveniently scheduled at a time such that she would be late to rounds at the hospital, which of course would beg the question, *Why is Patience late this time? Oh, let's see, I called that slut Jodi an asshole bitch for misrepresenting my idea as her own and she ratted on me to the medical school and now I'm expelled.*

She approached the receptionist outside the dean's office. "Hi, I have an appointment with Dean Perkins." Patience announced.

"Ah, yes. He's waiting for you."

"Get in there!" the receptionist whispered urgently, motioning towards the door behind her.

She entered the office to find Perkins sitting behind a large Lucite desk. He was a thin, vain looking older man with copious amounts of hair gel and an expensive suit to match the too-white caps his phony smile revealed.

"Ah, there she is," he said imperiously, extending a supine hand to the two chairs in front of his desk. "Have a seat."

Patience took the seat on the left. She smelled a whiff of peach schnapps and hoped the Dean couldn't.

Perkins looked down at a file and flipped through a few pages. "I see this is your second trip here within a year."

Patience sat there, silently.

"The last time I made arrangements for Dr. Oswald to be a mentor to you. I trust things are going well with the process?"

"Yes. Fine."

His eyes lingered on a page in her file. "You still want to be a pediatrician like you stated in your application?" he snorted sarcastically.

She didn't reply.

After an awkward moment, he got to the point.

"Yesterday my office received a phone call from a hysterical medical student. She was practically inconsolable. You wouldn't happen to know anything about this, would you?"

"I don't have the faintest idea what you're talking about," Patience said.

Perkins became more acerbic. "I'm pretty sure you know what I'm talking about, Student Doctor McMorris."

There was a pause and then he continued. "The call was from a Miss Jodi Livingston who was upset with the language you used in your…confrontation, shall we say?"

"Well, sir, I do have a rather wide range of vocabulary—could you be a little more…specific?" *Shall we say?*

"What I think would be useful would be if you formally apologize to Miss Livingston. We wouldn't want this to be a blemish on your permanent record."

Oh shit, not this frigging permanent record crap again. Patience was losing control, her voice becoming shrill. "Why should I have to be the one to apologize? She's the one who stole my f-" she held back from cursing, "—stole my idea."

"Did you tell her your theory?"

"Well, yes, but—"

"Did you speak up on rounds when she allegedly stole your idea?" Perkins interrupted.

"No, but that's not..." Patience let out a frustrated sigh. "Look I don't know *what* she told you, but I'm late for rounds. I'll take care of it, please excuse me." Patience hurried out the door.

Dean Perkins leaned back in his chair. "Patience, what are we going to ever do with you?"

Patience walked briskly through the humid air between the parking lot and the hospital entrance. It was a little after 8:00 AM, so her meeting with Dean Dickhead had only put her a short time behind. Morning rounds were scheduled daily at eight but this attending was usually late anyway. She could even spare a few minutes to check on her patient before heading over to rounds. Better a few minutes later than late and unprepared.

Hospital interns often see their patients briefly before morning rounds, and Patience was no different. The habit served to get an update on the patient's progress overnight so that the most up to date assessment could be provided during rounds with the team. The practice is referred to by many as "breathing rounds," because the main reason for visiting one's patients shortly before rounds was to ensure they were still breathing and none had died unexpectedly after responsibility had been passed to the on-call team the previous evening. "Breathing rounds" thus spared the embarrassment of reporting to the team that a patient was fine, only to find an empty bed as the team traveled around the hospital to each patient.

As a student, Patience was responsible for only one patient at a time and she made her way to Ms. Janice Williams, a forty-six year-old with asthma and high blood pressure who was admitted two days earlier with exacerbation of the former condition. She was receiving steroids and nebulizer treatments and hopefully was improving to the point where she could be discharged that day.

The door to Ms. William's room was open but Patience knocked on it anyway as she entered.

"Ms. Williams?" Her bed, nearest to the window of the two-bedded room, was obscured by the privacy curtain.

"Yes," a voice came from behind the curtain.

"It's student doctor McMorris, okay if I see you?"

"Yes."

Patience walked around the curtain to the right side of the bed. "How's your breathing this morning?" she asked.

"Better."

"Any problems overnight?"

"Not really. I couldn't sleep," Ms. Williams offered matter-of-factly.

It sounded to Patience like she would rather be home. To clarify this thought she asked "Couldn't sleep from your breathing, or the hospital?"

"The noise."

"Do you feel well enough to go home today?" Patience asked as she listened for wheezing with her stethoscope.

"Yes," Ms. Williams said between breaths.

"Here," Patience said cheerfully as she handed her patient the bedside peak flow meter, a device that measured how constricted one's breathing could be. Ms. Williams blew through it and showed Patience the gauge much like a child would display a thermometer to a parent. 160. Better.

"I'll tell the attending this and we'll see you when we round in a little while." Patience removed the clipboard form the foot of the bed to look at blood pressure, heart rate and body temperature. No fever, vital signs were similar to yesterday's. The student doctor pursed her lips and smiled at her patient. As she left the room, Patience noticed the left side of her head was throbbing. Time for another RockStar.

Coffee cup filled with energy drink in one hand, other hand thrust in pocket of her white coat, Patience entered the small room behind the nursing station where they held morning rounds. Her body language showed how she felt being late as she kept herself small and quietly slid to a position in the back of the room by the window. Patience sat on the ledge and drank, her eyes peering over the cup.

Yet she wasn't the only one late, the attending supervising physician hadn't arrived and the conversation between the team members, three interns, two residents and another medical student was focused on the crime, not patient care. The senior resident, a stocky woman in her forties, older than usual for someone in her third year of residency training, was making a point in her rapid cadence as Patience walked in.

"...I mean, I'm on call tonight, and to think there is a maniac roaming the hallway—"

"Still, you must acknowledge that most homicides are committed by an individual with whom the victim was familiar," interrupted the second-year resident, a short, slight male wearing a bowtie and sporting a pompous attitude to match. In contrast to the third year resident, he spoke slowly, deliberately. "Oh, Student Doctor McMorris, you're here. Are you aware one of the critical care nurses was murdered in the hospital last night?"

Patience's eyes widened.

"One of the nurses just told us. But not to worry," he looked back to the senior resident. "Random acts of violence, including *murder*, are exceedingly rare."

"Still, I don't want to be *exceedingly* dead," the senior resident replied dryly. Although shocked by the news, Patience snorted a nervous laugh at the joke.

"I heard that the nurse was one of these mercy-killing nurse serial killers," said an obviously overworked and exhausted intern, a tall, pale slouching figure dressed in wrinkled surgical scrubs. He was leaning back in his chair, tossing a foam heart model into the air and catching it repeatedly. The heart was of dense foam, designed to be used as something to squeeze a few times in order to relieve stress. It was provided by a pharmaceutical company as a promotional item.

"Oh? What's the motive then?" Dr. Bowtie inquired.

"I dunno." The intern kept tossing the heart. "Maybe he killed himself."

"Evidence would point away from that supposition. *My* sources tell me there were fingerprints on the unfortunate soul's neck. Strangling oneself is a physical impossibility."

The wrinkled intern wrinkled his nose but said nothing.

"And what about *you,* Patience?" the senior resident asked with a smirk. "Why are you late? Being questioned by the police?"

Patience blushed and didn't answer. A bizarre thought entered he mind. What if she did do it? She recently had an argument with one of the ICU nurses. Maybe she blacked out last night and took her revenge?

Trying to get the thought out of her mind, Patience decided to crack a joke of her own. "I heard our *attending* is the prime suspect in the murder, and he's late today because *he's* being questioned."

This statement should have received a round of laughter, but all there would be was an uncomfortable silence as the group noticed the attending standing in the doorway. Patience was sure he had heard her statement.

Tall, with dark curly hair, the supervising doctor was dressed in slacks, a sport coat and dress shirt open at the neck. His outfit was emblematic of his laid back style.

"Good mornin' everybody."   He sat in the remaining chair. "Who was on last night?"

"I was," said the thin, disheveled intern.

"Let's hear it."

"The patient is an eighty-six year-old female transferred from a nursing home for fever. The patient is a poor historian due to dementia…"

CHAPTER EIGHT

Elsewhere in the hospital, a meeting of hospital administrators was about to begin. Having arrived at about the same time, the executive vice president of operations, the senior vice president and the hospital's general counsel were outside the heavy dark wood door to the president's office. After greetings were exchanged, the VP of operations knocked on the door. Ten seconds later, the knock was answered by president's assistant. She opened the door to reveal the president, Adin Safford, behind a large mahogany desk. To the side sat Garret Quackenbush, the vice president of corporate affairs, a man in his early forties, dressed in a dark brown suit with wide lapels, white dress shirt and a colorful tie.

"Come in, come in," Safford said with a welcoming hand.

The president's assistant, Rebecca Crawford, a young woman with dirty blonde hair, no makeup and a tight fitting suit with a knee length skirt directed the arriving group to chairs to the right and in front of the desk, then resumed her seat to the left of the president.

Safford leaned forward in his chair and placed his elbows on the desktop. He was distinguished-looking in a blue pinstripe suit with a maroon silk tie. About sixty years old, the president had been at the post over the past twelve years and had a reputation for being reserved and professional. He had arrived at a time when Saint Twigleighct was in deep financial trouble resulting from the federal cuts in graduate medical education funding that had affected the balance sheet of many an American medical center. Safford, holding a medical degree and a graduate degree in business administration, was recruited from one of the large West Coast HMOs to turn the hospital around financially, and over the years he instituted cost saving changes by emphasizing outpatient treatment, cutting inpatient staffing, streamlining billing mechanisms and refocusing attention away from expensive research and towards patient care-oriented profits.

Today the talk was about the aftermath of the worst crime ever committed at any of the places in which the members of group had worked. "So…what's the latest news on the memorial service?" the president began.

The VP of operations answered. "Based on our last conversation, I know that some of us were against a formal service of any kind. Personally I think we should do *something* so I tentatively set up a service in the hospital chapel—"

"Let's make sure we keep this low key," Quackenbush interrupted in his usual pushy tone. "Send out a broadcast email one or two hours before the service is to begin to keep the advertising to a minimum. A make sure the service is scheduled for the lunch hour."

As he was taking this in, the VP of operations glanced out of the corner of his eye at president Safford. Safford had curled one corner of his mouth but otherwise showed no reaction. "I'll tell the pastor," the VP said, through his teeth, displeased with being cut off.

Has anyone heard how the investigation is coming?" Safford asked. "Michael, you spoke to the police?"

The senior VP had. "I talked with the Albany detective this morning. She's interviewing the staff-those who were the last to see Mr. Fisher alive, those sorts of things. It sounds like homicide investigation 101 to me. She's working on coming up with a motive but so far none has emerged."

"What do we know about this detective?" the president inquired.

"She seems...inexperienced. If you ask me, I don't so far have a lot of confidence in her. She's a young, skinny thing."

Rebecca Crawford grunted.

The VP of operations added, "Do you think we ought to hire our own PI?"

The VP of corporate affairs didn't like that idea. "I think I can speak for all of us when I say we want this to go away as soon as possible. Let's leave the detective work up to the Albany PD."

No one challenged Quackenbush on this statement but it was followed by an uncomfortable silence as his overbearing tone hung in the air.

The president broke the silence with a question for the general counsel, an attractive middle-aged woman who had a sexy look about her but was known for having a brilliant legal mind. "What's our legal exposure in this case? Will we get sued of lack of security?"

"I looked into that after our last meeting," she began. "There isn't much precedence. A hospital remains more or less a public place. The closest thing I can come up with is that several colleges have been sued after campus murders have occurred. Some cases have been lost based on the perception of adequate surgery. Colleges across the state have responded with informational briefings on safety to students and employees and infrastructural changes like the installation of panic buttons in common areas.

"Then of course there is the well-known case of young pregnant pathologist who was killed while working late at Bellevue Hospital in Manhattan in 1989. A former psychiatric patient broke into her office, raped and strangled her. The killer had been recently hospitalized there, but after being discharged returned to live out of a hospital supply closet. Her widow sued the hospital for wrongful death, but a jury exonerated Bellevue, convinced that the hospital had provided adequate security. Word has is that the hospital did offer an out-of-court settlement, however, but it was turned down."

"Should we do something to show we're concerned to try to stave off potential lawsuits?" the VP of operations suggested.

The senior VP added, "The killing was committed with a knife. We could install metal detectors."

The VP of corporate affairs didn't like that idea either. "He could have been killed by a scalpel," he said. "Having everybody pass through a metal detector sends the *wrong* message, not the right one. Besides, having metal detectors may not have prevented this crime."

"Bad for business," Rebecca muttered, looking down at the floor.

No one seemed to want to add anything so the president decided to move things along. "Very well," he said. "Good suggestions everybody, we'll give it some more thought. Anything else?"

"Yes," Quackenbush said. "Any word on when we can use the room where the murder was committed?"

"I'm not sure if the police are done processing the room. I will find out," the VP of operations offered.

"What are the radiologists doing in the meantime?" Safford asked.

"They're sharing space in the general radiology reading room."

"How is that working out?"

"The neuroradiologist is complaining but so far we haven't detected any productivity issues."

"So the films that were in the bone room are all read and reports are completed?"

"Yes," said the president's assistant, "I checked on that like you asked."

Quackenbush wasn't satisfied by this. "Even still, let's get the room back as soon as possible," he barked.

The VP of operations raised his brow to show his indignation at Quackenbush's tone.

"Well, if there's nothing else," the president said, "let's adjourn."   He looked at his assistant and nodded as the others rose to leave.

CHAPTER NINE

It was uncomfortably warm in the autopsy suite, and Selinda felt flushed. The large room was located in the basement of the government building and the detective had assumed the room would be cool. As she waited for the pathologist, Dr. William Pak, Selinda heard noises through the open windows located near the ceilings. Humid air seeped in along with the sounds of the morning. The room was equipped with black countertops and stainless steel autopsy tables over faded blue ceramic tile. Every few feet there were tarnished drains to collect formaldehyde, blood, and other body fluids.

Contrary to television depictions, most homicide detectives couldn't endure the sights and smells of the autopsy suite, preferring to wait for the coroner's paper report. Selinda Bruchart, however, thought observing an autopsy was a valuable way to spend time working up a case. She had already examined the body at the crime scene, but, to her, a crime scene inspection allowed a go-with-your guts journey into the state of mind of the killer during the commission of the crime, whereas the autopsy was a more cerebral, analytical event providing clues to help solve the mysteries of the crime. The interaction with the pathologist also provided a valuable dialogue that often generated hypotheses that could be difficult to reach alone.

So she stood in the swampy room anticipating this dialogue, slowly inhaling the sweet, nauseating mixture of preservative and inanimate flesh. She kept her distance from Caleb Fisher's body and peered at it as she considered the facts of the murder uncovered so far. She had conducted a number of interviews, with the mysterious doctor who discovered the body, the intensive care unit staff who were the last to see Fisher alive, and his roommate. She learned that the victim was a registered nurse in the intensive care unit and usually worked the eleven PM to seven AM shift. He had worked in Saint Twigleighct's intensive care unit for the past three years and had been on the medical/surgical wards for the prior five years. His primary duty in the intensive care unit was to care for the patients admitted there, monitoring the patient's condition through vital signs and blood tests, administering medications and nutrition, and preventing hospital-acquired problems like infections and skin pressure ulcers. Ordinarily intensive care nurses would care for two or three patients at a time, although recently, due to budget cuts, the nurses were being asked to be responsible for three or even four patients simultaneously.

Through her interviews and perusal of Fisher's personnel file, Selinda concluded that he seemed to do his job well with only a few incidents. Shortly after he had started to work in intensive care, he had gotten into a physical confrontation with the family of a patient who died while under his care. The cause of the altercation wasn't clear in the file as Fisher's coworkers had told conflicting stories. One nurse who was working at the time explained that a family member had blamed him of intentionally killing the patient and words led to blows. Another story was that a family member had heard Fisher laughing as she grieved at the bedside and had become enraged, mistakenly thinking that the nurse was making light of her situation. Whatever happened, however, the fight occurred three years ago and was therefore unlikely to be a motive in his murder.

The ICU staff had also described a more recent incident between Fisher and a medical student. None of the staff had known the student's last name but said her first name was memorable for a medical student because it was Patience. A nurse who had witnessed the dust-up told Selinda that Patience had asked Fisher to put a Foley catheter in place on one of the patients. When Fisher replied, "Hey, babe, why don't you do it yourself" or something similarly demeaning, Patience started a screaming match with Fisher.

Selinda had met Fisher's roommate, Elizabeth, at the apartment they had shared.

"So what was the nature of your relationship when he died?" Selinda had asked the skinny, pretty woman, after spying a picture of Elizabeth with Caleb's arm around her, the two looking like more than just roommates.

"Just friends."

Selinda had raised an eyebrow.

"Oh, we were going out for nearly two years," Elizabeth had added. "We broke up about three months ago but we're..." trailing off, appearing to be on the verge of crying. After blinking a few times her voice picked up speed.

"I'm sorry...I still had feelings for him and he came on to me the day before he— we ended up in bed but I knew we weren't getting back together..."

"I see," Selinda had said nonjudgmentally. "Why do you say that?"

"Because I knew he wasn't going to change." Elizabeth's tone had changed to that of frustration. "He's...was a self-centered jerk."

Was this enough to be suspicious? Selinda had asked herself.

Dr. William Pak entered the suite, interrupting Selinda's thoughts.

"How are you, Detective?"

"Fine. Hoping you will help me with this case."

The pathologist smiled in response. Selinda had worked with Pak on many cases and found him a trusted advisor with an understated style. Age seemed to be slowing him down, but in his forty year career he had amassed an enormous amount of experience that Selinda could count on.

Pak began speaking into a microphone hanging near his face. He spoke swiftly and softly dictating routine autopsy information as he had done thousands of times before. Rather than pay close attention to the routine introduction, Selinda's mind wandered. Her thoughts turned to a recurring dream the coroner's low talking reminiscent of the low male voice that always began her dream.

In the dream she is asked to identify her father's body. Although she was eight years old when he was killed by someone he was trying to apprehend, in the dream she is an adult. She knows she is an adult in the dream, but feels and walks awkwardly like an adolescent as she approaches the body on the stainless table in the Albany city morgue. Her father's corpse is covered to the neck by a white sheet spotted with crimson blood stain at the center of the chest. The smell isn't of death but the clean scent of her father's shaving foam Selinda would spread on her face as a child, standing beside him, pretending, to be preparing for a day's work as a police officer. Sometimes he would take a spot of foam on his finger and, with a rare smile, dab it on Selinda's nose.

In the dream Selinda expects him to remain still, but as she gets close to his body he gently opens his eyes and his head towards hers. With the same loving smile he speaks like she was still eight years old.

"I was hurt bad, Linney Bear," he said using a nickname he coined when Selinda was a toddler and would say *Selinney* when trying to pronounce her own name, "but I'm alive and when I get better I'll be back to take care of you." The anguish of her task would then crest like a wave and break into ecstatic relief. Her father's assurance feels like a caress down her cheek. At that point she would usually awaken, and cruelly, the ecstasy would carry though to her waking mood. For a moment she would feel as if her father were still alive, that her father's death was a thing of nightmares. Like swallowing a bitter liquid, Selinda would choke on the reality as she became fully awake, rapture replaced by disappointment.

Those feelings nearly overwhelmed Selinda as they punctuated the memory of the dream. She wore a painful scowl as she waited for Pak to finish his desultory remarks. Even though Selinda was distracted by the memory, she could sense Pak's voice change to a questioning tone.

"I'm sorry, what?" Selinda asked the pathologist to repeat his query.

"Detective, did you see this?" With his palm on the corpse's forehead, Pak turned the head away from Selinda to expose the neck. She moved closer to the body as if stepping out of her daydreaming state to observe what the pathologist was pointing out.

"The perpetrator is most likely right hand dominant as you probably have surmised." He spoke softly so Selinda tilted her head to focus her hearing on his voice. "The interesting thing is the cut. Most…slashings are conducted horizontally, across the neck." He paused. "In this case, the incision is vertical, as if to maximize the damage to the carotid artery."

"So you're saying this was done by a pro?" Selinda asked. *Or someone with a knowledge of anatomy. Like a doctor or a med student.*

Pak nodded. "If the artery were only nicked by a horizontal cut, pressure in the area by the victim, who I understand was an RN, might have allowed it to clot. The perpetrator was either lucky or located the precise location of the artery and sliced it in a parallel fashion. Death would be quick and nearly impossible to prevent."

"Does it suggest more than one killer?" Selinda asked.

"Not especially, but if it is one perpetrator, as I think it is, it does suggest it happened quickly, and the killer had the element of surprise. We will check blood and tissue for evidence of anesthetics or hypnotics."

"The other interesting observation to be made is that the cut looks like a surgical incision. Most knives used in homicides aren't very sharp and leave jagged, thicker wounds. This one looks as if it were made by a scalpel. Or if not, at least a very sharp knife"

Selinda considered this. There were lots of scalpels in a hospital—it would have been an easy murder weapon to dispose of without attracting attention.

Pak turned his attention towards the victim's limbs. "There don't appear to be any defensive wounds." He raised each hand to his face, getting a close look of the fingers. "There doesn't seem to be much under the fingernails for DNA." Even so he used a wooden blade to scrape underneath the nails for samples.

Selinda had seen enough autopsies to know that an internal inspection was about to follow. A large T-shaped incision would be made to open the chest, the organs would be inspected, and a large needle would be used to draw blood from the aorta for testing. Confident that the cause of Fisher's death was the neck wound and that Pak would notify her if the remainder of the grim task revealed evidence to the contrary, Selinda mumbled something about getting ready to leave.

"Okay, we'll do all the usual protocol, but for now, it looks like he bled out."

Death by exsanguination.

CHAPTER TEN

After rounds, Patience and her resident walked down the hall on the way to see their patient with cirrhosis. The resident, Dr. Jonathan Gordon, had forsaken his usual dress shirt and bowtie for surgical scrubs but his bombast was a permanent accessory. Despite his obnoxious tendencies, Patience didn't mind working with him; she regarded him as capable clinician and teacher, and not without sensitivity and compassion for patients and colleagues.

Mr. Garrison was one of the new patients presented on today's rounds to the supervising attending. During the discussion the team learned that Garrison was 50 years old, had a history of chronic hepatitis C that had most likely been contracted as a result of intravenous drug use. Hearing Mr. Garrison's story on rounds had stirred up old concerns for Patience that she could have caught hepatitis from the application of her tattoo. The ink, depicting a red rose entwined by barbs, had appeared on her shoulder blade during an alcoholic blackout she experienced the weekend she graduated from high school. For this medical student, "tattoo regret" took on a new meaning as she dreaded coming down with hepatitis or HIV infection from an alcohol-fueled youthful misstep.

The Interferon prescribed to treat Mr. Garrison's infection had led to intolerable fatigue so it was discontinued and his condition slowly progressed to a point where most of his healthy liver tissue was replaced with cirrhotic scar. Garrison's body, like most with cirrhosis, would compensate by creating small islands of functioning liver tissue but overall the organ would exist in a state of failure.

When the liver fails, fluid accumulates around it as blood can't properly flow through the organ. This accumulation, called ascites, causes the abdomen to distend, sometimes painfully, as the skin bulges outward. Pain from ascites can also be caused by a bacterial infection which can spontaneously erupt in the distended abdomen. To check the fluid for infection, a sample of the fluid was removed through a large needle the previous night while Mr. Garrison was in the emergency department. This technique can also be used to withdraw excess abdominal fluid to relieve the distention, as Patience, under Jonathan's supervision, intended.

"Let's first stop in the supply room to get a paracentesis kit," the resident said, using the formal name for the procedure. I hope we can finish expeditiously," he added. "I have to go to the E.D. to admit a GOME from the nursing home with fever. She was just discharged from this hospital two days ago."

Patience wasn't desensitized enough not to take offense to the insulting term the resident used to describe the patient. *GOME* or *GOMER* was an acronym for "Get out of my ER," used to label an elderly patient with dementia that were viewed by some as a nuisance. *And I hope you will be old and helpless one day too, Jonathan,* Patience thought.

Jonathan located the kit on the shelf of the supply room, pulled it down and handed it to Patience. "We'll also need gloves, extra four by fours, and Betadine," he instructed.

As she carried the items into Mr. Garrison's room, Patience spotted the patient in bed, on his back, head elevated about a thirty degree angle. He appeared completely immobile, except for his eyes, dull yellow orbs that tracked the pair as they entered the room and approached his side. His head didn't move and his eyes were angled downward, giving him a helpless, childlike appearance. He was paralyzed by pain from his abdomen and the inflammation of the lining of his bones that accompanied his condition.

The resident approached the piteous form and offered in an optimistic tone, "Hi, Mr. Garrison, we've returned to take some of that fluid off." He turned his body to include Patience in the conversation and continued, "I don't know if you've met student doctor McMorris, she is going to do the procedure under my supervision."

"Uh huh," Garrison said plainly.

Jonathan explained the risks of putting a sharp needle in one's abdominal cavity. Garrison winced as he moved his arm to sign the consent form.

"We're just going to talk a little about you and your condition as we work." The resident displayed a talent for sounding congenial and professional at the same time. "Don't worry if I use some medical terms that sound frightening. Feel free to stop me to ask questions."

Garrison said nothing but his jaundiced eyes shifted in Patience's direction.

Jonathan folded the sheets and blanket down to expose a protuberant abdomen that resembled a pregnant belly. The smell of sawdust and fecal matter wafted into Patience's nostrils as Jonathan moved the bedding.

"First we want to locate the landmarks for the site where will put the needle," Jonathan began, "We want to palpate for the rectus muscle and identify its borders. You can also see a good example of a caput medusa—engorged superficial veins resulting from portal hypertension." He waved his hand over worm-like bulges in the skin surrounding the patient's belly button. Getting over her uneasiness at the sight, Patience examined the area, also noticing small thin black lines twisting like a grotesque vine across Garrison's abdomen. "If you look closely," the resident continued, "you can see spider angiomata. These are small blood vessels that emerge in response to the increase in estrogen that occurs in cirrhosis."

Cruel friggin' disease, Patience thought. *Increasing estrogen in a man?*

"So one feels for the border of the rectus muscle; the needle is to be placed two to three centimeters lateral to the border to avoid the epigastric artery." Using a marker from the breast pocket of his scrubs, Jonathan drew a small x on the left side of the patient's abdomen. He deftly opened up two packs of gauze squares and squirted Betadine antiseptic into the packages to saturate the gauze. He had obviously done this procedure many times. After putting on gloves, with an expert hand he circled around the mark with the soaked pads twice.

It was time for Patience to take over. "While that's drying, let's get the other equipment together. Open up the kit," Jonathan instructed.

The kit was a plastic tray seal by paper to keep the contents sterile. When she tore the paper off, Patience fumbled the plastic tray, almost spilling all the contents and making her appear to be the opposite of expert. Her face blushed and she hoped her patient didn't notice.

Jonathan didn't acknowledge her embarrassment and kept things moving so Patience could regain her composure. "Let's just make sure the tubing is okay." The resident extended some plastic tubing, connected it to a liter glass bottle and placed the bottle on the floor. "Now put on sterile gloves and let's get started."

Patience opened a pair of sterile gloves. Within the package the gloves were wrapped in sterile paper. She placed the wrapped gloves on the window sill so she could open the wrapping while maintaining a sterile area. As she stretched the gloves over her hands, Patience peered out the window to see dark clouds off in the distance. Nearer to her the sky darkened and wind swept through the street next to St. Twigleighct, flipping the leaves on nearby oak trees, revealing their white undersides.

Once her gloves were on, Patience removed a drape from the blue plastic kit and placed it over Garrison's abdomen. Her hands trembled as she took out a small glass vial, broke the top with her thumb like she was cracking an egg with one hand, and withdrew the contents into a syringe. Her hands were shaking so badly she had trouble attaching a needle to the anesthetic-filled syringe. Patience glanced at Jonathan, who squinted his eyes a bit. Patience said innocently, "A little too much coffee this morning," although she knew the tremor was from alcohol instead.

Patience started as her pager began beeping loudly. Garrison continued to lie motionless.

Patience glanced at Jonathan with the frustration of a child.

Reading her expression, Jonathan said, "Allow me to answer for you. I wouldn't want you to break sterile technique."

Patience tilted her hip up to offer her pager and Jonathan plucked it from her scrub bottom.

"It's an outside line," he commented. Jonathan held the pager up so Patience could read the number. She recognized it. Zeke Oswald was checking up on her.

"Not important...I'll answer it as soon as we're done."

"Is it a personal call?" Jonathan asked.

"Well...no." *Stupid idiot, why didn't you just lie to him? And why can't stupid fuckin' Dr. OCD just leave it alone?*

Jonathan answered the question. "You should answer all your pages promptly, *Doctor*." Then he went to the phone beside their patient's bed to answer the page.

"Good Morning, it's Dr. Gordon, answering for Student Doctor McMorris. Yes, she's right here. The student doctor is scrubbed in on a procedure."

"Tell them I'll call them right back," Patience offered.

Jonathan ignored her. "Yes, she's performing splendidly."

But then Jonathan moved away and said in a low voice, "If she could just get her hands to stop shaking."

He then raised his voice again making it appear as if he had never said the previous statement. "Yes, of course Dr. Oswald, I will inform her of your call."

Patience was furious at what Jonathan said but too embarrassed to say anything. She turned back to her patient to focus on her work. Steadying the syringe with both hands, Patience pierced his skin underneath the landmark and injected a small amount of anesthetic. When she was done she walked over to the red plastic container mounted on the wall and deposited the syringe into it. She went back and stood at the patient's side, looking as if she didn't know what to do next.

"Okay, so get the needle," Jonathan nudged. "With the end of each step, start thinking about what comes next."

"I don't see it..." Patience had a little panic in her voice, like a teenager learning to drive. "Oh, here it is." She removed a five-inch needle covered in a plastic sheath, fumbling and almost dropping it. She removed the sheath.

"Now, bevel up." Jonathan was referring to the position of the needle. "You will want to go gently, parallel to the floor. There will be some resistance after the skin is punctured—that's the peritoneum. Just relax, after the resistance it will go in easily.

Jesus. He could be taking about sex, Patience joked to herself. *Must be hard up.* She pushed the needle through the skin and felt it pop through the tissue and advance. A dripping stream began to flow from the end of the needle.

"Attach this tube. I have to leave," Jonathan declared. "Draw out about one liter, remove the needle and hold pressure for five minutes."

During the time it took the bottle to fill, Patience considered this poor gentleman, who seemed nice enough and undeserving of such agony. While the fluid dripped into a plastic container, she would occasionally look at Garrison. If he caught her glance she sent him a small smile of empathy which was genuine and sincere. As the fluid left his abdomen, she could see his agony slowly transform in to relief.

"Feeling better?"   Patience asked after it was over.

"You have no idea...thank you, doctor. You're a saint. God bless you."

God apparently has other plans for me Patience thought as her temples began to throb again. The caffeine hadn't helped. This might very well turn out to be one of those days when only a couple of bottles of Potter's would provide relief from her headache, tremors, and the stress of the day.

CHAPTER ELEVEN

After considering the coroner's suggestion that Caleb Fisher was killed with a scalpel, Selinda called the hospital in the hopes of rounding up scalpels as evidence. The president's office directed her to the head of Environmental Services, who informed her they weren't responsible for collecting sharps for removal, it was the job of Laboratory Services. The director of Laboratory Services explained that used scalpels were dropped into plastic containers. These sharps containers, as they were called, were checked weekly, usually Mondays, and when determined to be two thirds full, placed by laboratory staff into larger containers. The larger containers were stored by the shipping dock until they were picked up by a medical waste company.

Selinda surmised that since the murder occurred early Wednesday, it was unlikely that if a scalpel was used for the killing and disposed of in a small wall-mounted container it would be found in a large container by the shipping dock. Furthermore, confiscating large amounts of medical waste located that far away from the crime scene could become a bureaucratic and logistical nightmare for the detective. To Selinda, at this point in the investigation, the effort involved in attempting to take the large containers into evidence and sorting through them wasn't worth the small chance that they contained the murder weapon. Her job often involved decisions such as this one where limited resources had to be prioritized. So while Patience McMorris was attending to her jaundiced charge and generating sharp waste of her own, Selinda returned to St. Twigleighct to collect small sharps containers as evidence and take them to the precinct's forensics lab.

Upon arrival to the hospital, Selinda met the director of laboratory services, a tall man wearing grey dress pants, a worn dress shirt with a frayed collar over a polyester tie, and unkempt greasy hair in need of a cut. His Hush Puppies squeaked as he walked the hospital corridor, pushing a metal cart to the area where the body was discovered. There was no sharps container in the bone room (it wasn't considered necessary) but Selinda picked the room as a starting point. In the doorway to the bone room, the yellow caution tape was dangling loose on the frame. She wasn't surprised by this finding but she decided to step in to the crime scene room to take a quick look. Looking around the room, the detective felt like something was different about the room she had inspected the morning of the murder. The grimacing corpse of Caleb Fisher of course was removed and the blood stain lightened to the point where it was barely recognizable on the floor, but there seemed to be something missing. After scanning the interior a few times, Selinda realized it was the cart that held the x-ray films that had been removed.

As Selinda made a mental note to ask the hospital administration the whereabouts of the x-ray cart, her cell phone rang. She slid the phone out of its belt clip and flipped it open.

"Detective Bruchart," she answered.

The nasal voice of the police station's operator responded. "Ma'am, you have an outside call from the Saint Twigleighct Medical Center administrator." The operator pronounced the hospital's name correctly.

Concerned that the lab director would become impatient, Selinda poked her head outside the door, covering the cell's microphone with her hand, she whispered, *"Be right with you."* Then, into the phone: "Put him through." Selinda waited and when the phone's background noise changed slightly, she greeted the person on the line.

"Hello, Detective Bruchart," a voice said confidently and cheerfully. "Anderson Morris here, Vice President of Operations at Saint Twigleighct. I'm calling to see when the radiology reading room can be put back into service."

Selinda was used to people getting right to the point, but she found it curious how he didn't ask how the investigation was going. "Typically we reserve crime scenes for a period of seventy-two hours in case something else comes up. I'm actually here at the reading room right now, and it looks like someone has been in here after we left." She omitted the fact that the caution tape was compromised—maybe he knew that already and would reveal this knowledge accidentally.

"Oh?"

The detective paused to see if Morris would offer any unsolicited information. After a moment of silence, she continued, "Could you tell me the whereabouts of the x-ray films that were here at the time of the murder?"

It was his turn to pause. I'm...not sure, but probably they were moved so the radiologist could interpret them."

Selinda wasn't sure if the films were important to the case and Morris's explanation seemed reasonable to explain their disappearance. She was also aware that the crime scene team had catalogued the names of the names of the patients on the x-rays. "We'll need the interpretations of the x-rays when they become available."

"I'll start working on getting the releases for them."

"Thank you," she said and then disconnected.

Selinda rejoined the lab director and they began to hunt for nearby sharps containers. When the couple located one, the lab director unfastened the box's retaining strap and pulled the red container up by the handles located on the top of the unit. He then placed it upright on the cart for transport. Searching for and locating ten of the containers nearest to the bone room, Selinda wondered how important this task would be to generating clues to help solve the case. She asked herself, would the killer really dispose of the murder weapon in the nearest container? Did she expect to find fingerprints on a scalpel handle? If the killing were premeditated, surely the perpetrator would have worn gloves or wiped it clean. What if she found many bloody knives? The lab director did say that since the reading room was located away from places in the hospital that used scalpels like the surgical department, most of the containers would hold used syringes and needles. But if Selinda did find excessive amounts of the instruments, how would she narrow the search to identify the murder weapon? That would be a lot of blood to identify. Out of this desperate question, Selinda arrived at a practical approach-start not by analyzing the blood remnants on the blades, but by checking the handles for fingerprints. Most hospital-used scalpels wouldn't have any fingerprints as sterile gloves would be used to handle them from start to finish. If the handle had prints, perhaps it was used for something else that didn't require sterility, like an incision designed to harm not heal. She would plan to have the handles dusted for prints. If any were positively identified, then the blood could be tested to see if it was a match for Caleb Fisher's. A long shot, of course, but one that could quickly turn this case in the right direction. *Quick and dirty,* Selinda's forensics teacher used to say, to describe an approach with low potential but huge upsides. But, as usual, Selinda's plans were plagued by self-doubt.

The young detective wasn't as seasoned as her teacher seemed to be, but she did have a sense that most crimes were not solved by casting such a wide net anyway. However, methodical attention to details had the capacity to produce useful leads.

Still, Selinda worried she was wasting time trying to chase down something that might not even be the weapon used to create a deadly slit in the victim's carotid artery. Although it was his idea that a scalpel had been used, Dr. Pak had also said that it could have also been a new razor or very sharp knife of another kind. But so far no leads have been obtained by what was considered the best method of murder investigation: interviewing potential witnesses and known associates.

Despite this worry, Selinda rolled the ten sharps containers out to her car and placed them in the trunk. While driving back to the precinct, she could hear the containers shifting as the car turned, producing a sound like the clinking of glasses during a champagne toast. She felt like she wouldn't be popping any champagne corks any time soon.

She pulled up to the precinct's front entrance and called for a technician to help transport the containers to the lab. Selinda and the technician loaded them into a rolling bin and she accompanied him to the lab where the chief lab technician, Les Graham, was waiting.

"You know, detective, my mother told me never to play with knives," Les said playfully as the technician rolled the bin into the lab. The room was lined with jet black counters and shelves holding clear and brown glass and plastic reagent bottles of various sizes. There were center islands of black countertops and several stainless steel tables.

Selinda was used to Les's adolescent jokes, to her he seemed like a teenager in a middle-aged man's body. "Yes, Les," Selinda replied, eyes rolling. She had heard similar quips from him many times before.

Referring to the city pathologist Dr. Pak, Les continued, "So the great and powerful Oz thinks the vic was done in by a scalpel. Has the old boy gone completely *senile?*"

"That's just one of the possibilities," Selinda added with mock authority.

Les examined the top of one of containers, then took a box cutter and cut off the top. He spilled the contents on to a steel table. The table had raised edges to prevent items and liquids from falling over the edge, and as the used medical waste spread out on the surface, the sound made by the combination of plastic, metal, and glass striking the table had a musical quality. The sound had a harsh intensity which dropped off suddenly, causing Selinda's ears to tingle as she eyed the pile. She spotted several green-handled blades.

"We'll see if we come up with anything," Les sighed at the potentially arduous task of forensically analyzing ten such piles, not sounding so cheerful this time.

"I was thinking," Selinda offered, "if scalpels are only supposed to be handled with gloves, they shouldn't have fingerprints. So, start by dusting the handles for prints. If you get a hit—"

"Thanks, but I don't think we'll be needing any more of your help," Les snapped, scowling at her. Selinda was well aware of this side of Les as well. His comment was full of sarcasm and revealed to Selinda what he thought her idea of analyzing the medical waste for clues. She was accustomed to condescending challenges from her colleagues; some of the challenges came in response to her inexperience, and some were a result of sexism.

Stick to your guns, Linney Bear, her father would say when she came to him with a problem. *If you believe what you're doing is right, stick to it.*

She figured, just like dealing with an adolescent, there was no use trying reason with Les. It also wouldn't benefit her to pull rank to exert her authority over his teenaged will. She found, because of her gender, even subordinates didn't exhibit the same amount of respect afforded her male counterparts. Selinda also wasn't looking to jeopardize her investigation by some childish showdown. Allow him to have his tantrum now, in the end Les would do the work and do it well.

"Okay," Selinda said mildly, turning away and walking out. She then headed to the laboratory where electronic equipment was analyzed. The door to the lab had frosted glass, and on the edge of the glass where there was a small sliver of clear glass, black construction paper prevented anyone from getting even a small glimpse inside. Certain the door was locked as usual, Selinda rapped her knuckles on the glass.

She heard shuffling noises from inside the lab and then the lock's chamber clacked and the door cracked open. A bespectacled green eye peered out from below her line of sight. She recognized it as belonging to Louden Andrews, Albany PD's hermetic information technology specialist.

"Who is it?" he asked.

"Louden, it's Detective Bruchart. I wanted to know the latest on the Fisher case."

"Hold on."

The door swung open to reveal a slight, fair-complexioned man dressed in a worn blue dress shirt and khaki pants. Selinda found his face to be cute in a nerdy sort of way. There was a lot of potential for a makeover. His sandy-colored oily hair was uncombed on one side. The detective would have suspected that he had just rolled out of bed if it weren't for the fact that this was Andrews's usual appearance. The technician stood there, motionless, staring at Selinda with a moonstruck expression.

"Louden?" Selinda asked, trying to break the state.

"Yes?" Andrews replied, the expression remaining.

"The Fisher case?"

"Oh yes...sorry." The spell broke. He spoke quickly, like a hyperactive child. "I have received a mobile telephone and a CPU from the victim's apartment." Andrews often spoke in technical jargon and would become inpatient when asked to explain his words, but from experience, Selinda knew that by "CPU," he meant the part of a personal computer that contained the processor and various forms of memory. The other parts, mouse, keyboard, and display weren't vital to his analysis.

Selinda followed him to a corner of the lab where he picked up a BlackBerry and held it up for display.

Andrews continued. "I'll work on getting the calls the victim recently made, make a list and hopefully get it to you by the end of the day. You'll probably want to start working on a court order to obtain the names and addresses..."

As he continued to talk, Selinda gently took the cell phone from his thin, waxy grip. *No time like the present,* she thought a she pressed an up arrow button to reveal prior calls. *Jeannie* was the last call made. The name was highlighted so Selinda pressed the send button.

Andrews made a plaintive noise as Selinda turned away from him, cocked her head with the phone at her ear, and paced in the other direction.

"Hello?" an insecure female voice said after five rings.

"Hello. This is Detective Selinda Bruchart from the Albany PD. Whom am I speaking to?"

"Jean Bradley. Oh my God, like, I didn't know what to think when I saw Caleb's caller ID came in," the voice said shakily. It was high pitched, like a young girl.

"What do you mean?" the detective asked in her least threatening voice.

There was a pause. "Like, it gave me the chills, like a call from a...*ghost.*" With the last word she exhaled a brief sob.

Selinda gave her a moment, then asked softly. "Ms. Bradley...Jean...how did you know Caleb Fisher?"

"He's dead, right? I heard he was dead."

"I'm afraid so. How did you hear the news?"

"From his...roommate." Her squeaky words then started to come more rapidly. "When I didn't hear from him, like, and I heard about the murder at the hospital, I called her and she told me."

"Were you close to him?"

"Yes," Jean sniffed in an effort to hold back tears. "I have to call his family to find out where the funeral is..." she gulped hard.

"I know this is difficult, but can I ask you a few questions, Jean? You might be able to help with the investigation." Selinda sat down at one of the benches, pinched the phone between her ear and her shoulder and removed he notepad and pen from her pocket as she glanced back to see Andrews skulking into a corner to work on something else.

Selinda didn't hear an answer but she decided to start asking anyway. "Did you talk to him that night?"

"No," Jean began sullenly. "He usually called me when he got to work but he didn't...that night."

"Was that unusual?"

She sounded on the verge of tears again. "No. Like, I guess he didn't *always* call. Now I wish he did," she finished in a small voice.

"Did you notice anything out of the ordinary with Caleb over the last week or so?"

"No, not really," Jean replied, but Selinda thought she sounded unsure of her declaration. "I mean, like, I thought he was sleeping with his roommate again."

"What makes you say that?"

"Nothing, really it's silly."

Selinda didn't interrupt.

"He started wearing the cologne again—the one I know *she* likes." The sentence was peppered with jealousy. "But I asked him," Jean sighed. "He said he wasn't, and I believed him."

"Were you mad? I mean, I would have been if my boyfriend was back with his ex." Jean didn't correct Selinda's use of the term "boyfriend." The fact was Selinda hadn't had a boyfriend since she was in the seventh grade. She rarely dated, hardly ever with the same guy more than once or twice. She was still a virgin, married only to her job.

"No, I thought I was just being paranoid."

"Do you know anyone who had a grudge against Caleb or was otherwise an enemy?"

"I didn't mean to say that I thought she did it."

I'll be the judge of that. "Of course not." Selinda attempted a soothing tone, but wasn't quite successful. "I meant former friends, business associates, people at the hospital."

"Oh, no."

"Did Caleb talk much about what was going on at work?"

"No. One time he told me he was trying to, like, improve some oxygen thingy in the intensive care unit, but most of the time he didn't talk about work."

"What did you two talk about, then?"

"He's...he was really into music. And computers, his computer, that's all he seemed to want to talk about lately. And he was spending a lot of time in chat rooms." The jealousy was back in her Jean's voice.

Selinda took note. "Do you know, was he close with his family?"

"I don't think so. His Mom and Dad still live in California, where Caleb grew up. I wouldn't be able to tell you, like, the last time he spoke to them." The statement sounded more like a question. "Oh, God, I have to call them..."

Selinda, done with her questions, relied on a detective's staple to close the interview. "If you can think of anything else-anything at all—please give me a call. Albany PD, homicide division, ask for Detective Bruchart."

"I remember. Selinda, that's a pretty name."

After pressing the disconnect button, Selinda looked up to find Louden Andrews absorbed in his work across the lab. "Thanks, Louden. I'll leave the phone here for you to work on." She placed the phone on the bench and showed herself out.

Walking to the vending machine to get a Diet Coke, Selinda reflected on her conversation. "His computer, that's all he seemed to want to talk about lately," Fisher's girlfriend had said. *So let's take a look at that computer.* Selinda began rubbing her temple, thinking about long hours at the victim's computer, searching for anything that could help solve his murder when another homicide detective, recent user of the vending machine, stopped her.

"Bad hair day?" he asked, with a tone that was half patronizing and half empathetic. Detective Joe Wellard had been part of the Albany homicide force for about five years. In his late thirties, he didn't appear the typical homicide detective, he was thin, attractive, with clear skin and a full head of thick wavy brown hair.

"Just another day in paradise," Selinda answered.

"Why don't we go out for drinks tonight? I excel at the art of foot massages, great for stress on the job," he said, trying to sound inviting.

Ugh, Selinda thought. "I don't drink," she told him. "And I don't think you wife would appreciate you saying that," she said walking past him to the soda machine.

"She doesn't have to know. What's the matter with you?" He asked, more teasing than accusatory, as if to say *Don't you like men?*

Selinda shot back. "Nothing's the matter with *me*. I don't date married men." She slipped a dollar into the front of the machine and pressed the button.

Being an attractive, young woman in a male dominated profession, Selinda had probably heard it all when it came to advances from her married colleagues. *My wife doesn't understand me, my wife's ill, we're separated, we have an open marriage.*

Wellard was trying a different approach. He came up behind her. "We're all worried that your...needs aren't being fulfilled."

"Thanks for all your consideration of my...needs," Selinda answered with mock sweetness, turning towards him and punctuating her statement by lifting the can of soda towards her licentious colleague and opening it with a loud *pop*. The action caused some of the spray to hit Wellard in the face. "Now if you'll excuse me, I have work to do."

While confident that she had handled the encounter appropriately, making herself clear and putting that creep in his place, the conversation did leave Selinda thinking about how nice a bubble bath and a neck massage from a handsome man would be. She raised the can to her mouth and drank, the sharp edges scratching her lips as the sweet taste flowed across her tongue.

CHAPTER TWELVE

1989

The burns healed and the scars faded but the thirst didn't. The sensitivity to light prevented Zeke from going out in the daylight (sunscreen didn't work) and he was restless at night, so he adopted a nocturnal existence, staying home during the day to sleep. He was able to replicate his work with the mice, but the project hardly seemed worth pursuing if the treatment traded alcoholism for a lust for blood. On the other hand, if Zeke could figure out the underlying of the strange craving, perhaps it could be eliminated through further research.

Nevertheless, Zeke was spending less time in the lab and more time in the hospital. The hospital provided him access to specialized testing to help him find the cause of his anemia and the thirst for blood was so strong that the hospital's blood bank beckoned with the promise of blood to drink. He picked up as many overnight shifts as he could.

Zeke had devised a plan to run tests on his blood by ordering them under the names of certain hospitalized patients. He sought out patients on alternative level of care, which was sort of a hospital limbo for patients awaiting a bed in a nursing home. When patients were too chronically ill to be discharged home with conditions like Alzheimer's dementia, but not acutely ill, this was a level of care that didn't require much attention and therefore didn't use many hospital resources. As a result, Zeke felt tests performed on such patients were likely to go unnoticed. He would find an unused patient label in the chart or in the patient's room, apply it to a tube of his blood, order the blood test, leaving the ordering doctors name blank. Most of the time the results were placed in the chart before his shift was over, so Zeke could remove them, leaving no evidence as this was still during a time before computerized reporting of tests was widespread.

Zeke had been running tests to try to identify the exact source of his anemia. He hadn't been able to recall the name of the disease that caused those affected to crave blood and it was so rare he couldn't find it in standard textbooks. He knew it was a type of porphyria, a disease characterized by the abnormal accumulation of porphyrins, chemicals that play a role in the body's manufacture of hemoglobin, the protein used to carry oxygen from the lungs through the blood to the tissues.

A build-up of porhyrins can cause a wide variety of maladies, including severe abdominal pain, vomiting, nerve damage, and skin blistering in sunlight. Anemia can result from red blood cell destruction. Porhyrins in excess poison the red cell, causing them to eventually burst apart. Certain types of porphyria are characterized by psychiatric disturbances like hallucinations, depression, anxiety and paranoia. George III, the British ruler during the American revolutionary period, may have suffered from the disease. Some cite porphyria as the cause of the King's mental deterioration.

A blood smear, where a drop of blood is spread on a glass slide for microscopic analysis, had revealed schistocytes in Zeke's blood. The irregularly shaped fragments of red cells were the shrapnel left behind as the cells explode. Chemical tests on his blood had confirmed an excess of porphyrins, specifically due to abnormally low activity of an enzyme used to make hemoglobin.

Uroporphyrinogen III cosynthase, or UROS for short. *There must be some similarity between UROS and the gene I was targeting, A2p2* Zeke had thought as he read the results. *The liposome treatment was designed to affect only the A2p2 gene, but my UROS supply must have been disabled by the treatment as well and now I've developed porphyria because of it.* Porphyria caused by a deficiency of UROS was also referred to as Gunther's disease, after the scientist who first characterized it. *Will it be permanent?* Zeke asked himself as he came up the theory to explain his sudden illness.

Permanent or not, Zeke felt he had to do something about the thirst. Water obviously wasn't going to work so he tried soda, sports drinks, coffee, black tea, herbal tea, tomato juice. He tried to quench it with red wine, even though he had no interest in drinking alcohol. One night he had brought home a bottle from the local liquor store he used to visit quite frequently.

Returning after a one month absence, Zeke had recognized the cashier as he approached the register to make his purchase. Placing the bottle on the counter to be bagged, Zeke had thought the employee looked at him as to say "Where have *you* been?" But in reality the cashier hadn't recognized him at all.

Back at his apartment, Zeke had hastily poured a few ounces of the cabernet in a water glass. He had sniffed the glass's contents but found it smelled more like cork than wine. Holding the glass up, he had examined the dark red liquid and pondered his fate, wondering where things would lead if the wine was effective in quenching his thirst. Would he introduce alcohol back into his life, would it now replace water? There was no reason to think it would help with porphyria.

He hadn't wondered for long, however, as a swig of the wine had produced an unpleasant numbness and taste on his lips, gums and teeth. It reminded Zeke of a time when he was hit in the mouth with a football as a kid.

After more trial and error, what Zeke had found to be effective was scalding hot water. In order to work the water had to be just at the point of boiling, so he would fill a teapot, place it on the stove and wait until it the pot just started to whistle faintly. He would look like a dog waiting for his dinner as he watched the teapot. When the water reached the correct temperature, he poured the steaming water into a clear glass mug (porcelain didn't work) and quickly downed about six ounces. It didn't burn, in fact drinking the hot liquid led to a release of his thirst that would last for several hours.

Zeke knew from his medical studies that drinking very hot liquids could cause cancer of the esophagus. In Argentina, it was well established that the cancer was commonly linked to drinking nearly-boiling tea through a metal spoon. However, in Zeke's current frame of mind he was only thinking about the moment and a hard-to-come-by solution to his thirst and not some remote risk. Getting control of the urge enabled Zeke to get through the days and almost get through the nights.

Zeke's evenings were full of disquiet. He had begun to dislike being alone; he longed to be out in public and no longer felt paralyzing social anxiety. Zeke found himself now able to initiate conversations with strangers without trouble and had developed of talking smoothly without a hint of self-consciousness.

On a hot Friday night in August, Zeke decided to go out to join the Baltimore nightlife. He chose to go to a club because he felt the loud music would distract his mind away from its feeling of restlessness. Also developing in Zeke was a desire for human interaction, a real departure from the social isolation with which he was so comfortable before...he changed.

Zeke began preparing for the night by showering. He left day-old stubble on his face—the style of the time made him appear less pale. He applied hair mousse, deodorant, and cologne. He dressed in a cream-colored silk button-down shirt, which also downplayed his pallor, brown slacks, and brown leather shoes. Stopping by in the mirror just before he left his apartment, Zeke unbuttoned one more button to expose more of his chest.

He ventured into a club on South Clinton Street, on a site made famous by frequent visits by Edgar Allan Poe when he lived in Baltimore in the mid nineteenth century. The club was named Usher House, after one of Poe's famous gothic tales.

Zeke walked confidently through the front door, heel to toe, shoulders back, neck extended, arms swinging casually. He stopped, arms comfortably at his sides, and scanned the club like a lion admiring his territory. He seemed to breathe in the beat of the music, pounding out speakers, creating musical haziness typical of a late eighties dance club.

In the front of club stood the bar, large, oblong shaped, circling the bartenders and a sizable liquor rack. The undulating lights from the dance floor flashed through the different colored bottles, creating a pleasant visual effect. Rather than being drawn to the bar to drink, Zeke bypassed the bar to the dance floor area. He was there for a different reason: to satisfy a need to socialize.

Zeke stood as if he were trying to locate someone, and took in the scene. The dance floor was crowded with couples and groups of women dancing to the beat of the Fine Young Cannibals. On the sides and behind the floor were semicircular booths with tables. To avoid appearing conspicuous, Zeke didn't pause for too long, moving to his left, passing the first booth which contained five or six college-age women. One was talking with another by leaning over cupping her neighbor's ear with her hand. The scent of hairspray filled Zeke's nose as he strode by.

The second booth was empty, and Zeke was considering sitting there when he noticed an odd number of people in the third: one man and two women, attractive, affluent-looking, in their mid-twenties. The man, dressed in an oxford button-down shirt and hair swept back, was sitting next to woman in a dark blue business suit. The woman had an abundance of make-up and hairspray—a severe kind of look that was typical of the day. The two were oriented slightly facing each other, while the other woman was facing slightly away and didn't appear to be part of their conversation. She resembled the first woman, like a relative, and wore an ivory-colored blouse with a high neckline and slightly more material at the shoulders. As he approached, Zeke could see she was also wearing a tight-fitting black skirt. Her dirty blonde hair was teased high over an alabaster face accentuated with heavy rouge. Her lips, Zeke noticed as she sipped from a small candy-red straw, were a lustrous burgundy. Through all the mature coloring, her hazel eyes were slightly wide, giving her face a child-like innocence.

Seeing as though the group might benefit by the addition of another person, Zeke stopped at the table and smiled.

"Hi, I'm supposed to meet some friends here but I don't see them, do you mind if I join you while I wait?" he asked in a tone loud enough to be heard over the music but not pressured. Perfect.

The man glanced at the empty table next to them then looked back at Zeke. He had a smug but gregarious appearance. "I don't see why not," he replied, sliding over to make room. Extending his hand to Zeke, he said, "I'm Kyle, and this is Emily and Jessie."

Zeke raised his brow and brightened his eyes. "Hi. Zeke."

"Hi," the two women said cheerfully in unison.

Emily, the woman seated next to Kyle, asked Zeke "Have you been waiting long? Where are your friends?"

Zeke was surprised at how relaxed he felt speaking to strangers. "I don't know exactly. I left the hospital a little later than them so I may be late—they may have left to go elsewhere by now." Lying now seemed effortless to him.

"Hospital?" Kyle asked. "What do you do? Doctor?"

"Yes. At Johns Hopkins." Zeke use to describe himself as a scientist but that didn't seem accurate anymore.

"What kind of doctor?" Emily said with a playful breathlessness. She gently elbowed Jessie as if to say, *did you hear that, Jessie?* Jessie, watching the conversation with unassuming eyes, didn't seem ready to speak.

When he replied, Zeke caught Jessie's eyes briefly, then spoke, lingering a bit on her eyes. "Internist. I'm a resident."

"Interesting!" Kyle said, in a tone that punctuated the conversation. "Well, what do you say Em, shall we hit the dance floor?"

"Uh..." She looked at Jessie, who seemed to give tacit approval. "Uh, sure."

"Can I get you a drink while I'm up?" Kyle offered. "We're drinking Long Island Iced Teas." Zeke's stomach turned at the thought and the look of temptation in Kyle's eyes. Zeke unconsciously wiped his lips with his hand, recalling the numb feeling from the cabernet.

"No thanks, I'm driving."

"How about you, Jess?"

"No thanks. I think I've had enough."

Kyle held out his hand to Emily. Zeke stood to allow the couple to leave the booth. He sat back down and slid closer to Jessie until he was about a foot and a half away. Turning her head, she followed the couple as they made their way to the dance floor. This motion exposed to her neck to Zeke, the sweet smell of her perfume, roses and orange blossoms, soap and hairspray wafting up to him. The scent, along with the sight of her neck, caused Zeke to feel warm in his chest and throat. He felt his heartbeat quicken with excitement.

"So," Zeke said casually, "that your sister and her husband?"

"You can tell, huh?" Jessie said with a cute half-smile. "Kyle's her boyfriend actually. They've been dating for, like, two years already." To go with her smile, she had a cute voice, high-pitched yet mature. "Think he'll marry her?" She broadened her smile.

Zeke let the conversation hang for a moment. "I dunno. They seem like a nice couple."

"Yes they are," Jessie agreed with a tone suggesting pretend impatience, as if she were tired of hearing it. "So," she said to Zeke, echoing the phrasing of his first question, "You're a doctor, huh? You like it?"

"It has its ups and downs. One thing is: it's never boring. How about you, what do you do?"

"I'm an administrative assistant." She paused. "It's *always* boring."

Zeke laughed, and Jessie seemed to like it. She giggled adorably. "You wanna dance?" she asked brightly.

"Love to."

On the dance floor, Zeke felt like he was in a euphoric dream. He couldn't recall that last time he danced sober. His head was clear and his body felt energized, dancing to the beat of a remake of Vicki Sue Robinson's "Turn the Beat Around" with a beautiful woman who declared "I love this one!" when she recognized the melody. Zeke could see Kyle and Emily at the other side of the dance floor smiling approvingly at the new couple.

Dancing to a few songs, Jessie's look turned sexy, her face flushed, not quite overheated, her hair slightly tousled. Zeke had a grin of satisfaction as he watched Jessie enjoying herself. Occasionally she would move closer to him, draping her wrists on his shoulders as she swayed her hips, soon breaking the contact and turning away, tilting her head back to look at Zeke's face.

"What's that perfume you're wearing?" Zeke asked.

"*Beautiful.* You like it?"

Zeke grinned in approval.

After a few more songs, Jessie put her mouth near Zeke's ear. "I have to go to the little girl's room."

"Okay," Zeke shouted over the music.

As he waited on the outskirts of the dance floor, his arms casually at his sides, Zeke waited. After a song finished, he began to wonder if he would see

Jessie again. Imagining she didn't return, however, Zeke felt no insecure resentment—only an appreciation for every moment of their encounter. He scanned the dance floor but could no longer find her sister and her sister's boyfriend. Despite this, felt a calm anticipation that he would continue this evening with her. He felt very attracted to Jessie, with her beautiful skin, expressive face, and intoxicating perfume which had become slightly musky with the sweat of their dancing.

Zeke smelled the scent again as she rejoined him.

"Hi!" she said sprightly, eyebrows raised.

"Hi." Zeke replied, with a warm smile.

"Hi," she repeated, tittering.

"Hi," he said again.

There was a pause as Jessie pursed her lips. "Soooo...do you want to go somewhere...more quiet?" she asked.

"Sure," Zeke said, nodding. Jessie looked relieved as if she were anxious about asking and her eyelids settled and fluttered with the look of desire.

Outside on the club's sidewalk, the music could still be heard but the two could communicate in a much more normal tone. In the dark night, the neon *Usher House* sign burned brightly and the air was humid but not stuffy like the inside of the club.

When it appeared she wasn't going to say anything, Zeke asked, "So, where to?"

Jessie gave him a long scrutinizing look. "Ugh, I *never* do this." She sighed and started walking. Zeke joined her, matching her stride. The two were now looking forward as they strolled at a lazy pace.

Without looking at Zeke, she offered, "Should we go back to my room? I'm staying at the

Marriot." By way of explanation she added, "I'm here on business. My sister lives in Baltimore." She sounded playful as she followed up her offer with a warning, "I'm not promising you anything, *Doctor.*"

Still looking forward, Zeke said softly but directly, raising his hand as if to pledge, "I know. No means no."

"Yes." She giggled her adorable, nervous laugh again. "I mean no," she corrected herself with a tone of mock prerogative."

"Now, what about your sister?' Zeke inquired.

"I told her in the bathroom that I was making it an early night. Oh here's my rental car. Or would you rather take your car?" The pure moment was tarnished by the reminder that Zeke lied about driving, leading him to lie again to this woman who obviously had given him her trust.

"No. That way you won't have to come back to pick it up. But I'll drive."

She seemed happy with the plan but cautious. "Okay, but be careful, the insurance only covers me. Oh, but you're sober. Good idea."

"I'll be careful with your car. And you. I promise."

Jessie tittered.

In Jessie's hotel room the seating arrangements were at first a little awkward. She sat on the edge of the twin bed, one leg folded underneath her, trying to appear casual. But she seemed nervous to Zeke, and her arms were folded across her chest like the room was too cold for her. Zeke took a nearby armchair.

After a few uncomfortable questions from Zeke about the weather which were met with one word replies, Jessie began, "Zeke, I like you. But like I said before I don't normally take men I've just met back to my hotel room…" She sighed. "I think I've had a little too much to drink…" Her voice trailed off as she was momentarily at a loss for words. "Can you tell me a little bit about yourself?" she asked, wrinkling her face in a painful expression, her voice high-pitched and unsure.

"Sure," Zeke said reassuringly.

"Do *you* do this often?"

"No."

"You're not married, are you?"

"Nope. Currently unattached."

"Have you had a lot of…girlfriends?"

"Two."

Jessie looked at Zeke for a long time, staring at his eyes and face.

"Tell me more," she said gently, her voice dropping in tone, the nervousness gone.

Zeke was thoroughly disarmed by the attention and the intimacy of the request. But he returned her gaze, wanting to share life's details with her. He talked to her about growing up in New Mexico, his relationship with his parents, how he ended up at Johns Hopkins. A heartwarming feeling, new to Zeke, began seeping in.

He stopped talking and both were silent. Even though Jessie was seated slightly higher than he, she tilted her head downward, her eyes glancing upward. Zeke's desire began to boil over as he watched her breathing slowly and deeply. But it was desire never experienced before. He wanted to kiss her, but also drink her in, to take control of her.

He rose from his chair and walked slowly over to the bed and sat close to her. Jessie leaned back against a pillow, not losing eye contact. Zeke took her hands gently and looked deeply into her eyes. She raised her chin slightly and brought her lips forward. Zeke moved his head in to meet her lips.

Jessie moaned a soft approval.

Zeke parted his lips and Jessie's followed. Their tongues brushed each other as they kissed more deeply but still softly. Her mouth was wet, Zeke was breathing her in, taking her into his lungs, heart and if he still had one, his soul.

Jessie moaned again as Zeke pulled at the nape of her neck with his mouth. He felt his excitement crest as he moved his lips up to her jawline, sensing her pulse and the scent of her perfume.

Zeke cradled her head in his hands as they kissed again. Jessie unbuttoned her blouse slowly and slid it off her pretty shoulders, revealing an ivory-colored silk bra. He took her left hand and kissed her palm, burying his nose and mouth in the curve. The scent of the skin of her hand excited him further, and his jaw began to tense, hardening his breathing. His lips moved up to kiss and nibble on the inside of her wrist.

Zeke felt his eyes narrow and Jessie, noticing the subtle change, murmured "What...?" when she saw his face.

Zeke's desire then turned murderous. This was a different kind of lust. His eyes widened, his ears went back, and his mouth opened into a violent grimace. His lips had settled in the fold of Jessie's arm, and the scent of her body was so powerful that he began to feel as if things could go out of control. He was terrified that wouldn't be able to fight the urge to tear at her flesh with his teeth, puncture a vessel and suck the intoxicating blood.

Zeke, panting, pushed himself away from the inviting woman he had just met tonight and away from the bed that should have become a place of bliss and not of a crime.

"Zeke...what's the matter?" Jessie called him by name in a sad, confused voice with a bittersweet familiarity. She crossed her arms again and rubbed the inside of her elbow with her hand.

"I'm sorry...*Fuck!* I have to go," Zeke muttered, ashamed.

"Zeke!" Jessie cried, but he said nothing more as he moved sideways towards the door, staring at the poor woman who had given him the human gift of trust. There was an intense feeling of contrition as he realized his abuse of this trust. He slammed the heavy metal door, pushing it with both hands, holding it shut as if to try to contain the miscreation that his life had become.

CHAPTER THIRTEEN

Present Day

Though that night in Baltimore in 1989 was now far removed from Zeke's present existence roaming the halls of St. Twigleighct, caring for the ill at night, he still struggled with the urge to quench his thirst with blood. So far he hadn't given in to the temptation in Albany, but he knew it would be just as easy to do it in this hospital as it was in the past.

Before, when he had less control over his cravings, he would take the blood from a hospital's blood bank by ordering extra units that wouldn't be used as it was intended, for transfusion. He would procure it by picking up the blood himself, telling the blood bank technician that the patient couldn't wait for delivery, or by lifting it from the patient's room. Already warmed by the blood bank (blood is banked in a refrigerator), Zeke would transfer the blood to a paper coffee cup, first pouring the thick liquid out and then squeezing the plastic bag to empty it completely. Confining himself to a randomly-selected on call room, outfitted with a cot, mattress, chair and phone, Zeke would sit on the edge of the mattress and swallow the blood slowly, savoring it like a single malt scotch. It burned the throat like whiskey, and, in addition to the quench, created a euphoric feeling similar to alcohol intoxication. It was unlikely that he would be discovered in such a room, which was designed for individual use for overnight physicians to sleep in less busy times, but the practice was risky as the blood was sometimes noticed to be missing.

After an email had circulated that some blood bank blood had been unaccounted for, and out of a fear of being discovered, Zeke had decided to abruptly leave Johns Hopkins. He'd quit his research fellowship, citing "personal reasons," abandoning the hope of discovering a genetic treatment for addiction and perhaps the clue to reversing the damage he inflicted upon himself. Working only during dark hours, keeping his illness a dark secret, the research work had suffered to the point of futility anyway. Maybe he could resume his work sometime in the future, at a different place. The threat of being caught and exposed was more dangerous than the disease itself. Besides, going to jail or having his privileges to practice medicine or conduct medical research revoked would perhaps irrevocably harm his cause.

Having finished the clinical portion of his training, the institution had allowed him to graduate and become an independently practicing physician. After the night in the Baltimore hotel with Jessie, Zeke had decided he would rather save a life than take one, and after he'd left Johns Hopkins, ruining the best opportunity of his life, Zeke began an almost desultory lifestyle. He sought out and took temporary jobs as a hospital-based doctor who cared for admitted patients overnight while most doctors were out of the hospital. Zeke worked in Louisiana, Washington, Montana, and then in New York, never staying more than three years to limit his potential exposure.

Throughout the years Zeke kept his secret. No one knew what had happened to him on that sultry night in 1989. Being a doctor addicted to blood was like an alcoholic who could only work as a bartender. True, he could avoid proximity to blood by becoming an administrator or academic, but his drive to care for the sick was too strong to give up the practice of medicine.

He had dealt with his thirst through bank blood theft and social isolation until he stumbled upon a Twelve Step program in Great Falls, Montana. He masqueraded as a heroin addict, rather than an alcoholic, and the motivations for this deceit were unclear to Zeke. Perhaps he'd reasoned, the fewer elements of truth to his story, the more difficult it would be for someone to put the pieces together, or perhaps he had been embarrassed to admit he couldn't control his drinking and somehow, an inability to control a narcotic addiction was more acceptable. Following the principles of the twelve steps, and the advice and support of his sponsor, Miles, Zeke had been able to abstain from drinking purloined blood, with a few exceptions. He'd come to realize that the thirst came in waves that he could ride out, managing his addiction one wave at a time.

With the ability to survive without quenching his thirst, Zeke had questioned himself more than once, wondering if he could have avoided a lot of trouble by trying a twelve step program prior to foolishly attempting to cure his alcoholism with the arrogant self-experimentation that had gone so wrong. And, had things been different, he could have avoided the ill begotten blood-for-blood fiasco of Montana. These thoughts continued to weigh heavily on his mind, particularly on long, hot summer nights when there wasn't enough hospital work to keep him occupied.

CHAPTER FOURTEEN

The figure that had been following Zeke's comings and goings was now waiting for him just inside the hospital loading dock, Zeke's usual way of entering the medical center for his shift. The door was a large opening about the size of a two car garage. The sliding aluminum door was up like it had been last night.

There was a smaller door to the side of the large one, but last night the doctor slipped in through the plastic flaps that created the barrier to the outside. Once the flaps started to move, the figure could quickly move into position. That, combined with the absence of security cameras, would make the job almost *routine*. He would pounce on the unsuspecting doctor, strangle him, dump the body in the nearby compactor. It would take him longer to strangle than to cut, but he wanted this one to be bloodless. He wanted the doctor to disappear without a trace. If somebody else came through those flaps, he had a planned excuse and would abort that night's attempt.

The figure opened and closed his gloved fists a few times then rubbed them together silently as he heard the bus pull into the stop across the street. The bus's brakes squeaked as it came to a stop and the doors hissed as they opened. He watched the flaps with a maniacal excitement in his eyes.

CHAPTER FIFTEEN

Selinda was happy to leave the precinct and continue her investigation away from the likes of Joe Wellard. Not only did she find his lewd advances to be repulsive, she also considered them disrespectful—especially coming from someone who should be a colleague.

"Immature jerk," Selinda said to herself as she pulled out of the station's parking lot.

Selinda was headed toward the hospital to find the medical student who reportedly had a verbal altercation with Caleb Fisher shortly before his death. She also had Zeke's clogs in the back seat of the sedan. Her plan was to use returning the clogs as an excuse to continue her questioning of the doctor. If she appeared to be returning the clogs as a favor, she couldn't be accused of harassment, now could she? Selinda would just sneak in a few more questions.

But first she wanted to eliminate the medical student as a suspect. The MICU staff had only known her first name, Patience, but because of that distinct name she was easy to track down. The hospital personnel department wouldn't furnish

Selinda with Patience's home address but did confirm there was a Patience McMorris currently working in the medical center as an internal medicine sub-intern, the term used to describe someone one step below intern. Inquiring where a medical sub-intern would be found at the security desk, Selinda had been informed that the place to start looking would be on the general medical wards. She started on ward eight A and worked her way up.

Stepping off the elevator and into the tan, beige and brown colors of the ward, Selinda approached the nursing station. There was a dry-erase board to the side of the station that read "Hello! Today is August 14th. The weather is sunny," accompanied by a picture of a beaming sun. "The next holiday is the Fourth of July. Make sure you ask the name of your doctor."

"I'm looking for a student named McMorris," Selinda told the clerk.

"You a family member, honey?" the clerk responded.

"No. Detective Bruchart. Albany PD. I need to ask her a few questions."

The clerk stared, mouth agape.

"You could page her, but she's usually very slow in returning her pages," one of the nurses called from the other side of the station. "I saw her on the floor before, I think she went to eight B."

"Is she in some kind of trouble?" the clerk asked Selinda.

Selinda didn't answer. "Okay, thank you," she called to the nurse. "Oh, by the way," she turned back towards the clerk, "why do they write that? Today is August fourteenth and so on?"

"Oh that's for the ol' timer's patients, honey," she replied, using a malaprop to refer to those with Alzheimer's.

"Plus, it's easy for anyone to get disoriented in a hospital," the nurse added.

"But, the next holiday isn't the Fourth of July. It's Labor Day."

"They don't care 'bout that, baby, they don't care," the clerk said with a chuckle.

At the eight B station, the clerk responded to Selinda's inquiry by saying, "Yes, I think she's here." The clerk rolled on her chair a few feet to the intercom. She picked up the receiver and pressed a button. "Dr. McMorris to the front please."

Patience appeared and raised her brow when she saw Selinda.

"This lady's here to see you."

"Yeah?" Patience said to Selinda.

"Are you Dr. McMorris?"

"*Student* Doctor, but yeah. Are you a relative?"

Due to the height difference, Selinda was looking down at Patience.

"No. Patience McMorris, correct? Patience, that's an appropriate name for a doctor—sorry, doctor to be." Selinda was trying to sound friendly.

Patience rolled her eyes at the statement.

Oh, boy, this one's going to be trouble Selinda thought. "Never heard that one before, huh? Is there some place we could talk?"

"What are you, some kind of drug rep?"

"A what?" Selinda asked.

"A sales rep. Are you here to tell me about some new medication your company developed?" It was a good guess as pharmaceutical companies do tend to hire young, attractive, overly friendly people to represent them and the drugs they were selling.

"No. I'm with the police. Detective Bruchart,"

"What's this about?" Patience said slowly, her tone and countenance changing from annoyed to fearful.

"Can you tell me your whereabouts last night?"

Patience hesitated, then blurted out, "I don't have to answer any of your questions without a lawyer."

"Oh, okay, that's fine, you call your lawyer and we'll all meet at the police station tomorrow morning. The hospital won't have any trouble giving you the time off on short notice if I tell them." Selinda's piercing violet eyes were staring at Patience. Selinda held her gaze for a moment as she turned to leave.

"Wait! Wait a second!" Patience said. "I was at the medical school library." She seemed to choke on the sentence, raising Selinda's suspicion that it was a lie.

"Did anyone see you there?"

"No—I mean I don't think so."

"Did you check any books out? Do you have to scan your ID to get into the library? Something to prove you were there?"

"No—wait a second, maybe I did check a book out. I can get a receipt from the library and give it to you."

"Okay, good. How well did you know Caleb Fisher?"

"The guy who was killed? I didn't KILL anyone. Shit—I mean shoot. I didn't know him at all"

"Are you sure about that, Patience?" *Because I have witnesses who saw you get into a heated argument recently.* Selinda could have added that fact but decided a better moment may come if she had to formally interrogate her.

Patience's expression went blank. "Yes," she replied unemotionally. "I'm sure."

"Ok then. Here's my card with my phone, fax and email. Please send me that receipt. Or contact me if you hear of anyone who may have wanted to do...Mr. Fisher...harm." Selinda spoke the last three words slowly for emphasis, her eyes locked on Patience's.

Patience averted her gaze. "I will."

CHAPTER SIXTEEN

The flaps stirred and a hand pushed through. Deftly, the figure lunged and grabbed the wrist, pulling Zeke in like a dance partner. The assailant kept Zeke's back to him as his other arm wrapped around to form a choke hold to start squeezing the life out of his victim.

But Zeke would have been dead long ago if he hadn't learned to fight. As if he wasn't surprised at all, Zeke slipped his wrist out of his assailant's vice-like grip. He threw a quick punishing blow backwards into the figure's abdomen. This loosened the headlock for a split second, enough time for Zeke to duck out of it. Springing back up he landed a lightning-quick uppercut square on his attacker's jaw.

The attacker's head snapped back, but he still threw his arm around, trying to grab Zeke again, but Zeke had already darted off to the side, finding cover behind a forklift. He looked around for something to use as a weapon. He spotted heavy metal hooks dangling from tracks so they could be used to move bulky objects. *Okay, come after me, you bastard, and I will bash your skull in with one of those. How would you like that?*

"Come, on doc, I just wanna talk to you," the figure spoke.

So the attacker hadn't seen him move. Zeke kept silent, thinking he would like to keep this advantage. He looked through the engine block and he saw the huge figure, arm raised. *What was that in his hand? A gun?*

Not liking his chances against someone armed, Zeke quickly moved further into the loading dock area, pushed the nearest hook to catch his stalker's eye, then ran in the opposite direction towards the street. The assailant was distracted for a second, but soon realized it was a feint. He quickly stowed his knife in an ankle sheath and headed towards the still swaying barrier flaps.

In addition to fighting, Zeke had a lot of experience evading thanks to his on-the-job training with his Russian mobster friends, and he quickly came up with a plan. Looking over his shoulder, seeing that the figure had located him and was starting to pursue, Zeke ran as fast as he could towards a nearby abandoned building that used to be the home of the hospital's research program.

He ran up the stairs and tried the door but it was securely locked. He needed to get inside somehow so he ducked around the corner to the back of the building to find double doors. The chains looked loose. *Yes! Thank God for the drug addicts or whoever broke in before.*

The door opened enough for Zeke to slip through under the chains. He threw his body back against the wall and listened, trying not to pant in the wake of his run. *Okay, with the size of him he'll never make it through there.*

But just as Zeke felt safe there was a large *smash* as his pursuer was using a large object to hit the chain. A few more hits like that and the door would be open.

In fact it was one more hit and Zeke heard the chain fall as he sped down the hallway. He had to find the underground tunnel that connected the building to the hospital. There was no light in the building but Zeke had good night vision so when he saw what looked like a stairwell he pushed the door open and bounded down the stairs. After descending one flight he spun around to amble down another and noticed a greenish glow to his left.

The tunnel! There must be some type of emergency power lighting it. A path to safety! He probably didn't even see me take the stairs but get ready to RUN.

But as he turned to sprint down the eerily-lit tunnel Zeke heard heavy steps above him. The attacker must have seen him go down the stairs.

Running as fast as he was able, Zeke twisted his body to look behind him. In the glow his pursuer was a hulking mass, his shadow splashing on the tunnel walls as he advanced past each light source. Zeke was fast so it didn't appear that the shadow was gaining on him, but he could only hope that the door at the tunnel's end wasn't locked.

He practically collided into the double doors at the end of his dash, violently pushing the bar. The door flew open and Zeke jumped into the familiar green hallway of what he hoped to be a crowded hospital.

Just wanna talk, huh? I don't think so Zeke thought, panting, trying to catch his breath as he walked quickly to find a populated area.

Was it a robbery attempt? Then why didn't the attacker just give up run away? No, he was out to kill. Zeke could smell it. This was about Montana. They had tracked him down.

CHAPTER SEVENTEEN

Zeke thought he left all this behind when left Montana for good. Now he was on edge again, the fear and anguish returning like it was yesterday. Can't go to the police with this, it would risk exposing him and ruining the fresh start he thought he had achieved in Albany. It was bad enough he had already attracted the attention of the authorities by stumbling across a murder victim. He was certain they were considering him as a suspect in the crime. And the police would *really* start poking around in his past if he reported that someone was out to kill him.

And, along with the anxiety came the craving for the intoxicating effects of blood. Sitting in the office, sign-out sheet in hand, heart and mind still racing from dodging his assailant, Zeke thought about how easy it would be to write for a few units of blood for one of the patients on the list. With the hospital distracted by a horrific crime, the last thing they would worry about is a few missing units of blood. Besides, hampered by their current financial problems, the hospital probably hadn't updated their inventory system in years. Who knew if they even kept track?

Zeke jumped as a knock on the door startled him. In case it was the person trying to kill him, Zeke didn't make a sound. If he kept quiet, hopefully whoever knocked would just go away. But what if it was one on the nurses with something important? He looked down and checked his pager. No pages. *They would have paged me if they were trying to reach me...*

"Dr. Oswald?" a voice came from outside the door. "It's Detective Bruchart from the Albany PD. The one investigating the Fisher murder? We met the other day. The guard told me I could find you in here."

While Zeke was relieved to find it wasn't the large figure that chased him into the hospital, he was in no mood to talk to her either. He stayed motionless.

"I have your clogs. I was here interviewing someone else and thought I drop them back to you." *She must have heard the chair when I started. She knows I'm in here.* Besides, if it was true that she had his clogs, she would probably leave them at the nearest nursing station. The security guard already knew she was looking for him and Zeke didn't need anyone else knowing. He rose from his chair and opened the door about halfway.

"Yes, Detective?" Rather than inviting Selinda in, Zeke held his stance in the partially opened doorway.

Selinda help up the clogs and said, "Here they are," with a small flourish. Her tone and manner then turned thoughtful. Pursing her lips, she said,

"Hmm...I hope I didn't interrupt. You look like you were...in the middle of something."

While it was possible she was reading the stress of earlier events on Zeke's face, he was pretty good at masking signs of distress. He thought Selinda was trying to trump something up. Either way, he had decided not to reveal that he had someone after him.

"No, that's quite alright," he said calmly, gently plucking the clogs from her grip.

"Tell me, Dr. Oswald, what made you think it was a good idea to clean the blood off your clogs? You didn't think you might be tampering with evidence?"

Zeke didn't reply.

"Are you some kind of neat freak?"

Zeke said nothing. When you have been interrogated by Russian mobsters, this seemed like questioning from a department store rent-a-cop.

"No too talkative tonight, huh, Doctor? Okay, I'll let you get back to work. Just one more thing—do you carry a scalpel?"

Zeke broke his silence. "No. Why?" he said, wrinkling his brow.

"The M.E. seems to think Fisher was killed with a scalpel." Selinda peered over Zeke's shoulder into the office. "You wouldn't happen to have any in there would you?"

Zeke didn't move. "No. Scalpels are stored in the supply room and, after they're used, disposed of in sharps containers."

"Sharps containers. I see. Oh well, thank you for your time."

What else could go wrong? Zeke thought, leaning against the inside of the door after he shut it. With someone out to kill him and the police thinking a scalpel-wielding doctor had killed a nurse in the hospital, he became preoccupied again with blood.

To find a patient with a problem that might require a transfusion, Zeke scanned the names on his sign-out sheet. The name *McMorris* caught his eye as the name of the trainee assigned to patient *Garrison*. The recognition of the name snapped Zeke from the preoccupying urge as he remembered was scheduled to meet with the student doctor he was mentoring. Or at least that's what the medical school was calling it. He knew about Patience's troubles with the dean, and the faint odors of peach and alcohol he sensed on her at times made him surmise that she was battling some of the same demons he was.

Yes, let me keep myself busy with this meeting and that will provide time for the craving to pass, Zeke thought, reaching for the phone. He then thought about what the resident said about her hands shaking during a procedure. *She may be worse off than I originally thought and I should try to help her, even with all my troubles* was the next thing to come into Zeke's mind as he dialed Patience's pager number.

Hoping for a busy night to take his mind off the past, Zeke was disappointed to find that, after meeting with his mentee, there was little hospital work for him to do. Keeping busy was the best way to avoid his impulsively stealing blood from the hospital, so after checking results of a few blood tests, he decided to keep moving by seeking an update on the case of the alcoholic writer with heart block. With the obvious things he shared in common with Mr. Ira Carswell, Zeke felt he could identify with him-countertransference, psychiatrists would label the feeling. Because of this, Zeke had an interest in seeing what happened with the patient whom he had seen in the Emergency Department the previous night. He started out towards the hospital ward which held the telemetry section, where heart function was continuously monitored through wireless electrodes, to check on Mr. Carswell's progress.

The telemetry ward was located on the sixth floor on the opposite side of the hospital, accessible by the same green corridor he walked the night of his gruesome discovery. It was necessary to take separate elevators as the medical center had been expanded by the addition of wings. As Zeke passed by the hallway leading to the bone room, an unsettling chill passed through his body as he relived the experience of discovering the murdered nurse. Shaking off the chill, he wondered if the police considered him a strong suspect, or if they had any leads pointing away from him. Maybe Zeke could spend his downtime looking for answers. What was a nurse who usually works in the ICU doing in the orthopedic radiology room? Maybe he was killed somewhere else and left there. Zeke guessed that couldn't provide a good explanation as to why there was so much blood pooling underneath the victim, no evidence that his body had been dragged to create a blood smear. Like a good physician who considers different diagnoses for a medical problem, Zeke considered other possible scenarios. What if the neck incision wasn't the cause of death? Was it possible he was killed some other way? But why kill him somewhere else, carry the body to the bone room for a blood-letting? Or perhaps he was incapacitated elsewhere then put in the room to finish it? Was he lured there or followed there? Zeke decided, if the night remained slow in terms of his work, he could return to the room to survey for clues. Specifically, Zeke could look for x-rays of patients who were in the ICU recently. If there were, it could provide a connection between an intensive care nurse and the reading room. The unfortunate victim could have been looking for x-ray results on a patient under his care.

"Sixth floor, going down," the deadpan female voice announced as the elevator doors swung open and Zeke stepped out.

"Hey, Dr. Oswald, how are you tonight?" A melodic voice greeted him from behind the nursing station. The middle aged, obese woman who was the nighttime clerk for the telemetry ward had a crush on Zeke, and took no steps to hide it. She often called out to other staff, "He's my boyfriend, that Dr. Zeke," as he walked by.

"Fine, Tanya, and you?" Dr. Zeke always made time to chat with the clerk no matter how busy or stressed he was.

"Just seeing you brightens my day. Can I get you some coffee, hon'?"

Zeke smiled crookedly at the suggestion of his brightening anything. "No thanks, Tanya," he said lightly. "I came by to check up on a patient I admitted last night, Mr. Carswell."

"Oh, he's been discharged. I think he's still in his room, though."

"In that case, let me see if I can catch him." A large thunder clap sounded as Zeke grabbed a worn three-ring binder from the chart rack. There was tape on the spine with *Carswell* written in marker. He opened it a leafed through it as he walked towards the patient's room.

"Oh I think there's a storm coming, Dr. Oswald," Tanya called after him.

"It would seem so," Zeke replied, not breaking his stride. He found the section of the chart containing progress notes and read the final note entitled "Cardiology".

Intermittent second degree heart block, normal physical exam, no significant bradycardia on tele, f/u with echo in the office in 1 week.

When he arrived at the door, Zeke spotted Carswell, facing the window, gazing at the dark street. Raindrops were making musical popping sounds as they hit the window's pane. Concerned he would startle the writer if he walked in and began speaking to him, Zeke knocked on the open door. Carswell turned around.

"Oh, hi, doctor," he said with pleasant recognition. "Don't be surprised, I remember you. We met last night in the Emergency Room."

"You have a good memory," Zeke observed. "Going home soon?"

"Yes, I was waiting to see if the rain would pass. The cardiologist, Dr. Sommers, finally saw me and said it was nothing to worry about. He will take a sonogram of my heart this Thursday in his office to be sure. I hope he won't find something terrible. I guess I will have to live with the uncertainty until then."

Zeke smiled supportively.

"'The only thing that makes life possible is permanent, intolerable uncertainty; not knowing what comes next.'" After a pause he added, "Ursula LeGuinn said that."

Zeke felt as if Carswell had more to say, and he would welcome the distraction of a good story, so he raised his eyebrows and nodded in encouragement.

"I met her once when I was a journalism student at Columbia. She had just won the National Book Award, for a novel I whose name I can't recall at the moment, it must have been 1972 or three, the Vietnam War was still going on. She came to give a talk and afterwards, a group of us went out to dinner with her. I remember to conversation to be very philosophical and that statement I have carried with me since.

"What is the *name* of that tome?" Carswell asked himself. "It's a famous tale, a classic Le Guin fantasy novel about a fictitious archipelago. All the people are taking ill and their Prince is trying to discover the cause of the illness. He crosses into the land of the dead and confronts the evil sorcerer who is apparently responsible for his constituents' plight. The sorcerer's motive was a desire to escape death and live forever—sort of what a doctor does," he smirked.

Sometimes with gene therapy Zeke thought.

"Oh, I think the rain has let up," Carswell said with a sense of urgency, looking out the window. "Better get going before it starts up again."

Zeke, who had been enjoying the story and Mr. Carswell's company asked, "How does the story turn out?"

Grabbing his discharge instructions, Carswell said quickly, "The prince brought along his own sorcerer, who gives up a lifetime of magical abilities in exchange for closing the connection between the evil sorcerer's world and that of the Prince's." He smiled and extended his hand. "Nice meeting you."

"Same here."

Carswell stopped in the doorway and turned back to face Zeke. "I remember now."

The Farthest Shore.

CHAPTER EIGHTEEN

Patience looked at her phone to check the time. It was 9:45 pm, fifteen minutes since the last time she'd checked. She was restless like she usually was after an hour of studying in the medical school library. With too many distractions at home, the storm had forced her to choose another venue besides the 649 for tonight's work.

Patience wasn't doing much studying anyway. She was too busy ruminating over the events of the day. Why did she tell that fucking bitch she would send her a receipt? She wasn't even at the library the night of the murder; she was just embarrassed to admit she was sitting in a cemetery alone. Maybe she should have told the detective the fox she saw trotting around the grounds could provide her an alibi.

And, she was still pissed off at that Dr. Oswald and the self-righteous questions he posed to her earlier in the evening.

He had been staring at her hands when he asked, "So, Patience, I noticed your hands shaking a little bit before."

No, asshole, I heard *my stupid fuckin' resident tell you my hands were shaking, so cut the bullshit.*

But his bullshit had continued, "I could probably help you with that. If you like…"

"I *don't* have a problem," Patience had interrupted. She had been trying to stay calm but sounded way too defensive. Catching herself, she had added quietly, "Just a little heavy on the caffeine."

Zeke had looked at her face until she had broken eye contact.

"Okay. Just saying."

He had left it at that, but Patience had felt the need to tell him, "I don't need your help," through clenched teeth.

A copy of *Cecil Essentials of Medicine* sat open in front of her. The book, an abridged version of the two-volume *Cecil Textbook of Medicine,* was nicknamed "Baby" Cecil by many medical students. *Cecil Essentials* was designed to make it possible for the average student to read it in its entirety during a typical twelve week course of General Medicine, although it still contained 1312 pages, roughly half of what the *Textbook* contained. A second relative to the textbook, a small handbook that one could carry in a lab coat pocket, was cutely referred to as "fetal" Cecil.

The book was open to the section on *Diseases of the Liver and Biliary System,* learning the details of all the horrible things that could go wrong with the liver. *Scary how you could only live a few days if your liver shuts down,* she thought as she read about primary sclerosing cholangitis, a particular nasty albeit rare disease in which the body turns on itself to attack the liver's bile drainage system, damaging the ducts to the point where the liver first drowns in bile, then expires due to cirrhosis. In the early stages, the disease was characterized by chronic fatigue, itchy skin, foul smelling oily diarrhea, and darkened urine. Student Doctor McMorris was sure that the next time she had an itch, she'd become concerned that she was coming down with primary sclerosing cholangitis. Imagining that you have a rare, fatal disease you only recently learned about was a common job hazard among medical students, and Patience was no exception to this rule. Ironically she chose to ignore the fact that her daily alcohol intake, regarded by Patience to be a panacea for the bile of life, was a bigger threat to her health and a much more likely way to damage her liver than the development of some rare disease.

"I could probably help you with that," she mumbled, haughtily mimicking Zeke's concern, drawing a sip of Potter's from her travel-style coffee mug. *Fuck you, Oswald, I used to think you were kinda cool. Thank you so much for your oh-so generous offer but I was put on this earth to help others, not to get help.*

A desire to care for others was her way of compensating for her self-neglecting behavior. Patience was much more comfortable in the role of caregiver than receiver, like an entertainer who prefers her side of the microphone to the other.

And, it's ridiculous to think I had killed that nurse. If it was an inside job, my money's on that creepy Oswald.

The library's study cubicles were arranged in groups, separated by partitions to reduce distractions and provide for better concentration. Although the partitions were effective because she liked to keep to herself, Patience occasionally looked up and out beyond the walls of the cubicle. Leaning back in her chair, she peered out beyond her space and suddenly blushed from embarrassment. She had looked over to one of the large tables adorned with green banker's lamps to see another female medical student, who looked up at the same time, meeting Patience's glance with pretty hazel eyes that flickered in the green light. She had auburn, shoulder-length hair and attractive angular facial features. She thought it was Maddie, and the memory of the night they met came flooding back to her.

Patience looked over again at the woman, more discreetly this time and realized it wasn't the same woman. Still, her heart started to thud with the memory. The woman noticed her attention again, smiled and raised her eyebrows in a sign of friendly acknowledgment. Patience returned her attention to her book, but found it difficult to restore her concentration as she recalled the evening.

Invited by a senior medical student during a medical school orientation session, Patience had been reluctant to accept. Not familiar with any other students, she'd been worried that the anxiety of attending a gathering of people she didn't know would have been so unpleasant that she wouldn't enjoy the time. But her past experiences entering high school and college had been marked with a pattern of a big beginning effort to socialize and meet new friends to expand her social network, followed by a slow self-destruction towards isolation, ending up with no long lasting healthy relationships. So when she had arrived at medical school orientation week, Patience had been eager to break this pattern as she had a fresh start with a new situation. She had promised herself this time would be different, she would make friends that would last a lifetime, starting with that party.

Patience had arrived at the rented house in a residential section of Albany fifteen minutes early, afraid she would be late. She'd waited in her car, anxiously chewing on her fingers until the party's starting time.

"Hi. I'm Maddie, I share the house with Veronica," the tall woman with hazel eyes had said as she greeted Patience at the door. She wore a denim miniskirt and an off-white peasant blouse with a purple scarf.

"Patience."

"Well, Patience, Ronnie's out picking up wine for the party. She's going to be fashionably late as usual." The pitch of her voice had lifted as she said the phrase "fashionably late," conveying a sense of familiarity with her mock annoyance. Seeing the look of stress on Patience's face, Maddie had tilted her head down and looked out over eyeglasses with thick black rectangular frames and raised her brow. "Oh, don't worry about it, sweetie, come on in. Can I get you a drink?"

Hell, yes you can. Patience had stepped across the threshold and stopped, looking around an empty living room. *I'm the first one here?* It was an older house, with light colored walls and dark wood door frames and molding. "Uh, what do you have?"

"The only thing we have right now is vodka and orange. I've had a couple already. Care for one?"

"Sure."

"Follow me."

Leading Patience into a huge kitchen where the carpet turned into a bland linoleum floor, Maddie had said, "Have a seat."

Patience had taken a seat on one of the stools around an island in the center of the room. In addition to the large plastic bottle of vodka on the counter, Patience had noticed that the appliances looked antique, with a white-coated metal sink and enormous gas stove with large black burner grates. Patience's eyes had widened as she watched her host pour half vodka, half orange juice into two tall glasses.

"I like to add a little peach liqueur to mine. You want me to put it in yours?"

Unbelievable. Maddie liked Peach liqueur too? Patience's mouth had begun to water.

"Yes, please." She would have a more pleading tone when she used this phrase with her new acquaintance later in the evening.

The scent of peach extract breezing through the kitchen, Patience had noticed Maddie's beautiful hands. "Cheers!" she'd said with a playful, listing tone when she placed Patience's drink on the counter in front of her. Maddie had taken a sip of her own drink and had remarked, "Mmm!" as she had leaned back against the countertop next to the refrigerator.

"So, Patience, you're a medical student at the same school as Ronnie?" Patience had also been pleased that Maddie didn't ask if she liked to be called *Patty,* like Ronnie for Veronica and Maddie for…what?

"Uh huh. Maddie. Is that short for something?" Patience had asked.

"No. Just…Maddie. Do you work in that hospital, what's its name, St. Something-or-other?"

"St. Twigleighct. Yeah."

"I'm worried about my grandma. We're very close. She was just sent home after a long stay and now she's back in hospital after only a few days. So soon!"

"Her name's Deborah Semple. Be a dear and look in on her for me if you get a chance."

"Ok, I'll tell Ronnie what I see?"

"Nonsense. I'll give you my cellphone number."

Maddie, just Maddie, had drawn a cigarette from a box and was lighting it when she said, "I know, I know, it's a bad habit. I guess I'm not as health-conscious as you doctor types."

Patience had thought it unusual for a medical student to be a smoker. "Oh, I just assumed you were a medical student too. What do you do?"

"Guess."

"I dunno, model?" Patience had said innocently.

"Oh, aren't you sweet. Thank you, but no. I mean, I did do some teen modeling, clothing catalogues and stuff, but now I'm a design student at ITT tech."

"How do you know Veronica?" Patience had asked.

But before Maddie could answer, Veronica's breathless voice had interrupted from the living room. "Okay, okay, I'm here, where is everybody?" followed by her entrance into the kitchen carrying a box from the liquor store. After hoisting the box onto the countertop she had said, with a pout, "Nobody here yet? Oh hi...Patty, right?"

"It's Patience," Patience and Maddie had replied in unison. They looked at each other and shared a laugh. *How did she know I didn't like being called that?* Patience had said to herself.

For the most part Patience had spent the night in a corner of the living room drinking the cheap wine Veronica had supplied. After a few awkward and thankfully short-lived conversations Patience had been thinking of slipping out when Maddie stepped up to her.

"Enjoying your wine?" Maddie had asked with a cute smirk.

"Not really."

"Didn't think so." She was heading towards the kitchen, looking back over her shoulder. "I know just the thing. Be right back."

A few minutes later she had returned with two vodka, orange, and peach concoctions.

"Cheers," Patience had said.

"I love Ronnie, but this party is pretty *lame.*"

Patience, not wanting to sound unappreciative, then offered, "Maybe we could switch the radio station?"

Maddie had paused, scrunching one side of her face in contemplation. "Would you like to go upstairs?"

Patience had just stared at her, uncertain how to respond.

"I have better music in my room."

"Okay." Patience had been dizzy from intoxication and had appreciated the offer to sit down for a while.

The stairs led to a large hallway. "If you have to pee, the bathroom is next door on the right."

"Oh, no thanks. I just went."

"Well then, come on in and have a seat, I just want to get some pants to change into."

"Oh, I can wait outside your room if you want privacy."

"Don't worry about it, sweetie, *I* have to pee, so I'll change in the bathroom."

Patience had chosen a large deep purple futon over Maddie's bed. Grabbing some clothes from a dresser, Maddie had started towards the door. "Be right back."

Patience had removed her shoes with her toes, enjoying the feel of the room's carpet through her socks.

Due to a combination of naiveté and alcohol, Patience had been oblivious to Maddie's attention directed towards her. She thought Maddie had a nice way about her, friendly and familiar, and was comfortable in her company, like they were old friends. While alone in her room Patience had looked around, noticing that, matching the futon, the color scheme of the room was mostly deep earthy colors. The walls were covered in tapestries, in paisley and impressionist style. It made for a cozy feeling.

"Cozy," Patience had said aloud in a throaty voice like a cat's purr, stretching her legs.

Maddie had returned after a short time, dressed in an oversized t-shirt and purple velour pants. Her glasses had ended up on her nightstand.

"You like purple I see," Patience had observed, slurring her words. "And peach," she had added, giggling, but it was soft and barely intelligible.

"Huh? Oh you noticed?" Maddie had used matches to light candles of varying heights around the room. "Let's see," she had said, surveying a shelf of CDs. "Good music, good music. Let's try this."

Maddie had put the CD in a player and soft music had begun to play. It was an acoustic guitar with a female vocalist singing a sweet ballad. Patience had thought it sounded like Sarah McLachlan.

With Maddie on the bed and Patience on the futon they had chatted though the first few songs, where're you from, how do you like school, that sort of thing. A new song had started when Maddie remarked, "Oh I love this one." They two had listened silently to the singer whose inflection sounded at times like she was in the throes of ecstasy. Patience had felt like the words in the song were directed at her, telling her not to feel that every time something went wrong it was a disaster.

After the vocals stopped and a musical bridge began, Maddie had slid next to Patience. The vocalist had added a soulful improvisation.

"You, know, Patience, you're awfully pretty," Maddie had said softly, gently touching her hair.

Patience had sat there, looking up at Maddie, her whole body blushing, starting to breathe a little quicker. Maddie had put a hand on Patience's face, slid it under her hair to cradle her, leaned over and kissed her lips.

But Patience had broken the kiss quickly, turning her head away. "You know, I'm...uh...I'm not..."

"Not into girls?"

"Yeah."

"We don't have to do anything, Patience. I like you," Maddie had said softly in a sincere, caring tone. She was kneeling next to her, hands on her thighs, almost submissively, awaiting a response.

The two had held their gaze for a long time. In the candlelight, Patience's brown eyes had looked like rich chocolate until they began to burn with desire.

"Kiss me again," Patience had whispered.

Sucking gently on the taste of sweet peaches and swirling her tongue around with her partner's, Patience had loved how Maddie kissed her softly and brushed her face against hers. Little moans had escaped as their lips parted and rejoined.

"Oh...my...God," Patience had whispered breathlessly, incredibly excited from anticipation as Maddie had broken their kiss and slowly moved her mouth downward. Patience had little experience to know what was coming next, but she had an idea.

In her study cubicle, Patience began squeezing her legs together as she replayed the scene in her head. She recalled how Maddie had lifted her shirt to give Patience butterfly kisses on her belly while unbuttoning Patience's jeans. The scent of arousal and desire had wafted upwards when Maddie pulled her jeans down. One leg of the jeans had gotten caught on an ankle, and the pair had giggled at the difficulty. But Maddie hadn't giggled for long as, after she had gently removed the jeans completely, her face had grown serious as she had lightly run her lips from Patience's calves to the inside of her knees, and then all the way up between her thighs. Maddie's lips had been gently pulling, pulling, pulling, then pushing, pushing, pushing on her flesh again and again until Patience had begged for more, *oh please oh please oh please.*

Patience squeezed and crossed her thighs faster and faster. Medical school was the furthest thing from her mind as she could feel the tension building in her belly as the thought of that night with Maddie drove her wild. To keep from crying out with the release Patience bit her lip and slumped forward over the desk, burying her mouth in her arms.

After letting out a huge breath, Patience rested her head on her textbook. She thought about how Maddie had called her a few days after the party and left a voicemail.

"Hey, I got your number from Ronnie, maybe we could get together for a cup of coffee? Call me."

I really should have called her back Patience thought.

"Wait, did she say Semple?" Patience raised her head and said aloud. Although she had spoken softly to herself, it was enough to attract the attention of the woman who had reminded her of Maddie. The Maddie look-alike glanced over and Patience mouthed "Sorry!"

I could have sworn I saw the name "Semple" on one of the wards. Maybe it's Maddie's grandma.

Patience had told Maddie that she would check on her grandma. Maybe this would give her another chance.

CHAPTER NINETEEN

Selinda was fully immersed in her work in the Albany PD's forensic lab. The light from her computer screen was casting an artificial glow on her face, the angles of her neck and ears visible now that her hair was pulled back into a ponytail.

She was mining for information on Caleb Fisher's personal computer that might place her investigation on a track other than random. It was tedious work, but many people had all aspects of their lives stored on a hard drive.

Selinda smirked as she popped open a can of Diet Coke and contemplated the sticker which had been placed on the frame of the display. The sticker contained a likeness of Nipper, the famous canine RCA mascot. The dog, who originally was the subject of the painting "His Late Master's Voice" in the late nineteenth century, was a well-known figure in Albany because of a four ton Nipper statue resting on the old RTA building on Broadway.

"Help Us Take a Nip Out of Crime" was written next to Nipper's likeness on the sticker, followed by the words "Albany Community Task Force." The slogan was part of a public relations effort which followed the shooting death by an Albany police office of an unarmed suspect. The effort was ill-received and short-lived after a letter from the National Crime Prevention Council complained that it was too similar to their *Take a Bite Out of Crime* campaign. Consequently, most of the 5000 stickers produced were not distributed to the community and were scattered around the precinct.

"Take a nip out of crime indeed," Selinda scoffed, taking a sip from the can.

"What's that? You're taking a nip? What do you have in that can? Scotch?"

Her married colleague again.

"Diet Coke," Selinda replied, not in the mood to flirt. Not that she ever was, even though her mother kept recommending that she should give it a try. During their phone call earlier that day Selinda's mother had repeated her usual reminder that her daughter wasn't getting any younger and should explore the dating scene. And Selinda's usual response was that she felt too busy with her job to fit that in her life. But was she married to her job, or afraid of getting attached to someone and risk losing him like she lost her father? Either way, she certainly wasn't going to find out the answer to this question by becoming a coworker's mistress.

"Working late?" Wellard asked. He moved in closer and looked over her shoulder. Selinda stifled the urge to elbow him in the gut.

"Uh-huh," she said in the most noncommittal tone she could manage.

"Well, hey me too, what a coincidence. Say, if you need a break, I could show you another kind of nip." He spoke slowly, trying his best to be seductive but really coming off creepy.

"No thanks," Selinda replied coolly.

She was trying to maintain a calm exterior but he was making her very uncomfortable.

"Okay. Have it your way." His voice flared with anger.

Just please go away. And after a moment he did.

Selinda preferred to perform the computer forensic analysis herself rather than allow the forensics team to do the analysis and submit to her a written report. Waiting for the team to perform the analysis would take precious time that Selinda felt she didn't have. Without any solid leads, she felt the trail was growing colder with every minute that passed. In fact, without leads, the trail wasn't even identified yet, it was obscured and diminishing with time like a path in the sand during rising tides.

Her experience in analyzing hard drives had shown Selinda that it often provided information that may be lost in a paper report. It could provide hard data like contact information, financial information, records of communications, but it also gave of view of a person's hobbies and interest. In other words, it could provide a look into the mind of a person—likes and dislikes, personality traits, and emotional states. Searching a person's personal computer was a way to really get to know someone—a kind of electronic autopsy.

Selinda shifted her weight in the chair and began clicking the mouse to explore the hard drive. She started by clicking the *My Music* icon, this would give the detective a glimpse into Fisher's preferences through his music choices and also provide some entertainment to ease the tedium. The window that opened was completely filled Selinda's eyes with MP3 files.

"So our victim was a music lover," Selinda commented, remembering that Fisher's girlfriend had also pointed this out. She scanned through files but didn't recognize many of the artists:

Muse, Radiohead, Franz Ferdinand, Gary Jules, The Strokes.

One track caught her eye so she opened the file to listen. It took a few seconds to load the computer's music player, then came a heavy baseline accompanied by electronic drums and a falsetto voice.

If this song was typical of his musical tastes, Fisher was into rock-influenced dance music, Selinda thought. She allowed it to continue playing while she turned her attention towards *My Pictures*. The computer would most likely continue to open the remaining music files when Muse was finished, accompanying Selinda on her search.

Fisher had organized his pictures into folders. Selinda opened one that was named *Mexico.* Inside were pictures that seemed to represent a vacation to the warm country. There was one of a young woman in a lounge chair, wearing a floral bikini. Wet black hair was swept away from her face, looking cute as she playfully stuck her tongue out for the camera, her brown eyes gentle and inviting. *Must be the girlfriend,* Selinda surmised, although her picture didn't look at all like how Selinda imagined her from their phone conversation.

Another photo depicted the same woman and the victim, portrait style, both dressed as if the couple was on their way to dinner at a restaurant with a dress code. Jean (Selinda presumed) was on Fisher's left side, in a halter-top dress of thin tan material, spaghetti straps over her shoulders, one running through, dividing a white orchid tattoo on her right shoulder.

Fisher stood close to her, his left arm disappearing behind her back. He was wearing a black jacket over a blue button-down shirt. In stark contrast to his appearance on the autopsy table, his skin was tan and healthy-looking, his hair was thick and wavy, overall looking fit and masculine. He was smiling, but it looked a bit posed to Selinda, and when she looked carefully at his eyes she thought she detected something in his eyes that seemed almost...predatory. Selinda of course had seen this look before in her line of work, and knew it couldn't be posed away. Strangely, after leaving his face to look again at his partner, Selinda couldn't see the aggressive expression in his eyes when she returned her glance to them. Did she imagine it? Her eyes narrowed at the possibility of her projecting her own diffident views of the male sex.

Predator or not, the picture of Fisher and his companion disheartened the young detective with the realization that this youthful life had been ended prematurely. She thought of the years that had been ahead of the victim and the tragedy of his death. This sentiment motivated Selinda to press on to try to solve the crime.

She methodically looked through every photo folder on Fisher's hard drive. There were pictures of what seemed to be a college reunion in a bucolic setting, family pictures of a holiday, probably Thanksgiving judging by the clothing and lack of decoration. There was nothing in picture form that stood out to Selinda as a clue to his demise.

As one song ended and another electronic rock track began, Selinda opened Fisher's web browser to view his favorite web sites and history of visited web pages. The home page appeared, a popular web portal draped in a gothic theme. It was personalized with sections on local sports scores, national and world newswires, movie releases. A *cartoon of the day* appeared on the right side, showing a dog at a job interview. He was talking to a man in a suit behind a desk.

"I used to be a fox, but I heard that dogs have a leg up at your company."

The top of the page read *Hi Caleb!* Followed by a quotation:

"Anything one man can imagine, other men can make real-Jules Verne"

Selinda clicked on the history button to expose the websites he had recently visited and a list appeared on the left side of the display. The most often visited site was Facebook. There were also visits to CNN, ESPN, HBO, and Edmunds.com. She directed the mouse to the last Facebook visit and reopened it. The browser directed her to Fisher's Facebook page. A picture appeared of the nurse in a tropical print shirt, raising a drink as if to propose a toast. Selinda recognized the photo from Fisher's *Mexico* folder.

In the "About" section on the page, his age was listed and his status was "single." He described his occupation as "critical care specialist," and his hobbies as fine arts, sports, and music. The few last posts seemed to detail his thoughts on the care of several critically ill patients. To Selinda, these cyber conversations seemed more like venting than anything else.

After looking through his contact list uploaded from his BlackBerry (his parents phone number was there), Selinda let out an exhausted sigh. She stretched her arms upwards, decompressing her spine and glanced at her watch. 1:13 AM. What time was it in California? Still too late to call Fisher's parents, Selinda thought. Besides, she felt she was getting punch drunk from exhaustion.

She stretched again and leaned back in the chair, reflecting on the investigation of Fisher's murder. Selinda felt as if she had gotten to know the victim well. She was familiar with his interests, vocation, and his social circle. His job, critical care nursing, seemed to occupy a top spot in his interests, followed by music and women. Although he seemed to show sincere concern about the welfare of the patients under his care, Selinda had a feeling Fisher was an overly self-centered individual. Still, no strong motive for his murder had emerged from her investigation; nothing particularly useful in developing a theory of why he was so brutally cut down.

Hi Caleb!

Feeling exhausted and discouraged, Selinda nearly missed the tan folder on the table next to the display. In it she found pages and pages of cyber conversations from the times Fisher spent in internet chat rooms. The lines of dialogue disappeared from the display once they were replaced by other text but the computer scientists knew how to recover them from the hard drive and would print the conversations for review.

Selinda began reading, leafing through many pages of conversations. It appeared that Fisher's screenname was *whiterain*. Mostly the conversations in which *whiterain* participated seemed flirtatious, almost like interchanges one would have at a singles bar or club. A good balance of self-promotion and flattery. Selinda didn't encounter any of the simulated sex messages that she had seen (and been disgusted by) in chat rooms in other investigations.

Aside from the chat pick-up attempts, there were several examples of platonic-type conversations with a person whose screenname was *brainboy*. One conversation started out

brainboy: r u @ the hospital
whiterain: no.

Seeing this, Selinda made a notation in her notebook to remember to check the hospital's computers to see if Fisher used them for electronic chats. Maybe he met his killer online and they met at the hospital where things went wrong. She would also request that the computer specialists try to determine the identity of *brainboy*.

Turning the final page, Selinda cocked her head to one side, staring at the floor. She rested her head in one hand in deep thought: was she resigned to failure? This case was growing cold fast, and soon she would be considering filing the elements of this case along the many other Albany PD homicide cases that were failing to generate significant leads.

Selinda felt as if she were fighting with herself. Overall she had confidence in her abilities as a homicide detective, yet she still had nagging self-esteem problems. The death of her father had stolen so many things from her. He was the one who provided her with a foundation of confidence when she was feeling shy or inadequate. Losing the relationship interrupted her psychosocial development as no one could fill the role and her self-esteem remained underdeveloped as a result. The detective was plagued by feelings of mediocrity; she never felt her work was good enough. But she also never thought she was capable of any better, and as a consequence, even her expectations were mediocre. The bone room murder was doing its best to uncover the rawness of Selinda's personal flaw, like a bandage removed too quickly from an abrasion. She considered herself no more than an ordinary detective, able to solve the easy cases but not talented enough for the challenging ones, and her colleagues thought no more of her than she did of herself.

Hoping for a breakthrough in this case was like longing for Mr. Right. Unfortunately most cases were like this one and most men were like that jerk Wellard. Would this be the one, the challenging case in which she rose above her feelings of mediocrity, solving what was considered to be insoluble by most, finally proving her worth to everyone and her father's memory? Although the solution to this mystery seemed to be slipping away from her, Selinda was still driven forward by an earnest hope to overcome her limitations.

CHAPTER TWENTY

During some of the worst weather that night in Albany, rain pouring down and thunder clapping though the streets, Beverly Duncan received a phone call. The ward manager was in her office at St. Twigleighct late working on a presentation that would be delivered the following morning. The thunder didn't startle her, but the way the indoor lighting dimmed and lightning flashed eerily throughout the room was unnerving, and Beverly jumped when her cell phone chirped.

"Mommy, when are you coming home?" asked her daughter, who at age ten was just starting to use the phone on her own.

"Soon, but after you've gone to bed. Iris knows when you're supposed to go to bed." Beverly tried not to get too angry at the call even though she was having enough trouble finishing her slides for the talk on the hospital lengths of stay. She held her temper back but was firm about bedtime. *You never know, I could die in a car crash coming home in this weather, so don't let your last words to your daughter be harsh.*

"But I want you to tuck me in," pled her daughter.

"Can't tonight, honey. But I'll check on you when I get home."

"Awww."

Beverly talked a little while longer and then guiltily disconnected. Back to work. As one of the hospital's nursing administrators, she was given the task of monitoring how long patients stayed in the hospital. Analyzing the length of stay, as it was called, became an important strategy for the American hospital system in the 1990s. Originally it was promoted as a strategy for cost reduction by managed care companies whose contracts called for paying hospitals by the day for the care of their patients. A shorter stay translated into lower costs for the managed care companies. But early on the process was unpopular with hospitals as it decreased their revenue.

But the financial environment in the American hospital system changed and hospitals now realized they could save money and increase revenue by decreasing hospital lengths of stay. Hospitals are reimbursed by government or private insurance programs by a system that assigns a diagnostic related group (DRG) to each admission. The DRG assignment takes into account a patient's diagnosis, age, sex, and complicating factors due to other illnesses. The sum the payer givens the hospital is based on the DRG, not how long the patient stays in the hospital. So, if a patient stays longer than the reimbursement will cover, the hospital's uncompensated operating costs will lead to shortage of revenue, and if the patient stays a shorter time, the hospital will be paid the same amount and be able to use the vacant bed for another DRG.

Beverly planned to present the data she compiled on the hospital's most common DRGs: normal newborn, vaginal delivery, heart failure, angina pectoris, pneumonia. Her data would be part of a discussion on how to improve lengths of stay and in turn, improve the hospital's bottom line. Some measures that had already been implemented at St. Twigleighct included mandating a documented estimated length of stay in the admission paperwork. These estimations were compared to published Medicare data. The measures also included a DRG-specific checklist of requirements to be met prior to discharge. Once these requirements were met, there were no apparent barriers to discharge.

Beverly had compiled data on the previous six months and used slidemaking software to represent the information in a bar chart to see if the average lengths of stay were consistent with published data. She also made slides comparing lengths between different wards for the same DRGs in order to identify any differences according to where the patients were admitted. The group which would include other nursing administrators, the hospital's chief of staff, Wayman Newby, President Safford's assistant Rebecca Crawford, and the St. Twigleighct's vice president of corporate affairs, Garret Quackenbush. Beverly knew of Quackenbush's brusque nature and his reputation for being focused only on the business aspects of running a hospital. There was talk among Beverly's coworkers that Quackenbush was against having a memorial service for the slain ICU nurse. Beverly, like most of the hospital's nursing staff, thought a memorial service was a good idea to pay tribute to one of their own and as a way to grieve the loss of a colleague.

Because of Quackenbush's reputation, Beverly wanted to be over-prepared for her talk in case he tried to attack her or her work. The group expected a half-hour speech and she had made 45 slides, estimating one slide per minute with extras in case she rushed out of nervousness. Beverly wanted to practice her presentation a few more times before leaving her office by paging through the slides and saying aloud her accompanying words.

"As you can see here, six B had the shortest length of stay across the range of DRGs. Six B, of course, no, no that doesn't sound right." She paused.

"For those of you don't know, six B is primarily a geriatrics ward, which, in the past, had been plagued by long lengths of stay..."

As Beverly collected her next thought, there was a creak outside her office door. If she were home, she would have thought the sound was of the house settling. But did hospital buildings settle?

Whenever she worked after dark, Beverly locked herself in to her office, adopting this practice after learning of the hospital murder of a pregnant doctor when Beverly was training in Manhattan. Already feeling apprehensive with the sudden crashes of thunder outside her window (not to mention an unsolved murder of a hospital employee), hearing the sound at her door reminded her she could also call the hospital's security team to escort her to her car when she was finished for the evening.

Pondering this, her eyes on the door, she thought she saw the door knob turn slightly. Did she *hear* it turn? Was she imagining it? Her brow furrowed and her heart began to palpitate with these questions. She thought to call out, "Who's there?" but she held her tongue. It was probably just a member of the security force checking to see if the door was locked.

Things changed when she heard the sound of a key gently sliding into the keyhole. There was nothing but silence as the key stopped, flush up against the metal of the lock. The silence was broken by a gust of wind out in the dark night, increasing the pounding of the rain.

There was another flash of light.

When the thunder clap cracked, the door burst open and a huge figure in black hospital scrubs pounced inside the room and rushed towards Beverly. The figure was wearing a grey cap pulled low over a pair mirrored sunglasses. Her eyes widened as she screamed against the sound of the pouring rain.

The desk was still in between the Beverly and the intruder, and when he broke left, she jumped to run in the other direction. He grinned at her misfortune as her knees smashed against the bottom of the desk, impeding her motion enough so he could catch her from behind. He grabbed her neck, choking her with a latex-gloved hand, his fingers wrapped around her larynx. With one uninterrupted motion he twisted her to expose her neck, placed an index finger on it to feel for the carotid pulse and swiftly brought a razor up and dragged it downward, bending his fingers to remove them from the path of the blade.

Her arms went up in defense but she couldn't budge his grip. He folded the razor against his hip and let it fall to the floor, taking the free hand and holding the back of her neck with his arms extended. Bright red blood spurted from the incision. As her body became limp her last thoughts were of her daughter.

I'll check on you when I get...

The killer positioned Beverly Duncan's lifeless body face down behind the desk so that someone opening the door to peek inside without entering might not notice the killer's work. He scanned his scrubs and noticed some blood splatter on the right leg; he retrieved the razor, opened it and wiped it clean on the cloth. He inspected the blade, then surveyed the room to look for anything that might lead back to him. He would be leaving some DNA behind through hair and skin cells, but no more than the average visitor to the room.

Hulking over to the door, the killer stood with his head cocked, listening for signs of movement in the hallway. When he was confident there was none, he opened the door, paused to look out and slipped out into the hallway, walking purposefully to avoid suspicion should he run into anyone. He entered the nearest stairwell and jogged up three flights to an unoccupied ward. Down the hallway he entered the room he had hidden in before, went into the bathroom and closed the door. The clothes he left there were in exactly the same spot. He turned the bolt to lock the door. He removed the scrubs and folded them compactly, then donned the bland earth-tone clothes he had worn into the hospital the night before. He sat on the floor, leaning against the tiled wall, putting his head on his knees to wait. He didn't belong in the hospital but wouldn't stay uninvited. He would wait a few hours then exit the hospital through the loading dock area and on to his next job, first stopping in the emergency department to toss the scrubs into a bin destined for the commercial laundry where the clothing would be washed in hot, 150-degree water.

CHAPTER TWENTY-ONE

The crime scene tape securing the door to the bone room had been removed, and Zeke tried the doorknob, turning it with his hand through the lower part of his white coat. Despite the horror that took place in Beverly Duncan's office, the hospital was slow most of the night, giving Zeke to opportunity to return to the scene to look for clues. If could find something substantial, he could give an anonymous tip to the detective, casting suspicion away from him.

He didn't want to leave any obviously new fingerprints, but he didn't feel wearing gloves was necessary as his fingerprints and DNA could be found in the room anyway. He also prepared a story about looking for a patient's x-rays to explain why he was in the room in case he was found by someone. Zeke felt his breathing and pulse quicken as the knob turned in his hand, his body recalling the horror of his discovery the last time. This time, however, the door opened without resistance.

He stepped inside and flipped the light switch with his knuckle. Flooded with bright light, the room appeared very clean, with no visible traces of blood. He searched the green linoleum floor, tile by tile, but found nothing except dust in one corner. He moved his attention to the walls to find a dry eraser board. Although it was blank, he looked closely at it to see if he could detect any writing that was recently erased. Nothing. The remaining walls were uncovered except for a large picture of a wooded area that looked as if it belonged in a hotel. *Would I find any answers in there?* Zeke asked himself pessimistically. Moving in closer to the picture, he could examine his reflection in the picture's glass cover. He stared introspectively at the image, wondering what went wrong with the way he reflected. Was it self-experimentation gone amiss or was he defective from the start, destined for self-destruction? His skin was pale, was his soul pale before the blood drained? Or was his soul like a threadbare quilt, faded from exposure, barely holding together?

Like an act of avoidance, Zeke turned his back on the picture and on his reflection to refocus his mind on his task. New to the forensic world, he wasn't even sure what he was looking for. And, the police likely removed any clues that were pertinent to their style of investigation. Perhaps Zeke could use his knowledge of how a hospital works to develop new ideas. So he probed. What was a critical care nurse doing in a radiology reading room? Assuming he wasn't incapacitated and moved to the bone room before he was slaughtered, did he plan a trip there and was followed for an opportune kill? But what was Fisher looking for? Was he looking for a radiologist, was he there for a tryst? Or was he looking for an x-ray film?

Considering the last question, Zeke approached the rolling metal cart that held the films. About a year ago, he had heard that the hospital would be soon transitioning to all digital image processing, making film copies obsolete. The images would appear on computer screens, instead, in the reading room, or the ICU, or even home on a secure server through a virtual private network connection. He wondered why the transition hadn't taken place yet. If it had, he could have viewed Ms. Christie's x-ray images on an ED computer and avoided all this.

As if he were putting the blame on the films, he nudged the cart with his knee. It was locked and didn't move, so he nudged harder. The cart moved a few inches, kicking up dust. Zeke noticed that the flooring had four lighter spots away from the cart's wheels, suggesting that the cart had been moved from a spot where it had been for some time. X-ray films are large, fourteen by seventeen inches and made of blue tinted plastic coated with photographic emulsion. They were stored in large brown paper envelopes, arranged in the cart like a filing cabinet, separated by tabbed dividers labeled with a section of the alphabet *A-D, E-G,* etc. *I guess there are more EFG's than ABCD's,* thought Zeke as he leafed through the envelopes.

As he was considering pulling each film and examining it (there were about thirty of them), Zeke noticed something wrong with the arrangement of the envelopes. One of the envelopes was misfiled. Deborah Semple, eighty-six year old female, was located behind the *R-Q* divider rather than in front of it as the rest of filing system went. It was dated two days prior to Caleb Fisher's murder. Did they remove films from the room each day? Zeke doubted it, as perusing the films showed dates varying over the past week.

Zeke pulled the misfiled envelope out of the cart. Inside the envelope he found a paper copy of the request for x-ray on Ms. Semple. The location of the order was MICU-8. So she was a patient in the MICU and x-rays of MICU patients were usually read as a priority. There was writing of the bottom of the sheet, probably in the radiologist's hand. *Osteo-ischium.*

Zeke held the film up and looked upwards at it, using the ceiling light to illuminate the x-ray image. On the innominate bone, the periostium which normally covered the bone tightly, was raised, a sign of the bone infection osteomyelitis.

"What would cause an infected hip bone?" Zeke murmured aloud.

This reflection was shattered by the shrill sound of the St. Twigleighct intercom.

"Dr. Oswald, Dr. Oswald. Please report to the ED, stat."

Someone must be crashing, he thought. Zeke scrambled to the emergency department to find a crowd of sweaty hospital personnel swarming around a gurney. As he approached, Zeke was in disbelief when he saw whom they were working on. He was shocked to see the staff performing CPR and preparing to intubate Mr. Carswell, his patient with heart block. The cardiac monitor showed a flat line.

"Welcome, Dr. Oswald, to our little get together. Pull up a chair and join us." Zeke wasn't familiar with the ED attending physician with the southern accent but he seemed to be competently in charge of the code, so at the next pause Zeke moved in the replace the nurse doing chest compressions.

What...the...hell...happened Zeke thought with each compression, manually squeezing the blood through the lungs as green scrubs swirled around him in a panic. By all medical standards, it had been safe to send him home. Zeke had even questioned why he was admitted in the first place. This could have been dealt with as an outpatient. Why would he suddenly go into cardiac arrest?

"Still asystole," the doctor running the code declared. "Continue compressions and give another epi. Dr. Oswald, you saw this patient when he was admitted, right?"

"Yeah."

"I called you down to see if there was anything unusual about the case."

"No, he's a healthy gentleman with what seemed like uncomplicated second degree heart block."

"'Cause I'm gettin' ready to call this thing."

Zeke tried to come up with additional recommendations but the emergency doctor had really done everything possible to try to save Carswell's life. At no point during the code was any electrical activity of the heart restored.

"Allrighty. I will call it unless anybody has any bright ideas. Anybody?"

Around the stretcher was silent except for the rhythmic sounds of the mechanical ventilator and Zeke's chest compressions.

"Allrighty. Let's call it. Time of death 3:03 AM." He turned and snapped his gloves off in disgust. "I *hate* mortalities."

"What happened? How did he come in?" Zeke asked the ED doctor.

"Damn if I know, I was hoping you could help with that. A buddy activated 911 when he collapsed at home. He came in asystolic." *Zero natural pacemaker activity.*

"If he returned within twenty four hours of discharge, that will trigger a post," he added.

A postmortem or autopsy. Feeling bewildered, Zeke thought it a good idea.

CHAPTER TWENTY-TWO

Selinda had been asleep for about an hour when the sound of her cell phone awakened her. Squinting, she checked the caller ID. The police station's operator.

This can't be good news, Selinda fretted to herself as she clumsily pushed the answer button. "Hello, Detective Bruchart," she answered, her voice small from exhaustion and trepidation.

"Good evening, Detective," the mirthless voice of the operator began. "I have a call for you, please hold."

"Hello?" a different voice asked.

"Yes, Detective Bruchart."

"This is Officer Brinkerhoff. I'm calling from the St. Twigleighct Medical center. There's another body found at the hospital. With her throat slashed. Same MO as the last one."

Selinda still wasn't fully awake. *Did he say another murder?* "Go on."

"Albany PD got a call that one of the nursing administrators didn't come home last night. We found her dead in her office about an hour ago."

"Anybody see anything?"

"No, but we're still interviewing potentials as they exit the hospital."

The detective's mind had already begun to analyze the news as a serial murder. "Was the doctor who found the first vic working in the hospital last night? Zeke Oswald?" she asked.

"Unknown. We'll check."

"If he's still in the hospital hold him 'til I get there. I'm on my way."

"Will do," the officer replied. "Detective Clevaland is already here."

This was unwelcome news to Selinda. Palmer Clevaland was a sexist, self-centered homicide detective that would stab you in the back to make himself look good. Clevaland's behavior was so bad he made Joe Wellard look like a feminist. *Ugh, how did that jerk catch the case?* she thought. Dealing with him at the crime scene was nothing to look forward to.

Selinda disconnected, used the bathroom, brushed her teeth and hair, and dressed in a white dress shirt and grey suit. Leaving her apartment, she double-checked her appearance. She had a feeling there might be camera crews at the hospital where two murders had been committed in a few days. *This was developing into a big story*, she thought.

Selinda's assumption about the television crews was correct. Pulling up to the hospital in her car, she saw several vans from the local stations. She flashed her badge to a uniformed officer who let her pass and park directly in front of the medical center. She joined several black and white patrol cars, their flashing lights coloring the dusk.

A warm breeze blew Selinda's hair in her face as she climbed out of her car. She brushed the hair from her face with one hand while the other displayed her badge to gain entrance to the hospital. She found a cop interviewing a scrubs-clad man at the door.

"Do you know where Detective Clevaland is?" Selinda asked the officer.

"He should still be at the scene. Sixth floor, off those elevators." The cop pointed across the lobby.

Selinda looked around as she crossed the lobby. No sign of Dr. Oswald, she noted as she stepped on the elevator.

On the sixth floor, she was greeted at Ms. Duncan's office door by another officer. As she nodded to the officer, she could hear Clevaland's obnoxious voice. "No, *she's* not here yet. Probably had to change her *tampon* or something."

"I'm here, Palmer." *Minus tampon.*

Selinda's short, stocky, balding colleague didn't miss a beat. Apparently unembarrassed by the possibility that Selinda may have overheard his tampon comment, he continued to be caustic.

"Glad to see you could make it, *Ms.* Bruchart."

Selinda preferred to stay cool, as she usually did.

"To what do I owe the pleasure, *Lieutenant?*" Selinda placed some emphasis on Clevaland's rank in order to highlight the fact that he condescendingly did not.

"I don't like getting up this early either. It wasn't my idea. The Cap thought you might need a hand, although I'm *sure* he has full and total confidence in your ability to handle both cases. He also suggested that, now that there are two murders with the same

MO, you meet with the hospital administration to see if they know of any connection between the two employees. One of the vice presidents, named Quackenberry or some shit like that, can meet with you sometime today."

She stared at him for a moment, then started to move towards the body behind the desk.

He continued. "The body was found..." Selinda interrupted Clevaland by holding up her hand, palm facing outward towards his voice.

"If you don't mind, I like to start with a fresh look without any preconceptions," she explained as mildly as possible to avoid being accused of being bitchy. Although he was probably thinking she was anyway.

"Okaaaay."

Selinda stood over the body to begin a survey. The body was prone, face down in a puddle of thick blood on the light brown carpet. "Any info on time of death?" she asked.

A uniformed officer supplied the answer. "She was still alive at ten o'clock last night. She spoke to her daughter on the telephone at that time."

"Is anyone taking care of her daughter?" Selinda asked as she knelt by the body. She held out her hand and the officer handed her gloves.

"Huh?" Clevaland asked.

"Her daughter—who is with the victim's daughter?"

The lieutenant stammered. Obviously the welfare of Duncan's child was the furthest thing from his mind.

"Her aunt is looking after her. She lives nearby," the officer interrupted.

"Uh huh," Selinda said, without looking up. As she lifted up the corpse's head to examine the neck, a *glop* sounded as the face separated from the blood puddle. The congealed blood stuck to the nose and looked like solidified chicken fat. A piece of the clot fell with a disgusting *splat*. Selinda couldn't see the wound, as the slashing was on the other side, nearer to the desk. Same right-handed style. The victim's hands, which were covered in dried blood, showed no signs of defensive struggle. It was probably the victim's blood, from an attempt to stop the blood-letting.

"Any DNA evidence found?"

"No."

Why are you doing this? Selinda wondered. Looking up to the desk, Selinda noticed the computer. *The victim was here late, what was she working on?*

"Anyone look at the computer?"

"Nope."

The detective leaned over the body and gently moved the mouse with a knuckle, just enough to wake up the monitor. The screensaver dissolved with a static sound into a PowerPoint slide titled "LOS data." Length of stay. So unless the killer changed something on the computer, the victim was probably working on a PowerPoint presentation when she was killed.

"Any sign of forced entry?"

Clevaland snickered.

Of the room, *you pervert. Do you take anything seriously?* Selinda thought in exasperation.

"No," the other detective finally answered.

"Do we know if she shared this office with someone?"

"As far as we know, she was the only one to use this office, right guys?"

The guys nodded.

Selinda paused to review what she knew so far about this new murder. It would definitely help to share this review with a colleague, but she kept her thoughts to herself; she didn't feel Clevaland would be helpful.

The administrator was working late at night, probably behind a locked door, preparing a talk which included information on hospital lengths of stay, whatever those were. The killer somehow gains entry without forcing his way in. Perhaps she knew her assailant, or it was a hospital employee, or the killer had a key to her office. Or she left the door unlocked or even open, either way, the killer somehow gets in, and the nurse probably jumps out of her seat to try to escape. The perp catches her from behind and slits her throat.

Selinda was compiling commonalities among the cases: both murders were perpetrated at night, both victims were nurses, and Dr. Oswald...

Selinda's concentration was broken by the buzz of one of the officer's radio.

"Go ahead."

"Detective B still there?"

"Yeah."

"Tell her Dr. Oswald was on duty last night but so far no sign of him."

"I got that," Selinda told the officer. "Please ask him to ask the hospital operator to page him to my cell phone."

"Did you get that?" the officer said into his radio.

"I'm on it," the voice replied.

CHAPTER TWENTY-THREE

Here we go again.

Zeke wasn't exactly surprised that they had found out where he lived, so when he returned to his apartment and the light switch didn't work, this was the first thing that entered his mind. His loading dock attacker was in his apartment waiting to finish the job. Calculating that he was poised behind the door as soon as Zeke flipped the disabled light switch, he pushed the door firmly and sprung into the kitchen area to grab the nearest weapon. But this guy was good at what he did; there were no knives in the drawer where Zeke usually kept them. But old habits die hard. Although Zeke no longer kept a gun around, he did keep a spare kitchen knife in the oven.

The figure appeared just Zeke as was turning around from retrieving the six inch knife from the oven. The bulb in the open oven cast just enough light for Zeke to see that his face was obscured by a black ski mask and that he had his own knife.

"Get out now and I won't kill you," Zeke said boldly. "Tell them to leave me alone."

His eyes widened but the figure said nothing.

"Say something!" Zeke shouted, trying to see if he could identify him from his voice or at least store the voice is his memory bank. If they both made it out of this alive. "Or are you afraid you will fail to finish the job again?"

But the figure just kept moving slowly towards Zeke.

Not wanting to get trapped in the kitchenette, Zeke knew he had to move fast. He darted forward trying to slash his opponent's arm that held the knife. Zeke missed and the figure connected with a left hook to Zeke's head. He was stunned from the blow but was able to duck under a swing of the killer's knife. Zeke spun around. Now that the two were facing each other they squared off. They were dancing around like two boxers in the ring and it became obvious that the Zeke's opponent was waiting for him to make the first move. Zeke was happy to oblige; he lunged toward him to try to stab him in the chest. The killer backed away and swung his blade, going for Zeke's neck, but Zeke had raised his arm in defense.

The killer's knife slashed Zeke's bare forearm. Recoiling from the pain, the killer knocked the knife out of Zeke's other hand. Zeke grabbed the attacker's arm and managed to wrestle him the ground.

With two quick moves, Zeke slammed the man's arm to the floor to knock the knife free and then elbowed him in the Adam's apple. Zeke struggled away and scampered towards the door. The killer picked his knife up and threw it at Zeke, aiming for his kidney. It missed him and lodged in the door frame. Zeke didn't look back, he ran down the stairwell.

It was nearly dawn but there was not enough light to burn him. There should be time enough the get back to the hospital, or there was a motel within walking distance. Better to return to the hospital. It seemed to be the only place where he was safe these days. But that couldn't be further from the truth.

The taxi dropped Zeke off at the hospital main entrance and he rushed in. First order of business was to get to a nursing station and tend to the laceration on his arm. Hopefully the taxi driver didn't notice and he left no blood in the cab.

Never mind the taxi driver. As he entered the hospital, there was a group of uniformed police gathered at the security desk. In the middle of the group stood Detective Bruchart. Her eyes met Zeke's. Zeke noticed how exhausted she looked. She had no makeup on except for dark red lipstick.

Shit! I should have told him to drop me at the loading dock.

"Dr. Oswald, a word please," Selinda called out to Zeke as he scurried by.

"Be right back," he replied over his shoulder.

He continued his fast walk to the emergency department. After going through the automatic doors, he stopped for a moment to collect himself. Was she there to arrest him? Are they going to accuse him of killing Carswell? Either way, he knew he had to return to the lobby quickly. He didn't want her putting out an all-points bulletin.

Zeke looked down at his arm. Fortunately the cut had stopped bleeding. But he wanted to cover it so he grabbed and white coat off one of the wall hooks and donned as he left the ED as quickly as he came.

Zeke appeared calm as he strolled up to the group. As he got near there was a faint odor that resembled *Beautiful,* the perfume Jessie had been wearing when they meet in that Baltimore club in 1989. Was he imagining that? Why would that come to his mind at a time like this?

CHAPTER TWENTY-FOUR

"So," Selinda began when they sat down in the lobby's overstuffed chairs, "I imagine you've already heard what happened in the hospital last night." She was referring to Duncan's murder rather than the unexpected death of Zeke's patient with heart block.

Zeke kept his face expressionless. Instead of taking the lead of her question, he asked, "No, what happened, detective?"

"Come on, Doctor Oswald, another murder occurs while you're on duty and you don't know about it?" she questioned him aggressively.

Zeke looked shocked which only helped him in the eyes of the detective.

"You didn't notice all the police as you left the hospital?" Selinda continued, still hoping to throw him off. Perhaps he'd say something incriminating.

"No, I didn't notice," Zeke said calmly, but the look on his face was enough to convince Selinda that Zeke didn't know about the nurse administrator's murder.

"Another employee was found dead, killed in the same manner as the one you...found." Selinda was intentionally short on details, hoping he would make a mistake and refer to the new victim by gender. With unknown gender, most people would say "he" reflexively. But if the suspect referred to the new victim as "she," she would have reason to believe he may know more than he was letting on.

But "Oh God," was all Zeke said. Then silence. Taking his reaction in, Selinda felt guilty about trying to manipulate him with her tone. Her violet eyes gazed intently into his.

Selinda cleared her throat as if to clear her emotions and to remind herself why she was there. She continued her questioning, less aggressively this time. "Where were you working last night?"

Zeke seemed to be recovering from the shock. "I work all over the hospital. Last night, uh, mostly the medical floors but I also spent time in telemetry, the MICU and the…" he swallowed. "…the ER."

"Did you notice anything out of the ordinary last night?

Zeke paused. "No. Who was killed?"

Selinda considered not telling him. The fewer details, the more she might be able to trip him up. "An administrator. So far no connection to…your murder."

"Something the matter with your arm?" She nodded towards it.

There was now a crimson stain on the white sleeve as blood continued to ooze from the wound.

"Oh, no, must be from one of the patients."

"I don't think so. It looks like it's coming from you."

"I'll have to change this coat as soon as we're done."

Selinda thought quickly. She knew she didn't have cause to force Zeke to take the coat off but she wanted to see what was underneath. She tried to make her voice sweet.

"Are you sure you're okay, doc? If you're hurt I could help."

"No, it must be from a patient."

"Okay." The detective stood. Now her voice was cold and professional. "Doctor Oswald, if you think of anything, you know where to reach me. I'll make myself available to you." Her back to him, Zeke couldn't see the involuntary wince on Selinda's face when she realized how her last statement sounded more like an invitation to her bedroom rather than the police station.

Leave it alone, Linney Bear.

CHAPTER TWENTY-FIVE

Waiting anxiously at a stop light on her way to the hospital, Patience tapped the steering wheel as "The Sharpest Lives" by My Chemical Romance was blaring out of the Altima's radio.

Late again, she was in such a rush that she didn't take notice the new billboard on the corner. "When you see a ball rolling in the street—think of the child running behind it."

Patience hadn't been sleepy when she arrived home from the library the night before. Watching the television in bed, she had continued to drink schnapps until she had passed out. A loud infomercial for a laundry product had awakened her around 4:40 AM, and in her stupor, Patience had inadvertently shut off her morning alarm. She hadn't recalled doing so when her eyes had opened at 9:00.

Patience still felt inebriated. She hoped the way she felt would improve as she was scheduled for an overnight call that day. Life for Patience McMorris was becoming slippery, like trying to bounce on a trampoline in the rain. Worrying over how she might sober up enough to survive the day (she might have to self-administer a liter of normal saline intravenously), she had no idea how significant tonight's call would be.

Patience had already missed morning rounds so she would have to page her resident in order to find out what was new with the team and what needed to be done that day. Before doing so she decided it would be best if she gathered some information herself to appear prepared. Sitting at a nursing station computer, she reviewed testing on her patients, and there was one other patient she wanted to look after.

"Semple," Patience said as she typed the name in a patient search area.

A window popped up to read "This medical record is protected by the Health Insurance Portability and Accountability Act (HIPAA). Do you wish to proceed?"

She knew that she was violating privacy rules by looking up someone else's patient without a medical necessity but why would anyone care if a medical student were checking on somebody's grandma? Although Patience didn't encounter this warning on all patients' computer records she figured it was just a random warning. Did anyone even monitor such things?

She clicked "Yes."

The computer listed a Deborah Semple located one of the general medical floors. Patience wrote down the room number so she could pay a visit to see if it was indeed Maddie's grandmother. Then she could contact Maddie to finally honor her request.

Patience had a nervous moment when she thought suddenly, *What if Maddie's there visiting when I walk into her room?*

Patience calmed herself down by realizing what a hell of a coincidence that would be. *Should probably check her labs before logging out.*

Everything looked in order until something unusual caught Patience's eye.

"A bone culture? Don't see too many of those," Patience said to herself when she saw the test that was done to identify the cause of a bone infection.

The results of the culture were even more surprising.

"*Enterobacter*?" Patience said, crinkling one side of her face. She recalled that most bone infections were caused by *Staph* bacteria. "That's a strange bug to cause osteo," using the nickname for osteomyelitis.

Deborah Semple's room was on the eighth floor. Pulling her chart from the rack at the nursing station, Patience turned to the first page. Semple's address was listed as Mighty Pines Extended Care, Albany, NY and her emergency contact was Hansen, Maddie.

Even with the current shape she was in, Patience's face lit up when she saw the contact was Maddie. "So it *isn't* short for something else," Patience chuckled as she had half-expected to see something like Madeline or Madison as Maddie's given name. Thinking of the playful exchanges they'd shared made Patience feel lighthearted and warm and she hoped she could help her new friend. Was "friend" even the right thing to call Maddie?

Patience jotted down the phone number in case it was different from the one she had at home.

Patience also learned from the chart that Maddie's grandmother had severe Alzheimer's disease. She was recently readmitted after a long stay at St. Twigleighct with fever. The source of fever was determined to be a bone infection which seemed to be responding to intravenous antibiotics.

"Okay, good," Patience said to herself. "Now let's go say hello."

After knocking on the open door, Patience entered her room.

"Ms. Semple?"

"Yes, dear?" Maddie's grandmother was thin with long grey hair pulled back and braided. She smiled sweetly at Patience.

Patience returned the smile. "Hi, I'm student doctor McMorris. I'm a friend of Maddie's." She used the word "friend" for lack of a better term. How else could she have introduced herself?

"Maddie? Did you come back to do my hair?"

Patience gently put a hand on Semple's shoulder. "No it's not Maddie. I'm a friend. I work in the hospital. Maddie asked me to check on you."

"You're not going to hurt my hip, are you?"

Why would I... "No, I'm just here to say hello." Patience was accustomed to dealing with patients with Alzheimer's. Their memories and attention spans were so poor it was best just to be gentle and understanding.

"How does my hair look?"

"It looks beautiful."

"Thank you, sweetie," Semple replied, using the same term of endearment Maddie had used with Patience.

Back at the nursing station, Patience paged her supervising resident to see if there were any hospital admissions for her. She apologized for her lateness, lying that her presence was mandatory at a meeting at the medical school. He didn't challenge her excuse, stating that it was slow so far, there was no work for her and she should check back with him later.

Patience locked herself in one of the on-call rooms, a quiet place for her to call Maddie.

I'll call her in a second, Patience thought as she stretched out on the cot. But, instead, she sighed slowly and fell into a deep sleep.

CHAPTER TWENTY-SIX

The hospital's administrators were gathering for another meeting in the President's office to discuss the latest chapter in hospital's current troubles.

"Is the Albany PD still here?" President Safford asked no one in particular.

"Yes," the VP of operations responded. "They're still working in the office where the murder took place."

"Have they said they have any leads?"

"No."

"Or if they do, they're not saying," Garret Quackenbush added.

After giving Quackenbush a look of disapproval, the VP of Operations addressed the president. "Adin, the media have been calling, asking if we will hold a press conference."

Rebecca Crawford added, "The Mayor's office also called, too, to see what we were doing about the crimes."

There was a pause as everyone waited for a response from the Safford. "I don't want a press conference," Safford said, looking at the VP of operations, "too much publicity, I don't want the hospital turning into a three ring circus."

"But we can't just do nothing," the hospital's counsel said. "Two murders within a week in the same hospital. This looks bad."

"Not to mention how it's going to affect our bottom line," Quackenbush said.

Everyone started talking at once. Safford held up a hand and said, "All right, hold on, everyone. Here's what we'll do. No press conference for now. I'm hoping there will be no more incidents. The sooner this all goes away, the better for the hospital. A press conference will just attract more attention and perpetuate our troubles."

The general counsel didn't agree. "No, you have to make some kind of statement. Something reflecting a definite, confident approach to the problem. That way, after that is done, it will be easier to move on."

Safford scowled in irritation but could see the value of the advice. He nodded toward the VP of operations and said rapidly with a hint of exasperation, "Work with the public relations office and prepare a *written* statement to give to the newspapers, TV stations, bloggers, whoever wants one. It should contain words like 'safety of our employees and patients are of utmost concern and so on and so forth.

"Because of this tragedy, we will be hiring private, *undercover* security—"

"Undercover?" the counsel interrupted. "Why not make a bold statement with uniformed, armed guards? That might help in any potential lawsuits, we could say we tried everything—"

"Because, I don't want anyone panicking or being driven away by the environment. This is a hospital not a prison. Instead, we will inform the public that undercover security will be placed in every area of the facility as a deterrent and to provide a safe and unobtrusive environment. One that will promote safety and be more conducive to…healing."

There was some additional murmuring which was broken by the hospital counsel. "I also think we should secure the exits, limit ingress to two or three places, make sure other ways of entry are locked and there are guards posted at all entrances."

Quackenbush grimaced. "Good idea; only, no guards."

Safford nodded in agreement. "Put that in the statement," he added, shifting his body forward and placing his hands on his thighs to indicate that he wanted to wrap the meeting.

"Dr. Safford, one other thing," Rebecca Crawford said. "There was another suspicious death last night. A patient that was discharged a day before came in DOA. There are rumors that this was also intentional and that these murders are being committed by an employee—like an 'Angel of death' serial killer. No names are being circulated, just that it's an inside job."

Quackenbush's eyes widened. "Who's starting these rumors?"

"I don't know," Crawford answered. "But, should we repeat background checks on all employees?"

Quackenbush started to say something but Safford interrupted him. "I don't think that's necessary based on the rumor mill," the president said calmly. "Besides, the police should be doing that and we don't need to be duplicating their work." He rose from his chair. "We'll have to end this here. I should return the mayor's call."

As the group was filing out, The VP of operations turned to the president and asked, "Should I find a good undercover security outfit?"

"No, no, I already have someone in mind. The owner is an old fraternity brother, I'll call him to initiate."

They all said their goodbyes, leaving Safford alone with his assistant. "Rebecca, please get the mayor's office on the line," he asked.

"Sure. And just give me the name or number of that security company contact, I'll get the ball rolling on that too."

"No, no, I'm not hiring any security," Safford said quietly. "I don't want the extra expense. This will all blow over."

CHAPTER TWENTY-SEVEN

Carswell's unexpected death disturbed Zeke in several ways. The conversation they had shared right before his discharge left a pleasant impression of the man. Because of this he felt sorry for the loss and knowing what killed him might provide some closure. Zeke was also the last doctor to see Carswell alive—this dubious distinction led to the impression that perhaps he had missed something, especially in the eyes of his peers. Was Carswell's death preventable? Had Zeke made a deadly, passive mistake? With the murders occurring in the hospital, he also wondered if somehow the writer's death was related. If so, could it provide clues leading to the killer?

But there was something else bothersome. Zeke was in the hospital for both murders and was one of the last to see Carswell alive and he was beginning to have doubts about his own innocence. He had blacked out before, was it possible that he was blacking out and committing the murders so he could drink blood?

And now, because someone was out to kill him, he was stuck in the hospital. As if the temptation of the blood bank wasn't enough. He thought about fleeing, but he felt relatively safe in the hospital and it was still the best place to be if he wanted to clear his name.

In the afternoon Zeke called the pathology department to inquire about Carswell's autopsy.

"Pathology," a female voice answered.

"Hi, it's Dr. Oswald, can I speak to the pathologist handling the Carswell case?"

"Hold on, that would be Dr. Miner."

After a few seconds the line reconnected. "Hello, Dr. Miner.

"Hi Law, Zeke Oswald here. I'm calling to see if there are any results to the Carswell post."

"What's your interest?" the pathologist asked.

"I took care of him when he was hospitalized."

"Oh. I afraid I still have no idea why he arrested—no evidence of MI, PE, CVA."

No heart attack, blood clot in the lungs, or stroke.

"I'll be moving to the microscopic analysis soon."

"Today?" Zeke asked with a hopeful tone. "Maybe," he said with a hint of irritation. Then, lighter: "The Pirates aren't playing tonight."

"Okay. Can I get the results as soon as they get in?"

"Boy, everyone's on my case about this one. I'll put you on the list."

CHAPTER TWENTY-EIGHT

Selinda met Garret Quackenbush in his office in the administration section of the medical center. She immediately noticed that the section was nicer in appearance than that of the patient care areas. There was burgundy-colored wall-to-wall cut pile carpeting, expensive-looking office furniture, and dark wood doors and frames.

Arriving at the VP's office, there was no receptionist at the desk outside his door so she approached the door in preparation to knock. It was open slightly, and she could hear a male voice inside, raised and staccato.

"No…he doesn't want that…no, not that either…Ask him yourself, then…I think someone's at the door…I'll get back to you." The sentence was punctuated by the clipping sound of a cellphone being closed.

Selinda knocked.

"Come in."

Selinda walked inside to find Quackenbush standing by his desk, looking out of place in his own office. She extended her hand as she walked towards him.

"Mr. Quackenbush, Detective Selinda Bruchart."

"Yes, yes. A pleasure to meet you. I've been expecting you. I was just on the phone discussing something with my wife. We're redecorating."

"I understand." She didn't really, but she thought it might facilitate the conversation. Besides, Selinda wondered who he was actually talking to. She had the feeling that he was lying because he feared she overheard the conversation. "I'd like to ask you a few questions about Ms. Duncan."

"Yes, she was a good employee. No, she didn't appear to have any enemies."

"I see you've anticipated some of them," Selinda said slowly. "May I sit?" She gestured towards a chair in front of Quackenbush's desk.

"Of course," he said.

To slow the meeting down to a pace where she was in control, Selinda took her seat slowly and deliberately, settling in with her back straight and shoulders back as she pretended to write something on her memo pad. She looked at him in silence, with an unassuming expression, to see if he would start talking first. He was handsome, in his mid-fifties, with tan skin and conservatively-cut silver hair. He was now seated behind his desk, looking calm, in a blue-grey business suit with a royal blue tie.

Obviously familiar with the detective's interview technique, Quackenbush was also silent with a slight, accommodating smile. Selinda broke the silence.

"How long did Ms. Duncan work at this hospital?"

"I don't know exactly, I'd like to say, ten years?"

"Do you know if she was close to any other employees? Socially?"

"Not sure. You should ask someone who's worked more closely with her—someone from QE."

"QE?"

"Quality enhancement."

"I see. Did she know the first victim, Caleb Fisher?'

"Don't say it like he was the first of many, detective. As far as I know, she didn't know the *other* victim. They were both nurses, but Nurse Fisher worked in the ICU, and Ms. Duncan was mostly administration, so it's unlikely their paths would cross much."

"Does Ms. Duncan have any family close by?"

"I know she has...had a daughter at home."

Recently orphaned, Selinda thought as she paused her questioning.

"Do you know what Ms. Duncan was working on?" Selinda then asked.

Quackenbush looked surprised at the question. *Did he just flinch?* Selinda asked herself. "I'm just trying to understand why she was here so late." The VP's expression had changed for only a split second, noticeable only to a trained eye like Selinda's. "We were to have a QE meeting today. It is my understanding that Bev—Ms. Duncan was to update us on current hospital length of stays. Oh, that reminds me, I need to speak to the rest of the QE committee. If there's nothing else, you'll have to excuse me."

"Of course." Selinda handed Quackenbush her card with the usual closing. "Oh, one more thing, can I get a list of those who were to attend the meeting?"

"I don't see why not. Please see my administrative assistant. If she can't help you, call or stop back to see me. I'll help you and the Albany PD in any way I can."

"Thank you."

CHAPTER TWENTY-NINE

Zeke was looking up laboratory values at an MICU computer station when he decided to investigate the hospital stay of Ms. Semple. He had found her x-ray misfiled in the bone room and it was the only film there taken of a patient in the MICU. Was that x-ray the reason why the murdered MICU nurse was in the bone room? Zeke couldn't be sure, after all, even if Caleb Fisher was looking for an x-ray, perhaps the one he was looking for had been removed already, or he was looking for an x-ray from a patient outside the ICU, or not looking for an x-ray at all. At least Ms. Semple's x-ray was *possibly* connected.

Zeke searched the hospital's database. The name Semple didn't appear on the active patient list; she must have been discharged. Zeke turned his attention towards finding her discharge summary, a synopsis of Semple's hospital stay. There was one discharge summary dated 5 days ago.

But the x-ray was dated 3 days ago. Either there was some mistake or she was readmitted. If she was no longer in the hospital, where was the summary of admission during which she had the x-ray? Even if she died in the hospital there would be a discharge summary associated with her stay. Although practitioners were usually good about completing the summaries in a timely manner, the most likely explanation was that it wasn't completed yet.

In the least, Zeke could find out if and why Ms. Semple was readmitted so soon after being discharge by searching the admission diagnosis database. Using her name as a key word, Zeke found an admitting diagnosis dated 3 days ago, the same day as the x-ray. She admitted with sepsis, the vague term for diffuse infection, two days after leaving the hospital.

What about the prior hospital stay? Was there any indication why Semple would be so quickly readmitted with an infection? By reading the discharge summary generated by her prior admission, Zeke learned that Ms. Semple was an eighty-six year old nursing home resident with dementia would was brought to St. Twigleighct for dehydration, which her doctor attributed to poor intake of food and liquids. If this were true, Zeke surmised that Ms. Semple had severe dementia, to the point where she was bedridden and totally dependent on the care of others. With what went on in some nursing homes, it was a common reason for admission and Ms. Semple responded well to intravenous hydration and was sent back to the nursing home in 3 days. Zeke read the summary twice; there was no mention of any infection.

Just then Zeke's pager began to alarm. He didn't recognize the number on the display, and he had the location of most extensions memorized.

He picked up the receiver next to the computer and dialed.

"Dr. Oswald," Zeke said when his call was answered.

"Zeke, it Law," the pathologist responded.

"Wow, you're working late," Zeke observed, a little too nervously.

"Yeah, the powers that be want the results of the Carswell post ASAP. He was a popular guy, I guess," he joked. "Actually, they were concerned I would find evidence of foul play. They were suspicious of the death of someone so soon after hospitalization for such a benign arrhythmia.

Probably didn't even need to be admitted, Zeke reminded himself.

"Anyway, since you called before, I figured you would want to know."

"And?" *Are you going to tell me I'm falling under suspicion for negligence or worse in Carswell's death?*

"Now, I've only read about this in textbooks and have never actually seen a case and will have to get expert confirmation, but it looks like an AV node mesothelioma."

A tumor of the heart's electrical conduction system? Zeke was shocked by the news. In a way it was good news for Zeke, there was no reason the suspect a rare cancer while Carswell was hospitalized, and therefore appropriate to discharge him to be follow up by the cardiologist in his office. And Miner didn't say there was any evidence Carswell died of severe anemia after having his blood drained.

So it doesn't look like a case of homicide by a bloodthirsty doctor in a black out Zeke thought.

But it was a horrible fate for the writer. A collection of abnormal cells located at a junction of the heart's electrical system, smaller than a pin tip, detectable only at autopsy, could cause death without warning. Mesothelioma of the atrioventricular node, so rare there was only a few dozen cases known, was known to pathologists as "the smallest tumor which causes sudden death."

So Carswell died from this tumor which was mistaken for a more benign condition usually treated by observation and sometimes a pacemaker. And the tumor was microscopic, so small it would evade detection by the usual tests.

Would he have lived his life differently if he knew it would be cut short? Zeke wondered. A cruel fate that insidiously creeps up, paying no attention to past foibles or successes. No cosmic or physiologic cause other than faulty programming in Carswell's genetic code, the fruit of life, his heart, spoiled like a bruised apple.

CHAPTER THIRTY

Life could spoil in different ways and Patience was a good illustration of this. Her dependence on alcohol had poisoned her, literally and figuratively, and was affecting her work and personal life. Oversleeping that day caused her to miss morning rounds and arrive late to the hospital, already behind on the day's work, if it hadn't been assigned to anyone else.

Patience was still sound asleep in the on call room when she was startled by her pager. Disoriented, Patience sat on the edge of the bed, hunched over, hugging her shins for a minute before reaching for the phone and dialing the return number.

When the call connected, Patience tried to speak but the phlegm caught the sound in her throat. She cleared it loudly. *Attractive,* she thought before retrying. "Student Doctor McMorris, I was paged."

"Hey, Patience." It was the bow-tied, compulsive resident Jonathan Gordon. "I'll be leaving soon, no admissions so far. I'd like to do walk rounds on our patients before I go."

Ugh. Patience looked at her watch. *At ten o'clock at night? Is this really friggin' necessary?* "Okay."

"We're meeting on eight C."

"I'm on my way," she said quietly, trying to hide her anger and adopt an air of professionalism.

Patience contemplated stopping to get a RockStar energy drink from a vending machine before meeting up with the team. She could have used the caffeine but decided she didn't have the luxury of enough time. The team would be kept waiting if she stopped, after missing rounds this morning, strolling in late to evening rounds drinking from a brightly colored can of energy drink could adversely affect her grade and her standing among her peers.

Still she was the last to arrive to the group, consisting of the resident and two interns. The resident looked impatient; the interns looked away. But at least no one could blame her lateness on her inconsiderately stopping for a soft drink.

"Okay. Now that we're all here, let's begin." Gordon led the team through the hallway to outside the door of one of the team's rooms. Darren Patterson, tall, skinny and dressed in wrinkled, faded scrubs, was the intern responsible for the patient's care. He began presenting.

"Mr. Baker is a thirty-four year old African American male-"

"Darren, is Mr. Baker's race truly germane to his hospitalization?" Gordon interrupted.

"Er...I...uh...no, it's not."

"Then kindly omit it from the HPI."

"Sorry. Mr. Baker is a thirty-four year old male—"

"Darren," Gordon interrupted again.

"*Yes.*" One could tell from the tone his response the intern was getting frustrated by not being able to finish even one sentence.

"If you refer to the patient as 'Mister,' it's redundant to say he is a thirty-four year-old *male.*"

Christ, this is going to be like pulling teeth. Patience thought during the awkward pause that followed Gordon's advice. *I wish I were at the 649 drinking Potter's with my fox buddy.*

"I'm not trying to give you a hard time," Gordon explained. "It's imperative to be concise, economical with one's words when presenting."

Dr. Patterson blinked and stared at Dr. Gordon blankly.

"Please continue."

"Mr. Baker is a thirty-four year old sickler—"

"Sickle cell patient."

"—Sickle cell patient who was admitted yesterday with a sickle cell pain crisis. Tests showed no significant drop in hemoglobin or platelets. He is receiving round-the-clock ketoprofen and hydration, doing well, feeling better today."

"Okay, shall we?" Gordon asked rhetorically.

They entered the room, with Patterson and Gordon taking positions on the opposite sides of the bed. The other intern and Patience remained at the foot of the bed. Patience backed into the wall to lean on it while Gordon spoke to the patient.

"Hi Mr. Baker," he said, trying to sound like a regular person, but to Patience it sounded put on, embarrassingly fraudulent. "We're just makin' our evening rounds."

Oh, come on, Jonathan, Patience said to herself of Gordon's affect.

Mr. Baker smiled at the resident but looked nervous. "Oh, I thought you were coming to tell me I had one month to live."

Gordon took the patient's joke seriously. Patience thought it was the right thing to do. Things that were so common to hospital staff can be frightening to patients. "No, we think you're doing well," Gordon reassured him. "We are just doing routine visits on all our patients. You don't mind if I do a little teaching with the team, do you?"

"No, I don't mind." Mr. Baker, reassured, now had one eye on his television anyway, watching one of the *Law and Order* series.

"You might hear us throwin' around a little medical jargon here and there. Please don't be alarmed."

"Okay."

"Patience," Gordon continued, with a little snap to his voice to focus the medical student's attention. "What's the underlying problem in sickle cell anemia?"

Patience's mind hadn't been focused when Gordon called on her and the question caught her off-guard. "The...the...the blood cells...sickle...uh...become deformed...uh..." she stammered.

Gordon smiled in a patronizing fashion. "Uh..." he said, mimicking her response and prompting a snort from the presenting intern, "...why?"

"Um...uh..."

Looking strangely at Patience, the intern standing next to her, small, mousy woman named

Laura Keller, took over. "It's caused by a substitution mutation in the hemoglobin chain. Glu-6-val," genetic shorthand for the replacement of amino acids valine for glutamic acid at the sixth position of the protein. "The mutated protein causes the red cells to harden and assume the shape of a sickle."

"Which is a curved metal blade," Gordon said, over-enunciating the final three words pompously. "Now, what are the complications of sickle cell disease?"

This time Patterson answered from the patient's bedside, not allowing Patience a chance to answer. "Hemolysis, hypersplenism, stroke, aseptic bone necrosis, osteomyelitis, pulmonary hypertension..."

"Okay, good." Gordon said, satisfied with the answer. "Don't forget priapism," he added, referring to a prolonged, painful erection.

"No," the intern replied.

"What's that?" Mr. Baker asked, taking his eye off the television.

"Just some medical jargon. You'd know it if you had it."

"Oh," the patient said.

Dickhead, Patience thought.

"Okay." The resident moved on. "May I examine you briefly?" he asked Mr. Baker.

The patient nodded. Gordon listened to his chest and back with a stethoscope. "Are you getting up out of bed a few times during the day?" The resident asked as he ran his hands down his legs, looking for swelling.

"Yes."

"Well, sir, it looks like you're on the launching pad for tomorrow." Gordon extended his hand to shake the patient's.

"Okay, good."

"Good. Mr. Baker, have restful night, and we'll see you in the morning."

Out in the hallway walking the team to the next room, Gordon asked Patience "So, why did I pay so much attention to Mr. Baker's legs and asked if he was ambulating?"

She was prepared to answer this one, but still she phrased her answer in a question. "You're worried about deep vein thrombosis?"

"That's right, doctor," Gordon said approvingly, trying to reward Patience for the recovery over her disastrous first attempt to answer one of his questions. When he wanted to be complimentary, Gordon addressed medical students as doctor, even though they hadn't yet received their degree. "Hospital patients on too much bedrest can develop DVT. We wouldn't want to discharge him home tomorrow to have him code from a saddle embolus."

Patience perceived the resident's concern about a fatal lung embolism to be rhetorical so she added nothing.

They arrived at the next patient's doorway and the mousy intern, Dr. Keller, began presenting. "Mr. Cummings is a fifty-four year old patient with end stage renal disease on hemodialysis. He was admitted two days ago from the dialysis unit with hyperphosphatemia. It is slowly improving with phosphate restriction and lanthanum."

"And when is his next dialysis appointment?" Gordon asked.

"He's due tomorrow so I called today to book it."

"Good work," Gordon said.

Oh, aren't you just so perfect, Patience snickered to herself contemptuously.

The team entered the patient's room and Gordon gave the same speech about they were just making rounds, please excuse the jargon, and so on. Feeling like it was unusually hot in the room, Patience experienced a wave of lightheadedness while Gordon was talking. She widened her stance and clasped her hands behind her back for stability.

Fortunately for Patience, the resident decided to pick on someone else. "Dr. Patterson, what are the causes of hyperphosphatemia?" He asked.

"Renal failure (of course), tumor lysis, rhabdomyolysis, lactic acidosis, acromegaly, vitamin D toxicity, hyperparathyroidism, pseudohypoparathyroidism-"

"To distinguish it from pseudopseudohypoparathyroidism, phosphate levels are normal," the resident interrupted.

Keller turned to Patience and whispered, "I was just about to say that."

Oh God, Patience thought, *could this get more friggin' boring?* She swooned again and began to feel drowsy, so she moved backwards to lean against the wall. Her back was supported by a red plastic sharps disposal container.

But when she leaned back harder, she heard a *POP* followed by a sharp pain in her upper back.

Fully awake and alert in a split second, Patience jumped away from the wall and fell forward.

"*OW!*" she screamed as she felt something pinching and then tearing her skin as she moved away from the box.

"Patience, what the..." Gordon began in a scolding tone, but his sentence was cut short when Patience turned around to reveal that a needle had punched through and was sticking straight out of the plastic container. It was smeared with blood. Gordon and the two interns stared in horror as the realization set in that she had been stuck deeply with a used needle. At first Patience was dumfounded looking at the needle, but soon she broke down and began to cry.

Oh shit oh shit oh shit kept repeating in Patience's mind and she was probably crying it out loud too. *Oh shit oh shit oh shit what am I gonna do* she thought. *The needle could have HIV, hepatitis, cancer cells oh shit oh shit oh SHIT!*

She must have been saying some of it out loud because her resident said, trying to be gentle, "Patience, calm down." He was about to add that she might be upsetting the patient when she started screaming at him.

"*DON'T YOU TELL ME TO FUCKING CALM DOWN! It could be an AIDS needle,*" Patience shouted.

"I don't have AIDS," the patient said in a small voice.

"We know that, sir." The mousey intern was trying to be helpful, but the nasal intonation of her voice made her sound more like a nerd than an authority. Then, even less helpful, she added: "You could be in a window phase, er, recently contracted HIV and not know it."

Patience, neck and temples throbbing, glared at her.

"Or it could be a needle used on someone else," Patterson stated dryly.

"I don't have AIDS," the patient repeated, more forcefully this time.

"I thought we were using needleless systems in this hospital," Patterson said to no one in particular, referring to catheter and syringe systems that connected only with a plastic interface.

His detached manner of speaking set Patience off again. "Oh what does it *matter?*" she said hysterically. "It could be hepatitis, who gives a FUCK about needleless systems now—it was a fucking needle*full* system. What the hell am I gonna do?"

"Patience, hold on," the resident said calmly. For all his problems with interpersonal skills, Gordon was a good doctor and would be a good doctor to his hysterical medical student. "I know what to do because I suffered a needle stick injury when I was an intern. He looked at the other interns. "Almost every doctor gets a needle stick at one time or another."

Patience sniffed. "What do I do?" she asked, this time in a weak, teary voice.

Gordon moved closer and put his hand on her shoulder. Ordinarily Patience would violently shrug off such an offer of consolation, but this time she needed it.

"Call the nursing supervisor. He or she will tell you what do to next. He/she will have all the information," Gordon told her.

Patience almost laughed when he said "he-slash-she." *What a dork,* she sniffed to herself.

She felt paralyzed, unmotivated, but knew she had to follow Gordon's instructions. After the initial hysteria began to die down, Patience started to think more clearly. *It's just a little needle, a stab, a pinch, I won't catch anything from that, it probably didn't even reach my blood stream. We don't even know if the needle came in contact with any blood. It may have been used to inject a medication into another bottle or bag to dilute it. Try not to fear the worst.*

"Patience," Gordon gently prodded. "You have to act right away so you can make a decision on whether to start antiretrovirals."

"You mean...protease inhibitors?" Patience asked fearfully, meaning class of medication that were used to treat AIDS that could also be used to prevent the disease from accidental exposure to the virus.

"Come on, follow me," Gordon said to Patience, sensing her reticence. He led her down the hall, behind the nursing station to the conference room when morning rounds started.

Oh, God, was this the room I was supposed to be in this morning? Is this punishment for missing rounds and lying about it? Patience questioned herself. Rather than reaching for the phone, she sat down at the table and stared blankly forward.

"Here, I'll dial for you and hand it over once I'm connected," Gordon suggested.

"Okay." Her eyes were wide, moist.

Gordon dialed 0. "Hello. This is Dr. Gordon, could you please connect me to the nursing supervisor? ...Good evening, Dr. Gordon here. I have my medical student here, Patience McMorris, who needs to report a needle stick." He stretched the receiver over to Patience. "Here you go Patience."

Patience took the receiver and spoke into it, emotionless. "I'm student doctor McMorris. I was stuck with a needle though a sharps container."

"When did it happen?" said a female voice, equally unfeeling.

"A few minutes ago."

"What's the location?"

"What?" Patience asked.

"Where...did it happen?" The voice rephrased the question impatiently.

"In a patient's room on eight C."

"Have you cleansed the area with soap and water?

"No."

"Was it known to be a needle used in the care of an HIV positive patient?" The nursing supervisor seemed to be reading from a checklist of questions.

"No...I mean I don't know."

There was a pause in the conversation as Patience realized what it was like to be in the position of someone needing care rather than caregiver.

"You'll have to be evaluated by the on-call doctor. Tell me your extension, let me look up who it is and I'll page the doctor to your number."

"Okay." With a grudging tone, Patience told the nursing supervisor the number. She hung up the phone and began to experience self-pity. *Why does this have to happen to me? Why can't I just be normal and enjoy life, like the warmth of sunlight on the skin?*

Patience waited alone as Jon Gordon went to complete rounds once he knew that the hospitalist was on his way to meet her. The resident had assessed her state of mind and determined she was no longer hysterical and could be trusted to wait alone without incident. Gordon had also asked Patience if she wanted him to stay and she sounded sincere when she replied it wasn't necessary.

While it was true that her thoughts were no longer dominated by repetitive curses, panic had given way to raw anxiety in Patience. *What if I get AIDS?* She worried. *No one will ever want to be with me, marry me. What if I wanted to start a family? Who am I fucking kidding, no one would want me anyway.*

Should I start antiretrovirals?

Better wait until the on-call doctor comes, he'll be able to advise.

Even if Patience didn't contract HIV, there were other viruses to worry about. Hepatitis B or C could be transmitted by needles. These were nasty viral infections of the liver without cures. At least there were good treatments for HIV disease; in hepatitis, treatments were limited and could at times the side effects of treatment could be worse than the disease.

How could you be so stupid! Leaning up against a sharps container! Why are you so out of control?

As Patience asked herself this question, her unconscious had an answer. She wondered next: *Can I drink on interferon? Or an anti-HIV cocktail?*

How about stopping either way?

Maybe this disaster was a sign that Patience needed to get under better control. And that meant doing something about the drinking. Had she not been so hungover today, maybe she wouldn't felt it necessary to lean against a flimsy plastic sharps container. *Stupid!*

Okay, Patience thought, *it's time to make a clichéd deal with God. Please, if I am saved from this predicament, I promise to give it up. Either way, protease inhibitors or not, AIDS or not, hepatitis or not, I will change my life.*

"Patience?" a voice asked at the door. Patience looked over to find Zeke Oswald leaning on the door frame. "What happened?"

Oh great, my self-righteous babysitter is on call tonight. I can't wait to hear what he has to say about this.

"They didn't tell you?" Patience said in an exasperated tone. "I got stuck by a needle."

May I come in?"

"Sure," she said with a questioning tone, wondering why he felt a need to ask.

Zeke passed through the doorway and sat at the table next to Patience, not uncomfortably close to her nor too far. "Yes I was told. But I wanted to hear it in your own words," he said calmly.

Unaccustomed to being in the role of patient, Patience didn't know whether to feel patronized or at ease by Zeke. Preparing to answer, she looked up at his face. In addition to a calm demeanor, Patience identified something she never noticed before. His face had a quiet confidence, but also something else: a soul troubled by the past, an expression of burnt out aggravation.

Patience recounted the details of her accident to Zeke, leaving out the feelings of self-blame she felt about her lifestyle, for now. Zeke listened carefully and when she was finished, called a nurse into the conference room to accompany them while he examined the puncture. Patience would have to lift her scrub top and Lycra t-shirt to make the wound accessible, and it was customary for Zeke to request a female chaperone when was with a female patient.

Patience pulled up her scrubs and t-shirt, exposing her back and embarrassingly revealing that she wore no bra. (It wasn't necessary.)

Her embarrassment was also unnecessary. Out of professionalism, Zeke didn't even pay attention to such things. "How old is this tattoo?" He asked.

"College," Patience replied, relieved that Zeke wasn't facing her to see her blushing skin.

"Have you had a recent tetanus booster?" he asked as he looked closely at the wound.

"Before med school," Patience answered.

"So three or four years ago?"

"Uh huh."

"It looks pretty clean, I don't think you need any antibiotics. Did anyone take the needle?"

"No. As far as I know," she added insecurely.

"So, let's go, show me the room so I can take a look."

The pair walked down the hall and into the room in silence. Patience, looking like a guilty child, bowed her head, shrugged one shoulder and pointed to the container on the wall. The needle was sticking straight out from the plastic. Zeke moved in close to the sharp metal, looking at it from the side, his ear almost brushing the plastic. His nose was about three inches from the needle, and from an observer's viewpoint from the other side it appeared to pierce the side of his eye. Zeke saw that the needle was now dry, without any signs of blood or fluid contamination. He still thought it wise to have it analyzed by the lab. The lab could attempt to recover any genetic material that could be used to identify HIV or hepatitis virus. The lab would also perform routine bacteriologic cultures by sliding or immersing the needle in growing media to see if it was contaminated by any drug-resistant strains of bacteria.

Zeke backed away from the container and moved towards the patient's side. Zeke introduced himself and stated the purpose of the visit.

"Mr. Cummings, how long have you been in the hospital?"

"Two days."

"Then we can't even be sure the needle was used…" Zeke was having trouble finding the right words "…used for your care. Do you mind if we take some blood to look for viruses?"

"Like I told the others, I don't have anything like that." He then glanced at Patience and saw the look on her face and the redness in her eyes from the tears. After a moment said, in a more forgiving tone, "But of course, do what you need to do."

"Thanks," Zeke and Patience said together, but her voice barely audible.

"The nurse or tech will come sometime tonight."

"Okay."

When they arrived back at the conference room, they resumed their seats. Zeke leaned in towards Patience for added privacy, looked with concern into her brown, worried eyes and began to speak.

"Patience, based on the size of the needle and the lack of evidence of contamination, I'm going to classify this as a low-risk needle stick injury. I will still look through the ward's records over the last week or so to look for any transmissible diseases that may have made their way into that sharps container. I will leave the decision up to you whether to start on protease inhibitor. You can have access to them right away if you feel you need them."

She broke eye contact first. "I don't think I need them." She raised her head to look at Zeke again. "Do you?" she asked, raising her brow a bit.

"No." There was a pause as Patience took in the recommendation, followed by his asking "Do you have a pager?"

She gave him the number "649," mistakenly naming the address of the cemetery in which she spent many nights, studying and drinking schnapps. "Sorry," she apologized, looking down in humiliation, "I mean 886. 886," she repeated.

"Got it. If you don't hear from me, don't forget to go to occupational health first thing in the morning for blood tests."

"I wouldn't be positive already, right?" Patience questioned.

"No. They want to make sure you don't have AIDS or hepatitis already."

"Oh."

Zeke left her in the conference room to decide if she should rejoin her team and complete her call or head home to most likely confront and defeat her cravings for alcohol for the first time in a long time.

CHAPTER THIRTY-ONE

Selinda had enjoyed her share of successes in the past two years, but none of these had required any talent as an investigator. In those successes, the perpetrator was usually handed to her easily by a witness or obvious blunder on the part of the suspect. One had left his wallet at the scene, another disposed of the murder weapon in an obvious place. These murders at St. Twigleighct had become challenging not only from an intellectual standpoint but also from an emotional one. Selinda had nagging doubts about her abilities. Her feelings of mediocrity plagued her. Would she feel this ineffective for the rest of her career? When Selinda felt this insight come to the surface, she would often think of how, when she was a child, she would play checkers with her father. She was learning the game, and like most parents, he would allow her to win to prevent her from becoming discouraged. But he wouldn't allow her to win always, as he wanted also to teach her that winning didn't always come easily. And he would use her moves on the checkerboard to scrutinize her character. "You know, Linney Bear, sometimes it seems that you're trying too hard not to lose instead of trying to win. Try thinking about it the other way around."

Selinda didn't know what that meant when she was eight years old, but she did now. Her insecurities led to an overly cautious approach, and she often felt like a child in class, too unsure of herself to raise her hand with the correct answer out of fear of anxiety and embarrassment. She had also developed a resistance to being proactive when presented with a challenge. She felt that once she was on the path of defeat, she could not alter it.

Selinda realized that this was an immature response and that realistically she had to take a proactive approach to solve a homicide case, no matter how hard her heart thumped and her throat choked when she had to assert herself in a potentially uncomfortable situation. She would remind herself of her father's comments on how she played board games when she needed motivation. *Try thinking of it the other way around.* Added to this motivation was a desire to catch a killer that had now left a child motherless, a child who would never receive guidance from her mother again. What would motivate someone to kill two apparently unrelated hospital employees?

Selinda spent the afternoon interviewing members from the list of those who were to attend the St. Twigleighct Quality Enhancement meeting. The first person on the list, Margaret Hannah, was a nurse on one of the medical wards. Selinda called the nursing supervisor to find out Hannah was working on ward eight B that day. She found the nurse working on a computer at the eight B nursing station.

"Excuse me," Selinda said to get her attention. Hannah didn't look up from her work.

"You'll have to speak with the clerk," Hannah said sharply, not taking her eyes from the computer but pointing towards the other side of the station.

"Ms. Margaret Hannah?" Selinda took out her badge but didn't flash it. The nurse's face was still glued to the computer screen and Selinda didn't want to appear awkward, standing there holding her badge.

"Yes?" Hannah's eyes glanced over and the detective raised her badge. Her expression was disengaged, but the eyes widened when she became aware of the silver shield. "What? Oh I'm sorry, what can I do for you, officer?"

"Your name was given to me as someone scheduled to attend today's QE meeting—"

"It was cancelled because of that woman's...death," Hannah interrupted nervously.

"Yes I know." Selinda asked her next question quickly to minimize the time Hannah had to think. "Did you know Ms. Duncan well?"

"Huh? Oh, no not really." There was a pause. "Am I a suspect?" she asked with trepidation.

"I'm interviewing everyone who was due at the meeting," Selinda said without inflection.

"Do I need a lawyer?"

Selinda didn't answer. She wasn't in the business of providing legal advice. "Do you know who she was close to?"

The woman replied quickly. "She and John are friends. John Smith, he's also on the committee."

So he was. Selinda asked a few more questions but soon realized that she had gotten all the useful information she was likely to receive from the conversation. Because he was on the list, she had planned to interview John Smith, and now she had an angle.

John Smith, like most mid-level administrators at St. Twigleighct, was a nurse by training. He had spent his entire career at the same hospital, starting as a surgical scrub nurse thirty years earlier. After practicing for many years, the hospital administration decided Smith could run the surgical department. Taking night courses to obtain a master's degree in nursing and business, he became the surgical administrator and had stayed in the position for fifteen years.

Smith had an office on the surgical ward and was expecting the detective when she found him there. "President Safford told me you would be coming..." he told her after introductions.

The president gave you a courtesy call? Selinda thought, raising her brow. As he stood up to shake her hand, Selinda could see that John Smith was a tall man, dark-skinned with large hands and facial features. When he smiled, she noticed his teeth were unnaturally white. He was an intimidating figure but Selinda tried thinking of it the other way around. Maybe she was the intimidating figure in this exchange.

He spoke again. "Terrible thing. How is her daughter?"

"I can't give you any details other than to say she's fine and with family."

"Yes, yes, of course I understand. Working in a hospital we deal with privacy issues all the time. But that's good to hear," Smith added.

"So, people tell me you and Ms. Duncan were close."

The question didn't seem to throw him at all. "Yes, I knew Bev very well. We had lunch together quite often."

"Did you ever socialize other than lunch or outside the hospital?"

"No, nothing aside from hospital-sponsored holiday parties catered at restaurants. We haven't had one of those in a while."

"So it was mostly a professional relationship," Selinda concluded.

"Yes. But we did discuss our personal lives as well, it's fair to say. She was a single mother, you know. And it was tough at times, but she did her jobs well, both here and at home."

"I see. Do you know what she was working on in preparation for today's meeting?" This line of questioning would reveal to him that she was still working on the motive, but it was an important question that Selinda had a hunch Smith could answer.

It turned she was right. "Yes, very well. She always had a little performance anxiety..." He paused. Was he getting emotional? "...so I would help her with her presentations sometimes."

"Can you tell me more about it?" Selinda asked, not wanting to reveal that she had some idea.

"Bev was working on length of stay issues. She found that our efforts to significantly reduce hospital lengths of stay were paying dividends. She also found that readmission rates, especially for our patients from skilled nursing facilities, were up. This was an important piece of information we would have discussed at the meeting. Were our policies aimed at decreasing hospital stay leading to greater readmission rates by discharging patients prematurely? I'm sure there would have been a great debate."

"A friendly debate?" Selinda wanted to know.

"Oh yes," Smith chuckled. "These meetings were never confrontational, if that's what you were getting at. Everyone seemed to get along. No major personality clashes."

"Would this information have embarrassed anyone or put them in a difficult situation?"

"Actually, I don't think so. I never shared this with the members, but I sort of predicted this. It only stands to reason: if you rush patients out of the hospital, they might end up back soon."

Selinda raised an eyebrow.

"Don't get me wrong; the policies were designed to increase efficiency, not to cut corners. The hospital *will* increase its profit margin by decreasing length of stay. Plus, ironically, readmissions can also make money for the hospital, but that's only if the patient is admitted with a diagnosis that is different from the one they were just discharged with."

Selinda decided to change course. "You said you discussed personal matters with Ms. Duncan. Was she acquainted with the other murder victim, Caleb Fisher?"

"Not that I know of."

"Do you know of any close friends in the hospital? Boyfriends?"

"Not really."

"What about her daughter's father?"

"They're divorced. She didn't mention him much. He did pop in from time to time. A couple years ago they were fighting about something. She even called me to her house for help."

"Was she afraid for her safety?"

"Not sure. It seemed she needed help negotiating—not self-defense. Still I guess he's someone you should track down."

"Thanks for the tip," Selinda said matter-of-factly.

Anticipating the next question Smith added, "Bev's family will know how to reach him." He paused, catching his breath. "I wonder if he knows yet."

Hopefully, uniformed officers were interviewing her ex-husband sometime that day. Selinda left her card with John Smith. After she left his office he ran his fingers over the typeset of the card with a contemplative frown. He set the card on his desk and leaned back in his chair, placed his hands together, up to his lips. Smith picked up the phone to call Duncan's office.

"Hi, it's John Smith, I wanted to know if you could download or email me a copy of Beverly Duncan's PowerPoint slides from her presentation."

"I can't," the assistant responded.

"I see. You mind telling me why not?"

"The police took the computer as evidence."

Selinda used the hospital operator to page the remaining name on the QE meeting list, Linwood Bruner. He was a pulmonologist, specializing in diseases of the lungs. When he was connected to her, Selinda could hear beeping noises in the background. She introduced herself and he said that he could meet with her right away in the MICU.

"I'll be the best looking one at the nursing station," Dr. Bruner offered so that Selinda could recognize him.

Amidst the beeps, she could also hear another male voice say, "Very funny, *doctor*."

This guy is really impressed with himself, Selinda noted as she replaced the receiver in the phone's cradle.

She made her way to the section of the hospital where Caleb Fisher worked to find that Bruner's opinion of himself, although conceited, was accurate. He was seated at one of the computers in an expensive-looking suit and floral tie. Somewhere in his mid-twenties, he had brown hair, greased and brushed back away from his face, handsome with strong features and a square jaw. He flashed a smile as Selinda approached him and extended his hand.

"Dr. Bruner?"

"Call me Linwood. *You're* the detective?" he asked, eyeing her up and down as they shook hands.

"Yes," Selinda replied, not flattered in any way.

His grip on her hand lingered. "Say, you're cute." He turned his hand over, exposing a wedding band.

"And you're married, I see." The computer screen at which he had been looking displayed an instant messaging window. "Is that your wife you're chatting with?" Selinda asked, nodding in the direction of the computer.

Bruner moved quickly to close down the window. "Oh, that's not her, just a buddy," he said. He was smiling, but his expression seemed artificial. "The hospital blocked access to Facebook, but somebody figure out Google messenger works."

"I see. So, Doctor—"

"Linwood," he corrected.

"Doctor. What was your role in the QE meeting?"

He seemed fidgety. Was this baseline behavior for him or did the question make him nervous? Selinda wasn't sure. "I'm the physician representative on the committee. Mainly I communicate to the other physicians what I see as avenues for improvement." Bruner brightened his eyes and smiled again. "Say, do you like Thai food? Perhaps we can have this conversation over some dinner." To the smile he added a goofy look to his face, like a child asking a favor, which Selinda found detestable rather than charming.

She ignored his advance and asked him how well he knew Beverly Duncan, whether he knew of any enemies, and the like before Bruner was paged away to another part of the hospital.

While no directly useful information had been supplied by the flirty doctor, something he'd said gave Selinda an idea. Bruner had shut the instant messaging window he'd been using to chat on the computer but she noticed that the instant messaging icon still resided in the desktop tray. Selinda wondered if Caleb Fisher had used this computer for similar communications. Thinking that any messages sent or received by Fisher could provide useful information and potentially help unlock the mystery of his killing, Selinda used the mouse to click on the icon in an attempt to access old messages.

The program opened to a login screen and she couldn't go any further without a username and password. *Everything done on a computer is saved somewhere,* Selinda remembered hearing from the department's information technology guys.

"Can I use this phone?" she asked the clerk.

The clerk ignored her. Selinda picked up the receiver and started dialing. Almost immediately, a busy signal pulsed in her ear, so she used her finger to end the attempt and tried again, this time starting by dialing a 9.

"Albany PD."

"Please connect me to IF."

"Hello, Information Forensics." Selinda recognized the voice of Louden Andrews's, the IT specialist who provided her Caleb Fisher's cell phone.

"Hi, Louden? It's Selinda Bruchart."

"Yes?" Andrews asked hopefully.

"I need a little remote IT help."

"Oh." He sounded deflated, like he expected Selinda was calling just to chat.

Sorry, just trying to solve a murder here. Instead of saying it aloud Selinda made a small noise like a polite chuckle. "I'm here at St. Twigleighct Medical Center working of the Fisher case, trying to get some information from one of their PCs and I thought of something you said once."

"Really?" The hope in Andrews's voice was back.

"Remember you were telling me that everything people do on a computer is saved somewhere?"

"Well, not everything, but sure. Even things that are deleted by the user."

"How about instant messages?"

"Oh, sure."

It was Selinda's turn to sound hopeful. "Great, now I need your help. I can't log in to the computer's messaging program."

"Well, you would only be able to see your own messages and responses that way."

"Oh right. And I don't use instant messages."

"Pity," Andrews commented.

Was it? Selinda didn't agree; she preferred to talk face to face or pick a phone to communicate. "So, how do I retrieve someone else's?"

"Just bring it in and I'll do it."

Selinda thought about the delays associated with the extra effort of paperwork and phone calls involved in getting a subpoena. "I may do just that, Louden," she said, lowering her voice, trying to sound seductive in order to prepare him for her next question. Not as experienced with the art of flirtation as the good Dr. Bruner, Selinda sounded more froggy than flirty. "Is there anything I can do here, right now, to get a head start?"

"Hmm, well. Do you see a nanny program installed?"

"A what?"

"A nanny program. They're used to keep track of what your kids are doing online or to monitor an employee's use of a computer. We use one at the station. Recently, I won't use names, one of your colleagues was busted for looking at porn sites."

You don't need to use names, I can imagine who it was, Selinda thought. "So how do I check to see if this computer has one?"

"Just look for an icon. It should be running in the task bar."

Selinda started searching.

"The most common ones are Spector, Eblaster, and PC Pair," Andrews added to help her search.

Selinda rolled over a picture of a half-closed eye. A box appeared that said "PC Pair is watching."

"Got it." She double-clicked it. Login screen. "Ah," Selinda muttered discouragingly.

Selinda's utterance finally got the clerk's attention. She glared at the detective. Selinda, feeling like she upset the staff at the local library, lowered her voice. "I don't know the login," she whispered in frustration.

"Don't fret, detective," Andrews whispered back. Then in full voice: "Most IT guys in the hospital are lazy and the want to make it easy for their colleagues. Did the user name appear automatically?"

"Yes." *Twig* was written in the user box.

"Most of the time the password is the same as the user name."

Selinda typed *twig* in the password box and pressed enter. The program opened.

"Wow, I'm in," Selinda said quietly, the amazement audible in her voice.

"Good. Now look for something that says 'chat' or 'messaging.'"

Selinda looked but didn't see anything like that. "How about 'history'?" she asked.

"Yeah, try that."

She clicked on it and a new window opened with a list.

Pages, Chat, Downloads, Streaming

Selinda's violet eyes sparkled with the glow of the monitor and the enthusiasm for a potential new lead. She clicked *Chat* and a list of users opened.

Scanning the list, one name stood out in her mind: *whiterain,* the name Fisher had used to identify himself on his own computer. There was a plus sign next to the name, indicating that the name could be expanded to outline form, and when Selinda clicked on that, a date appeared under the screen name, indented.

It was the date of the murder.

Selecting that date revealed an instant messaging dialogue, which was more of a monologue.

Whiterain: brainboy, u there?

Whiterain: think im on 2 smthng

Whiterain: wat we talked bout

Whiterain: brb alarms…

BRB. *Be right back.*

But Selinda could find nothing to follow.

"Anything?" Andrews asked.

"Yes, but why can't I see the other person's entries. The one he was chatting with?"

"You should be able to. Maybe that program doesn't save responses."

Although disappointed that she was unable to see the response, Selinda felt this could be a lead. If *whiterain* was "on 2 smthng," perhaps that smthng was what got him killed.

And she had a name. Or at least a nickname. "Louden, I need you to search the Fisher computer again. Try to find out if he knew a *brainboy,* and if there's anything that gives up his identity."

"*Brainboy,* huh?" Andrews mused. "Sounds like a superhero. This'll cost you extra."

"Put it on my tab. Goodbyyye, Louden." Selinda disconnected so that Andrews couldn't respond with his nerdy wit.

"And we have our first lead," Selinda declared.

CHAPTER THIRTY-TWO

Sitting in the conference room alone, Patience felt frozen in a state of shock. She wanted to leave the hospital, escape, go home to the comfortable burn and buzz of her schnapps. She knew that alcohol wouldn't be wise if she caught hepatitis as both were toxic to the liver. Schnapps wouldn't mix well with any medications for hepatitis or HIV. And hadn't she made a promise to herself to stop drinking? Still, didn't the doctor state her injury was low risk for transmission of these horrible diseases? She had an urge to call him for reassurance but didn't act upon it.

Rationally, Patience figured it was better to stay in the hospital that night and finish her call. Keeping busy was the best way to deal with worry. Still, her need to escape overrode this line of thinking and, in an almost zombie-like way, Patience left the hospital and drove home.

As soon as she entered her apartment and heard the sound of her keys strike the small table by the door and pierce the silence of her solitude, a wave of loneliness passed over her. Patience ran into her bedroom, and although she lived alone, shut herself in by closing the door. Feeling like a breakdown was coming, she sat on the bed and hugged a pillow. She began to rock and soon the tears came, flowing down her face, a high-pitched whine releasing each sob. Patience's isolated life, dominated by the use and thinking about the use of alcohol, left her no one to call, no emotional support, no one to talk to. She had become emotionally estranged from her family, and the relationship she developed over the years became victims of the sacrifice needed to get through the rigors of medical school. Friends who tried to stay in touch were rebuffed, both actively and passively. Many attempts by acquaintances to maintain contact were unreciprocated; friends tired of the groggy, uninterested phone conversations and eventually the phone stopped ringing, and Patience's email inbox filled with spam.

Patience spent the small remaining hours of the night lying on her bed, on her back, eyes lightly closed or staring at the ceiling, occasionally welling up with tearful sorrow. *Oh please oh please oh please, let me be okay. Maybe I'll go into substance abuse treatment as a career,* Patience bargained during these periods of sadness. While she wept, overwhelmed with feelings of self-pity, the tears ran down the side of her face, turning cold as they rolled to wet her ears and the bed sheets. Patience felt unable to swallow, to choke down the feeling of hopelessness, convinced that she would feel this way forever.

The following morning Patience was dazed but sober and functional. Her mood was volatile; she still felt on the verge of tears yet managed to chuckle as she drove the Altima over a pothole and heard the tinkle of empty bottles in the trunk. She rationalized that because she didn't have any new patients to present on rounds, it was unnecessary to inform her supervising resident that she would be missing rounds that morning. Upon her arrival at St. Twigleighct, Patience went straight to the Occupational Health office where the doctor asked her all the same questions she'd answered the night before, came to the same conclusion and drew some blood samples. Patience's eyes welled up with tears when the doctor asked "Are you married?" as part of her history-taking and Patience nearly choked when answering the next question, "Do you have any children?"

Along with these teary reactions, Patience had also begun developing feelings of anger over her situation. She left the Occupational Health office scowling, in a foul mood on her way to the hospital. Patience was angry over what had happened to her and the disruption it had caused, feeling at times like life's roadkill. But she also directed some of the anger towards herself. It was her own stupid fault, leaning into a flimsy sharps container.

She should have called to tell them she would be late to rounds. But she was her passive self as usual, preferring to choose entropy over action. Motivating herself for every action seemed a struggle. Now she was anxious about walking in on the group, worrying about what she would say as they all stared at her. They could keep their fucking sympathy as far as she was concerned.

But her mind also felt sharp, more quick-witted than it had been in a long time. Was this the clarity alcoholics spoke of? The cycle of inebriation, followed by hangover recovery, withdrawal then inebriation again kept Patience occupied, allowing her avoid things she'd rather not deal with, like emotions. Breaking the cycle cleared the way for her emotions to come to the surface again, and she was overwhelmed.

Patience found some courage in this new clarity and made her way to the conference room on eight B. The attending physician was not there so it seemed as if rounds had ended and the team was going over their work for the day. Jon Gordon was going over the plans with Darren Patterson, Laura Keller, and Jodi, the medical student who Patience detested for upstaging her on rounds.

"Hey, Patience, how are you?" Gordon asked earnestly.

Patience expected a hostile response to his question but Gordon's tone had actually expressed the right amount of concern without coming off as patronizing. "Fine," she replied, curtly but politely. "Sorry I didn't call but I had to go to Occupational Health first thing."

Jodi's eyebrows raised in curiosity. *Drop dead,* Patience thought.

Patterson and Keller were watching carefully for Gordon's response. "Don't worry about it. If I can be of any help, let me know," he said.

"Thanks."

"Ready to get to work?" Gordon asked nicely. "Remember, we're on the code team today."

Patience nodded. Through this experience, her opinion of Gordon had changed to one of respect. She felt she had misjudged him in the past as an uptight asshole in a bowtie. Life-altering events like getting stuck with a used needle sure changed one's perspective.

Gordon turned his attention towards Patterson to explain something about a patient's care, and while this occurred, Laura Keller drew closer to Patience to ask, "The nurses called about one of your patients on rounds, Mrs. Waverly. Her IV is out, they tried to place a new one, *blah, blah, blah*, they couldn't get it, the doctor needs to do it. You want to try? I'll go with you."

"Uh, sure," Patience said.

On their way to the patient's room, Keller broke the uncomfortable silence. "So, how are you doing?" the intern asked Patience, her voice, not casual but full of meaning.

Patience felt her temper rising like water on the verge of boiling. After a pause she became livid. "Look, *Laura*, if Jon sent you to babysit the fragile medical student, believe me, I'M FINE and I don't need any help."

Patience underestimated the impact her angry words would have on her colleague. Keller stammered a defensive but timid response. "He didn't ask…I'm just trying to help…everybody gets…"

"I know, *I know*," Patience said through her teeth, trying to keep her voice down in the hallway. Keller looked scared and hurt. Patience's voice became an angry whisper, mimicking their attempts to console. "Everybody gets stuck, we've all been through it, whatever we can do to help. I heard enough...*enough.* You people don't give a shit."

"Okay," Keller whispered back, in a tone that pleaded Patience would stop. She got her wish as the two continued towards the patient's room: Keller appeared defeated: shuffling, eyes down; Patience: tense, arms straight, hands in fists.

They entered the room and made their introductions. Keller surveyed the room and began to mutter. "Do ya think they could have at least set up an IV and flush—"

One her pagers interrupted her complaining. "It's the code pager," Keller commented, although Patience knew this. The intern trotted over to the doorway and she cocked her ear to better hear the announcement.

"Code blue eight C, code blue eight C," the pager crackled.

"One floor up," Keller said. "Come on Patience, let take the stairs."

The look on her colleague's face while she was yelling at her made Patience feel guilty about her outburst and her fury had melted into insecurity. "Okay."

Hearing the emergency call, Patience was now relieved she wasn't alone. She hated cardiac arrest codes, attending them she felt lost, helpless, and in the way. The chaotic nature of the code left her feeling that she couldn't follow what was going on to enable her to have a sense of what should happen next. Would this feeling change with more experience or would she never get it? Patience worried about this.

They jogged up the stairs, the sound of their footsteps echoing in the cavernous stairwell. Both kept their hands against the pockets of their lab coats to keep the contents from spilling out from the jogging motion. At one point Keller placed her hand over breast pocket to secure what was inside, looking like she was making a running pledge.

They arrived at the room to find the Gordon and an intern from another medical team at the bedside of an unconscious elderly man, attached to a ventilator. Patience remained in the doorway while Keller ran to the bedside.

"Ah, hi Laura, please take over chest compressions," Gordon told her. The intern stepped aside as Keller moved in to start CPR. "David, let the rest of the team in on the details of the code."

"I was called because he desatted," the intern explained, using the nickname to describe a sudden loss of oxygen in the blood. "So I increased the PEEP—"

"What were the peak and plateau pressures?" Gordon asked.

"The...?" The intern's trailed voice trailed off in a way that indicated he had no idea what the resident was asking.

"The peak and plateau pressures from the ventilator *when you were called.*" Gordon rephrased.

David didn't have a chance to respond as a nurse's loud voice interrupted their conversation from the doorway.

"Excuse us, *doctor.*" The nursing staff had arrived with the code cart, a rolling box that resembled a large tool box, used to transport equipment needed for various medical emergencies. The nurse was speaking to Patience, who was blocking their entrance. Patience jumped, and moved quickly inside the room to a wall away from the action. And away from the sharps container. Patience took the time to look out the window to notice the beautiful weather; sunlight streaming through the glass like it did when one was underwater.

With the obstruction relieved, the nurse pushed the cart through the doorway. The cart stopped short, hung up on the floor's divider. She pushed again, harder, and the cart lifted up over the divider and came down with a loud crash that Patience could feel with her teeth.

"Okay, let's get a quick look," Gordon said. He placed the defibrillator paddles on the patient's chest and watched the monitor. "There's a rhythm. No pulse?"

"No pulse," David called out after palpating the patient's leg for the femoral artery.

"Fudgecakes!" Gordon's substitution for an expletive added an air of absurdity to the grave situation. "It's P.E.A.!"

Patience removed a reference card from her pocket. It contained common abbreviations use in a cardiac arrest. P.E.A. stood for "pulseless electrical activity." This poor gentleman's heart was firing electrically, but the electrical impulse wasn't being converted into a heartbeat.

"David, take him off the ventilator and bag him. He may be having a pneumo."

Patience didn't need her card for that one. Gordon was talking about a pneumothorax, a condition where a lung explodes and deflates like a flat tire and allows air to rush into the chest cavity.

Gordon continued. "Raising the PEEP could cause a tension pneumo." The extra air pressure could crush the patient's heart." Gordon glared at the intern who slowly began sinking into his scrubs. "That's why you check the peak and plateau pressures when desats are reported." Gordon said emphatically, taking his stethoscope from around his neck and putting the earpieces in his ear as he leaned over the patient and listened to the lungs.

"Decreased breath sounds on the left," Gordon declared. "I need a chest needle."

Frantically, the nurses began rummaging around the drawers of the code cart. Witnessing the action and Gordon's words made Patience's chest tighten with anxiety.

"Doc, there's no chest needle in here."

"What?!"

"We can't find—"

"I heard you, I just don't believe it," Gordon exclaimed. He went over to the cart to look for himself.

"Ahhhh," the resident said in frustration. "Patience! Procure a paracentesis kit from the supply room." Even in the heat of the moment Gordon managed to sound like a nerd.

Patience froze.

"I can use the needle from the kit. GO!" Gordon shouted the command.

Patience's eyes widened as she nodded and ran out of the room while the team continued the attempts to resuscitate. She could feel her heart pounding *(no P.E.A. here* she thought) but her mind was clear and focused as she trotted down the hallway. She tried the door to the supply room and found it locked.

"Shit! I need the key!" Patience shouted down the hallway. She could see supplies on metal racks through the thick wire-embedded glass. She had no idea where to find a paracentesis kit.

Looking down the hallway and seeing no one, Patience ran back to the nursing station. But there was no one there either, and the room with the dying patient was all the way at the end. She began to run towards the room but stopped as she noticed a nurse exiting a closer room.

"Hi!" Patience startled the nurse. Breathlessly, she asked the nurse "I need...the key to the supply room...FOR THE CODE."

The nurse was older and walked with a limp, yet they moved quickly back to the supply room door. After it was unlocked Patience pushed the door open and rushed inside, thanking her helper on the way in without looking back. She started scanning the silver metal racks for the kit.

What am I looking for? What does a friggin' paracentesis kit look like?

Patience was panicking, but then she answered her own frantic question.

Wait, I just used a kit the other day to do a belly tap on that cirrhotic patient. It was in a blue plastic tray.

The search was still challenging, there were many blue items to look over. It reminded Patience of searching for an item in a long supermarket aisle. In a supermarket, Patience would abandon her search quickly if unsuccessful. That wasn't an option for her in this case, however, and Patience felt a duty not to hasten this man's death.

Then an image caught her eye. It was a picture, part of a logo on a box of surgical tape. It depicted a grinning brown fox, his tongue hanging out to one side over his sharp white teeth. Under his picture it read

FOX BRAND SURGICAL

To Patience, the fox appeared to be panting, laughing, his eyes sparkling and mischievous. He seemed to find her attempts to locate the kit amusing, smugly peering at her. *You're stupid, inadequate, and you couldn't care less about saving this guy's life! I'm with Fox Brand Surgical! Who are* you *with?* She imagined him saying.

Patience glowered at the fox for a moment then continued her search.

Blue plastic tray!

As she extended her arm to pull the box off the shelf, Patience felt a sharp pain in her back where she was stuck with the needle. Confirming it was a paracentesis kit, Patience ran back to the room and handed it to Gordon.

"Good job, Patience," Gordon exclaimed. "Now take over the job of chest compressions and when I give you the signal, stop. Laura, count out."

"Okay, one and two and one and two and switch," Keller said to Patience, who, smoothly and not missing a beat, stepped in, measured three fingers from the bottom of the patient's sternum, and pushed the heel of one hand with the other on the bone, depressing it 1 1/2 inches deep, counting her compressions softly. The success of her quest to find the paracentesis kit, asserting herself, and the praise from her supervisor boosted her confidence and made her feel like a valuable member of the team. Concentrating on the chest compressions, her anxiety faded like the final moments of a melting cube of ice, replaced by the satisfaction of competently performing a critically important task. But, boy! Did she have a friggin' headache.

With his hands on the patient's chest, Gordon marked an area between the ribs with his index finger. He readied the needle and said, "Okay, stop compressions." Patience did as she was told and Gordon guided the needle into the patient's chest. He slowly removed the plunger from the attached syringe. There was a popping sound as the rubber end exited the syringe.

"Check for a pulse," Gordon said.

Keller felt for one and smiled. "I've got a pulse."

Gordon looked like he would cheer. "Get a blood pressure. Hang some normal saline. Wide open!" he said triumphantly, referring to the rate of infusion.

Holy shit, I just helped save this guy's life! Patience thought when she realized that the pneumothorax would have killed the patient if she hadn't found the paracentesis kit. She felt exhilarated and it seemed as if sobriety was agreeing with her. But what to do when the excitement was over and the next craving for peach schnapps came? Maybe she should accept Oswald's offer of help?

The intern who had caused the pneumothorax in the first place didn't look so happy. "I could've killed the patient," he said.

His statement just hung in the air as no one had anything to add.

CHAPTER THIRTY-THREE

Brainboy.

Selinda had fallen asleep sitting up in bed while reviewing her notes on the St. Twigleighct murders, wondering how someone came up with such a moniker. Still in the same position, she awoke to her alarm at 6:30 and her first thoughts weren't of Caleb Fisher's IM partner but of a hot shower.

Selinda lathered herself, then ran hot water on her face and neck for a few minutes before shutting the water off. Donning a terry robe, she walked in to the kitchen to put on a pot of coffee. Her hair was still wet, the water dripping down her neck onto the robe's collar. As she was pouring the water into the coffee maker her cell phone rang.

"I know it's early, but I have brainboy's number," the voice on the phone said.

"Louden? Are you at work already?" Selinda asked.

"Yeah. I couldn't look on the vic's PC last night but it sounded like you were onto something so I came in early. You want it now?"

"Just leave it on my desk; I'll be in shortly."

"Okay," he replied enthusiastically.

"Louden?"

"Yes?"

"Thanks for the extra effort."

He sounded pleased to hear the compliment. "Sure," he said, his voice absent of the usual sarcastic tone.

After disconnecting, Selinda dried her hair, dressed, applied lipstick and one spray of perfume. After filling a *I heart Albany* travel mug with coffee and sugar and grabbing a protein bar, she left for the precinct.

One her desk was a sealed tan envelope with "For S. Bruchart's eyes only" written on it. The envelope contained a single white piece of paper that read *BB* and a ten digit phone number.

What area code is that? Selinda asked herself as she picked up her desk phone's receiver. After hearing six rings, she was about to give up when a sleepy voice answered.

"Hello?"

"It's the Albany, New York police department calling," Selinda responded.

There was a pause then the voice asked, "Yes?"

"I'm looking for someone acquainted with a Caleb Fisher from New York." Selinda offered.

"He's not here. Is he in some sort of trouble?"

"Who am I speaking to?"

Who Selinda presumed to be *Brainboy* sounded annoyed. "Hey, man, you didn't identify yourself, *officer.*"

Man? "Detective Selinda Bruchart, Albany PD."

"Okay, Detective, if that's who you say you are, I will get the Albany 'PD' phone number and call it in order to speak to your boss to confirm your identity."

"Fine," Selinda said brusquely "Ask for the homicide division. Goodbye." She didn't disconnect right away, waiting for the phrase *homicide division* to have an effect.

"Wait, wait, wait! Christ, is Caleb dead?"

"I'm afraid so," Selinda answered gently.

"Jesus, I was just online with him the other night." The voice was much smaller now.

Selinda was aware of that fact but didn't want to admit it to Brainboy just yet. There was nothing suspicious about his reaction to the news about Fisher's demise; he seemed genuinely surprised to hear it. The way a person responded to a general question like "do you know so and so" could raise suspicion. Still, Selinda's technique was to keep things open-ended in case the person being questioned would give something away in the future.

"Homicide?" Brainboy asked.

"Yes," Selinda said quietly. "How did you know Mr. Fisher?"

There was a sigh on the other end of the phone line before Brainboy responded. "We were college buddies." After nursing school, he stayed near where he grew up and I moved here to Seattle. I'm a neurosurgical scrub nurse.

Oh, Brainboy. That makes sense. "We only know you as Brainboy. What's your actual name?"

"Frost. Alex Frost."

"Mr. Frost, when did you say you were online with Mr. Fisher?"

"I didn't say exactly. But if you know my screen name, I sure you know the answer to your own question."

Selinda did know, it was the night Fisher was killed, yet she didn't reveal that either. Perhaps she discovered the nickname some way other than looking through an instant message session without a warrant.

"How did he seem to you when you were online?"

There was a pause. Selinda assumed Frost was hesitating because he didn't want to get involved or he was afraid of becoming a suspect with his choice of words.

"I was here in Seattle that night," Frost finally said.

"Mr. Frost, you're not a suspect, but thanks for the alibi," Selinda countered. "It's standard procedure to talk to individuals who...communicated with Mr. Fisher shortly before he was killed."

"Was he killed in the hospital?"

The detective continued to remain stingy when it came to details. "Why do you ask?"

Another pause.

"Look, Mr. Frost, like it or not you are already involved. We *will* subpoena all your communications with Mr. Fisher (and I do mean *all* of them) and bring you to Albany if we have to."

Frost sighed and mumbled, "Idiot! What did you get me into?" The line hissed with static.

"Mr. Frost?"

After a moment, he began to speak, this time in a normal tone. "He said he was getting close."

"Close to what?" Selinda said in an encouraging manner.

"I don't know why he was doing this but Caleb noticed some strange goings-on in that hospital."

"Uh-huh."

Without any more hesitation in his voice, Frost went on. "He noticed a pattern in admissions to the MICU. Caleb told me he thought there were an unusual amount of nursing home patients being readmitted to the hospital within a few days of being discharged."

"Nursing home patients?" Selinda asked skeptically. "I would think that they would frequently get admitted anyway."

"Yeah, I know, detective, but they don't all have infections. The patients Caleb was talking about all had the similar infections. He felt he was onto something when he was checking a patient in the MICU for pressure ulcers, he noticed a needle mark on the hip of someone diagnosed with osteomyelitis."

"Osteo-what?" Selinda needed the medial jargon translated.

"A bone infection."

"Would that show up on an x-ray?" Selinda asked.

"Sometimes. With this patient they couldn't find the source of infection so they did a bone scan; it uses radioactive tracers that hone in on inflammation-the ischium lit up."

Selinda processed this information in her mind. *So Fisher was probably in the bone radiology room looking for proof of a bone infection in the area where he saw a needle mark* she thought. *Proof of foul play.*

"Why would someone intentionally cause an infection? Just for fun?" Selinda asked aloud.

"Caleb thought the hospital was behind it. Increased hospital admissions means increased profits. Inject a patient with bacteria just before discharge and boom! They spike a fever 24-48 hours later and take the revolving door back into the hospital with a different diagnosis, septicemia, and the clock on the new DRG starts ticking."

"Do you know if Mr. Fisher shared this theory with anyone else?"

Frost was more relaxed now. "He must have. *I* didn't have him killed."

Now, if only Selinda could figure out who did.

CHAPTER THIRTY-FOUR

Rather than face the anticipated crying fits or the temptation of a half case of schnapps under her sink Patience decided stay at the hospital after her work day was over. After shadowing the on call intern for a few hours and running across the street in the warm summer night air to grab dinner, she returned to ward eight B. She placed her sandwich and spring water on the conference room table and scanned the titles of the textbooks that were kept on the bookshelf for reference. The only thing Patience knew about PEEP was that it stood for "positive end-expiratory pressure." If she read up about it, she could turn an intern's mistake into a positive learning experience.

Patience spotted a pulmonology text on the top shelf. When she tried to remove it from the shelf, she was struck by a severe pain in her upper back. It was the same place where the needle had plunged into her skin, but this time it felt she had been knifed in the back. The pain was sharp and severe, making her cry out, "Ouch!" as it shot around her body to the side of her breast.

Patience felt for the area by reaching behind herself with the opposite arm. Her fingertips couldn't quite reach the area where the needle stuck her, but Patience thought she could feel the edge of what seemed to be a soft lump.

It's probably nothing, she thought. *Just healing. My sober brain is probably going to exaggerate every little ache and pain.* Patience took a small mirror from her bag and took it in the bathroom reserved for staff behind the nursing station. She switched the light on as she closed the door behind her. The light flickered and began to buzz as it illuminated the small bathroom. With her back to the bathroom mirror, Patience removed her scrub top and positioned the hand mirror in front of her face to view the reflection in the mirror. The action reminded her of how, when she was small, she would to hold a hand mirror up to her mother's vanity mirror and delight in the infinitely repeating reflections.

The angle of the small mirror first revealed the lower part of her back, the small contours of the vertebrae leading downward as her hips curved outward. Patience changed the position of the mirror to view her upper back, and she began to panic as swollen, red skin slid into view. It was a large, raised welt over the area where the needle had entered the skin.

What the hell? Worried about the worst, the pain grew sharper as Patience replaced her scrub top and returned to the conference room, ringing her hands and pacing as she considered what to do next. Someone who could remain objective needed to look at it, but she didn't want to return to those impersonal assholes at occupational health. Besides, she didn't want to wait until the following morning. What if it were necrotizing fasciitis, the flesh-eating disease? With that rapidly progressive infection, she could be dead by morning.

She could go to the emergency department, but was embarrassed about the possibility of retelling her story. *I contracted a flesh-eating bacteria from stupidly leaning up against a sharps container when I was too hung over to stand up.*

Wait! What about Dr. Oswald? Didn't he say he was working all this week? He already knows the embarrassing details and seems like someone I can trust.

Patience asked the hospital operator to page him, and in a few minutes the phone was ringing. "Please be in, please be in, please be in" she pleaded.

"Dr. Oswald," he said when she answered.

"Dr. Oswald?" Patience began, speaking way too quickly. "It's Patience—Patience McMorris. Can you…help me?"

"Yes, yes, of course. What do you need?"

Patience thought he sounded on edge. *Oh, shit, was this a mistake?*

"I'm having a problem with the wound." Patience felt as if she would start crying again. "I think it's…infected."

There was a pause. Through the hiss of the phone line Patience expected a terse response directing her to the emergency department. Instead, he asked, "Where are you?"

"On eight B. In the conference room."

"I'll be right there." The doctor didn't criticize her and he didn't ask what she was doing in the hospital two nights in a row. He didn't treat her like a misbehaving child. His unassuming demeanor was a relief.

After an anxious five minutes, Zeke arrived at the conference room. With the aid of a penlight, he peered down the back of Patience's shirt.

"Yeah, you're right, Doctor, it looks infected."

"Just call me Patience," she asked, wincing at the news.

"I'll give you a prescription for clindamycin but I think it should be drained. I'll be right back." Zeke left, probably to go to the supply room which housed the laughing fox.

Looking carefully at his face as he returned to the room, Patience didn't think Zeke had returned from a recent laughing fit. His face appeared tense but emotionless as he arrived with a hospital gown, iodine disinfectant, a scalpel and bandages.

"So let me take a closer look. If it is an abscess, do you want me to lance it?"

Patience nodded. She trusted the hospitalist with the secret.

"Here or somewhere else."

"Here is fine."

"Go into the bathroom and put this gown on." Zeke suggested.

"I can just put it over my top, right?" Patience asked, blushing at the fact that she was wearing no bra again.

"Sure, that will work."

Instead of going to the bathroom, Patience pulled on the gown, over her arms, leaving it open in the back.

"Okay, Patience, I'm not going to use a local anesthetic. As you know, it wouldn't work well in infected skin and this will just be a quick pinch anyway."

"Okay," she said as she reached behind her and pulled up her scrub top.

Patience appreciated that Zeke spoke to her as if she were a patient and not a medical student. "First, some Betadine to clean the skin. It may feel cold. Ready?"

"Yup." She knew this about the disinfectant yet she was happy he prepared her for the clammy feeling as he spread it in a circular motion. After allowing it to dry, he quickly jabbed the blade at the center of the abscess. There was a pinch, then relief of the dull pain. It felt like blood as the warm grey pus dripped down the skin of shoulder blade.

"I'll send a sample to the lab for culture and ID," Zeke explained. "I'll put a loose bandage on it, don't be surprised if it continues to drain for a while. As long as it feels okay, someone should check it in a few days."

Patience turned around and glanced at Zeke with a look of childlike submission. "Can you do it?"

Zeke looked away. "Sure. Page me in two nights. I'll call the antibiotic prescription in to the twenty-four hour pharmacy around the corner." He looked into Patience's eyes which were now beginning to widen. "Okay?"

Zeke's kindness and the stress of her situation proved to be too much for Patience. "I'm sorry I'm so much trouble," she said. Crestfallen, Patience began to cry.

"Oh, Dr. Oswald, how could I be so stupid? Getting stuck with a needle like that."

Zeke, taking a seat, encouraged Patience to do the same but didn't answer her question. Instead, he looked at Patience calmly.

Patience continued. "I *know* why it happened. My life is outta control." She sniffled.

Zeke took a box of tissues from the window sill and offered it to Patience. She drew one out of the box and dabbed her eyes.

"Deep down, I always knew I was wrong to drink five or six bottles of schnapps every night but it was what I did and therefore a part of me. Because it was a part of me I didn't think it was something to be changed. I'm not making any sense, I know."

"No, no, Patience, I understand," Zeke said. "Please go on."

"The fact of the matter is that the accident happened because I was hung over, tired, and not paying attention."

She hyperventilated slightly as anxiety started to creep in. "But I was also not interested in protecting myself..." she trailed off.

"Then, with all these blood tests for AIDS and hepatitis I'm so worried—not so much about getting sick but how about I ruined my life. If I got sick, how would I be able to start a family?" Patience released a snort. "Not that anyone's beating down the door to be that father of my children," she said lightly, which prompted a gentle laugh from Zeke.

Patience stopped talking. And blinked. She could feel her eyes welling up again.

"I…uh…I…just feel…" she choked on her emotion. "That my life is endless…darkness. Unloved and unworthy of love," Patience declared, barely audibly.

Her brown eyes were crying now but still composed, the tears rolling down her pretty face as she continued to speak.

"I live in darkness but I'm afraid of the light. I'm afraid of success—afraid to accept the light of someone's love." Her voice began to tremble. "I'm ashamed of who I am but shame myself every day. And I worry that one day the darkness will take control and…win."

Patience cleared her throat gently and swallowed. Zeke sat patiently. "When I'm feeling overwhelmed," Patience continued, "it feels like I'm underwater. I remember feeling that way as a kid when my parents would take me to the public pool by our house. They hated it when I did it, but I would try to see how long I could stay under water by holding my breath. After a while it would feel like I was suffocating, opening up my eyes and looking up at the surface, the sunlight streaming through the water. They would get so *mad*, thinking I was missing or drowning because they couldn't see me. I wanted to touch the sunlight even though I was trying to stay underwater."

Patience then broke down, sobbing, tears streaming down to her chin, unable to complete sentences. "Mom and Dad…split up when I was young…they never talked to me about it…I heard the fighting…one day it was just…over.

"Did they split up because of me? If I didn't hide underwater, would they still be together? Did my

Mom drink because I was so much trouble?" Her usually husky voice was now high-pitched, like a child's. Patience closed her eyes and buried her head in her hands.

"Patience, it's okay," was all Zeke said.

CHAPTER THIRTY-FIVE

Selinda had decided to turn her attention towards developing leads in the murder case of the Saint Twigleighct hospital administrator. At her desk in the precinct, she phoned Beverly Duncan's ex-husband. He had remarried and moved to Los Angeles about a year before and was now employed as a maintenance worker, known as an environmental management specialist to the politically correct, at large hospital center.

He told Selinda that he was informed by the local police that his ex-wife was dead, he was sorry to hear it but he hadn't seen her in two years. He made a point of telling the local authorities that he was on the job the night she died and that his supervisor would vouch for his whereabouts. Selinda would have to confirm this but it sounded to her like he neither had the motive nor opportunity to be involved. True, he could have contracted the killing, but her intuition doubted it.

She disconnected with him and was about to go for coffee in the break room when her computer signaled an incoming email from *it.homicide@apd.gov* with the subject *Equipment*

Review. There was no message, just an encrypted attachment. Selinda clicked on the attachment and entered her password to open it. A word processing file appeared with the title *Equipment Review B. Duncan Personal Computer.*

At the request of Detective S. Bruchart an electronic forensic analysis was performed on the extant file QELOS.ppt, recovered from the office computer located at the scene of the murder of Beverly Duncan. Detective Bruchart wrote in his request (Selinda scoffed as she read the mistaken gender) *that this file was to be part of a presentation by the decedent to a hospital quality improvement review board. The file contains information on lengths of stay or time hospitalized for patient at Saint Twigleighct Medical Center, Albany, New York.*

The major conclusions are 1. Trends for length of stay at the hospital were decreasing over the last six months. 2. Hospital admissions were significantly increased over the same time specifically to the geriatrics service eight C.

The last sentence caused Selinda to catch her breath. *Geriatrics service?* That meant...nursing home patients. Caleb Fisher's friend Alex *Brainboy* Frost had said Caleb was suspicious of the repeat admissions of nursing home patients for coincidently similar infections. He thought it was the hospital's way of increasing admissions and profits. Beverly Duncan was about to present data on how hospital admissions were on the rise for nursing home patients. Was this knowledge enough to get Duncan killed? Selinda had seen some killed for less, and in her experience the decision to kill depended on how much needed to be protected. One would murder for ten dollars if it meant protecting a way of life.

Selinda's pulse quickened as she realized she had a theory for motive that linked the two murder cases. Both Caleb Fisher and Beverly Duncan could have been murdered because they had information that would have exposed a conspiracy to make people sick for profit.

It was time to work out the details, to try to fill in the blanks, to pursue the theory like a miner tapping a vein of gold. Selinda composed an email message in reply to the one she had received from *it.homicide.*

Great work! Could you please check the hard drive for a list of the patients' names that were used in the data for increased trend in hospitalization?

Selinda clicked the send button and watched her email being sent as she leaned back in her chair, feeling satisfied in her work for the first time in a long while. But there still were a lot of unanswered questions, a lot of work yet to be done. Somehow, someone was purposefully causing infections in frail, elderly patients in such a way that they were quickly readmitted to St. Twigleighct. The method of infection was probably occurring in the hospital just prior to discharge. With a list of patients that were readmitted with infections, Selinda could begin to look for commonalities in the patients' care, like in the employees who cared for them while hospitalized. Reviewing their hospitalizations might reveal clues with regards to the method of delivering the infection. It looked like Fisher and

Duncan had uncovered some of these details and been killed over what they knew.

·

CHAPTER THIRTY-SIX

Zeke's evening began in the usual manner, with his checking the list of his assigned hospital patients. When he logged into the computer to see bloodwork results, an alert appeared on the screen. The alert indicated urgent lab results available for McMorris, Patience. *Must be some computer error,* Zeke surmised, *why would I get blood work results from her occupational health visit?*

He clicked on the alert and overrode a pop-up warning against unauthorized access to an employee file. He was then directed to Patience's computer medical record in the form of a cover sheet. Within a section labeled *alerts* blinked a line of red type indicating abnormal microbiology results. Zeke was still puzzled, it was too soon to expect HIV or hepatitis test results on blood drawn this morning, it would take a few days at least. He clicked on the line and was brought to a lab results page.

His brow rose quizzically when he saw the surprising results: *bacterial culture, enterobacter* +++. These results were from the needle and syringe retrieved from the sharps container involved in the accident. To make a culture from the needle the technicians in the lab would have scraped the needle and ejected any contents from the syringe on a jelly-like growth medium and then placed the medium in an incubator.

These results didn't make sense to Zeke. He hadn't seen any blood or other contamination on the needle that was involved in the injury; it should have been sterile, or at least free from a significant amount of bacteria. +++ meant that there was a large amount of bacteria found in the sample, unlikely if there was a miniscule contamination from the sharps container. How did a needle in an ordinary hospital room become contaminated with a large amount of *enterobacter?* Would the abscess culture also reveal the same bacteria?

These questions would have to wait as Zeke realized he needed to switch the antibiotic he prescribed for Patience. Clindamycin wouldn't be as effective as penicillin. He paged her and in a few minutes she responded.

"Hi, Patience, it's Dr. Owsald." Anticipating an anxious reaction, he added, "Everthing's fine, I just wanted to switch your antibiotics. How's the pain?"

"It's okay, feels like it's getting better."

"Good. I'm going to switch you to penicillin, based on the results of the..." he paused to search for the right words, "...syringe culture. I see you called from a hospital extension. Do you want me to call it in to the twenty-four hour pharmacy across the street like I did with the clinda?"

"Uh-huh," Patience answered. "Penicillin? What did the culture show?"

"It grew *enterobacter.*"

"*Enterobacter?* Should that be growing in a clean needle? Wait, did you say *enterobacter*?" Patience blurted out before Zeke could answer.

"Yes, why do you ask?"

"It's funny...I was checking on one of my..." now it was Patience appeared to be word-searching, "...friend's family members who is in the hospital for osteomyelitis. She's a sweet old lady, pleasantly demented as they say. She has the infection in her hip, poor thing. I thought was unusual that it was caused by *enterobacter*. That doesn't typically cause osteomyelitis, right?"

"Yes," Zeke answered, but hearing that it was a hip infection he had to ask, "If you don't mind telling me, what was the name of the patient?"

"Semple."

Zeke's eyes widened and his jaw dropped at the sudden realization that it was the name of the patient whose x-ray he had found misfiled in the bone room. It was the only MICU x-ray in the bone room and Zeke had already been thinking it was linked to Caleb Fisher's murder. Something was telling him he should look in to this infection further. Law Miner was probably still in the hospital, working late on the Carswell post. Being a pathologist he would probably know all there was to know about *enterobacter*.

"Dr. Oswald? You still there?"

"Yes, Patience, I just realized I have to make a call."

After Zeke called in Patience's prescription, he dialed the pathology lab. The phone rang so many times that Zeke thought everyone had left for the day. He was just about to abandon the call when Miner picked up.

"Hello?" Zeke recognized the irritated voice.

"Law, I'm glad I caught you."

"I'm just putting the Carswell autopsy report on the computer. It should be there shortly," Miner said curtly.

"Oh no, that's fine. Actually I was calling about something else."

"Oh, okay. Shoot. Quickly."

"What do you know about *enterobacter*?" Zeke asked.

"I *thought* I saw your name on that."

Zeke was puzzled. "My name on what?"

"I got this instrument culture under the name McMorris. You were the referring doctor. I'm in charge of all hospital-acquired infections. They flag results for me when a strange bug is found."

"Yes, I thought it was a strange to find bacteria in a syringe."

"Oh it's *stranger than that*," Miner said suggestively. "The specimen you sent grew *enterobacter IIH3*."

Zeke didn't understand the significance. "Well, that's not surprising. The wound was a result of a needle stick."

"No, it's *very* surprising," Miner said with a serious tone that Zeke found uncharacteristic for his usually flippant colleague. "It's not iatrogenic. *Enterobacter IIH3* is a research strain. It's not found in hospital-acquired infections. It's only found in research laboratories, used in experiments on antibiotic-resistant bacterial strains. It's sensitive only to beta lactams."

"A *research* strain," Zeke repeated.

"Yes," Miner said. "And get this. This wasn't the first time we found *IIH3* in this hospital. There was a recent osteomyelitis case in the MICU that was due to *enterobacter*. The lab hadn't disposed of the culture yet so I had them do a strain analysis on it and guess what? The infection was due to same experimental strain. A random mutation or a lab error could explain one exotic infection, but two? It's more than a coincidence."

Zeke could guess the answer to his next question, but he needed to confirm his suspicions. "Do you remember the patient's name with the other *enterobacter IIH3* infection?"

"I may have it here in the file. Hold it, it was…Semple, Deborah Semple. Why do you ask?"

Zeke didn't answer his question. "Oh, that's the ED calling," he lied. "Gotta go. Thanks, Law. I'll switch Dr. McMorris to penicillin."

"Good call," the pathologist said sarcastically. Zeke had managed to end the conversation. He didn't want a colleague to get involved by admitting he discovered the misfiled x-ray film belonging to Deborah Semple at Caleb Fisher's murder scene. The film could have been what Fisher was looking for in the bone room when he was killed. Perhaps he knew why an elderly patient usually confined to a nursing home was infected with a research strain of bacteria, and maybe the x-ray was proof of some misdoing. Looking for it either tipped someone off the fact that Caleb had damaging knowledge, or he ran into someone who was also looking for the evidence-to destroy it. Was someone inoculating patients with needles laced with *enterobacter IIH3* and then disposing the syringes in the hospital sharps container? Why would someone do such a thing?

Zeke was determined to find out-to clear his name and hopefully put a stop to what had to be a deranged person. Without any pressing clinical duties, he walked over to eight B, the ward which contained the room in which Patience McMorris was injured with a needle. At the nursing station he found a nurse and a clerk. "Do you know who's taking care of room twenty-three?"

"Uh, yeah, it's Jane," the RN said.

"Is she around?" Zeke asked.

"Think so." The nurse walked over the clerk's area, picked up a phone receiver and pressed a button. "Jane, come to the front, there's a doctor here to see you," she said into the receiver.

A few minutes later Jane arrived at the nursing station. She was short, stocky, with short grey hair. Oversized scrubs hid her pudgy middle aged figure. Zeke recognized the nurse as the one in the room when he responded to Patience's needle stick injury. Jane recognized Zeke too.

"Hi Dr. Oswald."

"Hi, Jane. I'm still trying to find out which patient the needle that stuck that medical student came from. Do you always have that room?"

"Yes, for the last two weeks. But I was thinking about that too. You know we only use needle-less systems on this floor." She paused to let Zeke apply the logic of her statement. "So I didn't put it there."

"No. I understand that." Zeke tried to sound non-accusatory. "I wasn't implying that you did."

But there was only Mr. Cummings, the patient who was present when the med student was stuck, and one other patient for most of the month."

The nurse relaxed a bit. "Yes I remember. Hickman was the patient before him. He was there for almost three weeks for abdominal pain. He was on isolation because a nasal swab showed methicillin-resistant *staph.* Patients from Shady Oaks rarely get private rooms otherwise."

"And why is that?" Zeke asked her.

"That's one of the cheap nursing homes. Residents would be able to afford the extra cost of a private room."

"Did he ever have visitors?"

"Hardly ever," Jane said confidently. "Not even his doctor. (I won't say who but I'm sure you can figure it out.) Although I'm sure he billed Mr. Hickman's insurance for daily visits."

She became even more animated. "In fact, I remember the day he was discharged, his doctor didn't even see him then, he just phoned to say he was discharged. The day nurse was bitching to me it took her all day to arrange for the discharge and Hickman didn't leave for Shady Oaks until the evening shift. I'm sure the hospital would have kept him overnight if they knew they were getting paid for another day." The cynicism in Jane's voice left the conversation hanging for a moment. "That's why when I saw the phlebotomist coming out of his room that night I nearly freaked out. But when I asked her why she drew bloods on someone who was already discharged, she said it was a mistake, she didn't draw any labs."

Zeke thought that was interesting. "Do you know who the tech was?"

"Yes, it was Sharon. Why, do you think that's important?"

Zeke thought quickly. "I don't know. Maybe she disposed of some needles from somewhere else."

"She shouldn't."

"Yes, I know."

Or maybe she injected the patient with enterobacter *before he left and then put the needle in the sharps container.* Zeke kept this thought to himself. This phlebotomist was definitely someone the police should be talking to.

Jane added: "Imagine my surprise when I heard Mr. Hickman was being admitted again tonight with fever. You shouldn't stay in the hospital for three weeks. He must have picked up some infection."

Oh?

"Gotta go and do an admission in the ED. Thanks, Jane. By the way, do you know if Sharon is working tonight?"

"Uh, yeah, I saw her already tonight," Jane said.

Zeke left the ward, but he wasn't going to the emergency department. After the elevator bell rang and the door closed behind him, the ward clerk, who had been in earshot of Zeke's conversation with the nurse, picked up the phone and started dialing.

CHAPTER THIRTY-SEVEN

Later that night, Zeke decided to drink blood. The internal debate that lead to the decision was similar to how it was like when he was drinking alcohol. It was as if he was purposefully forgetting to consider the negative consequences, like it was part of a natural sequence of events. It seemed when a certain time of day arrived, having five or six shots of vodka was part of a normal plan. It was like Zeke was powerless to a self-fulfilling prophecy.

So making a trip to the blood bank appeared to Zeke to be a routine part of his scheduled tasks that night. Excited with anticipation, he could feel the pulse throbbing in his neck as he ordered a unit of blood on the computer. He selected *pick up in blood bank* as the delivery option. The blood would be ready in an hour.

The blood bank appeared empty when he arrived. The lights were dimmed, and as he entered the bank, they automatically brightened to reveal an immaculately clean room with white porcelain and sparkling stainless steel. In the center of the room stood a wide island designed to increase the workspace. Zeke swallowed as he spotted a row of refrigerators lining the back wall. The doors were made of steel and glass, and Zeke peered at the crimson bags stacked from the floor to the ceiling through the glass.

Nobody here? I can find the blood myself and take it without being noticed Zeke thought. If someone noticed the blood missing later, he could say a nurse picked up the blood instead. It was an untruth no one was ever likely to reveal.

It wasn't that unusual to find a part of St. Twigleighct unstaffed during an overnight shift. There, of course, would be at least one employee to cover the blood bank in case of a nighttime emergency. Like most urban hospitals, St. Twigleighct employed some ex-cons or convicts on work release to staff the hospital at night, and these weren't always the most reliable of workers, often disappearing for long stretches of time, ignoring their pagers. Zeke wondered if Sharon, the phlebotomy tech, had a criminal background. He was sure Detective Bruchart would find out after receiving Zeke's anonymous phone tip. After his conversation with Jane, the nurse on eight B, when he found out the phlebotomy tech had made a questionable trip to a patient's room a few days before a needle containing a research strain of bacteria was found there, he called the Albany PD switchboard. He gave the operator a message for the detective working on the Fisher case that informed the police a lab technician named Sharon was seen in the room of a patient shortly before he was discharged and that he was readmitted a few days later with fever. She may have information on hospital-acquired infections that Caleb Fisher may have been investigating before his death.

And how funny it was that a random injury to a distressed medical student shed light on all of this. How else would he have found out about *enterobacter IIH3* if Patience hadn't been so hung over that she leaned on the wrong sharps container? The lab doesn't usually put the specific strain of bacteria on the computer report—just the species name and antibiotic sensitivity. Zeke planned on contemplating this sequence of events as he sipped blood in one of the on call rooms.

Zeke felt like he was walking on a spongy surface as he ambled towards the bank of refrigeration units. It reminded him of how, many years ago, he had walked across the room where his experimental mice had been kept, on his way to discover that the mice treated with the gene had stopped drinking alcohol. As he closed in on the refrigerators, he could smell the sweet, salty odor of whole blood, mingled with the chemical scent of preservatives and plastic. He wondered about fresh drawn blood—it had been so long since he had a taste. But to feed from a living vessel was off the table, and had been for many years.

Zeke was reaching for the steel handle on the door of the refrigerator when he sensed something moving quickly, silently, behind him. He could see a reflection of a large object moving towards him in the door's glass, and he instinctively dodged to the right to avoid a collision. The figure crashed into the unit where Zeke had been standing, and it rocked a few times, jostling the blood in their soft plastic bags. In the blur of the impact, Zeke also saw a flash of metal and a *clank* sounded as the metal object struck against the glass. Zeke scattered to the other side of the center island and crouched down. He thought of making a break for the door but didn't know where his potential assailant was. He peered over the top of the island, ready to duck again if he saw a firearm.

"Take it easy doc, I told you before. I just wanna talk," the figure said. Zeke didn't see any gun, just a glint of a sharp object in figure's hand.

Then why did you try to jump me and stab with a knife? Zeke thought. The figure turned out to be a large man with a broad face, black hair and beard, and a deranged twinkle in his almost black eyes. *If I can see his face...*Zeke didn't have to finish the thought to know his life was in danger. He could make a break for it if he got close, but maybe he'd catch him the second time. *He said he wanted to talk...maybe I could find out the reason behind all this.* Zeke stood slowly.

"Okay, so talk," Zeke said, trying not to sound as terrified as he was.

"We could use your services," the man said in a gravelly voice as he moved slowly forward. "You could make a lot of money."

Zeke said nothing in response. The man's eyes, instead of having a cajoling look, narrowed and become more sinister. Zeke noticed the man's pupils were dilated, evidence that he was probably preparing an attack.

Zeke decided to try a bluff. But who could be behind this? "Look, I just got off the phone with the doctor. I accepted his offer to help."

"Nobody told *me* that."

Zeke spied a cell phone attached to the man's belt. "You'd better call him before you hurt me," Zeke said, trying to sound calm.

The man stared at Zeke. "No. *You* call him and hand me your cell phone. You must have his number, you said you just spoke with him."

Zeke had to think quickly. "He paged me through the operator, they don't give out the number."

The man stared at Zeke again, going over his options in his mind. After what seemed a very long time, he grabbed his cell phone from the holster, and, without talking his eyes off of Zeke, pressed two buttons.

He had engaged the phone's speaker and held the phone at arm's length. After two rings a male voice answered. "Hello?"

The voice sounded familiar to Zeke but he wasn't sure who it belonged to.

"Don't say anything doc, you're on speaker. I've got that doctor here, for that problem you wanted me to look into, and he says you called him to ask him to help *you* with the problem."

"He said *what?*" The voice on the phone sounded like it was about to lose its temper. Then, more composed: "No, no, go ahead with the plan." The speaker disconnected, and he put his cell phone down on the island.

"Nice try, asshole," the man said to Zeke, slowly moving towards him.

"So there was no deal. You were hired to kill me like you killed that ICU nurse."

The killer smiled proudly. "And that other dumb bitch nurse too." Then his face became rageful as he lunged at Zeke. Zeke lifted his forearm in defense as the man raised his hand, his weapon glinting in the artificial light, his eyes bulging, his mouth open, teeth bared as if preparing to bite. "This is going to be the best day of all."

The man sent to kill him had him trapped between the island and the wall. *This is it. This is where it ends.*

Suddenly there was the *crack* of a gunshot and another crash. The killer dropped his weapon, startled. Blood was splattered over his surprised face. But the blood wasn't his or Zeke's. The bullet had passed by them both and shattered the glass door of the refrigerator and the donated blood exploded outward.

While the killer was stunned, Zeke scampered around him to the corner of the island opposite to the killer. In the breeze he created with his movement he detected the faint smell of roses and sandalwood. *Beautiful.*

"NOBODY MOVE!" A female voice shouted. Selinda Bruchart stood in the doorway, her father's Glock trained at the killer.

"I heard everything." The scents of perfume, blood, and gunpowder hung in the room. "Very interesting conversation. After receiving an anonymous tip I came to the hospital to interview a person of interest in a murder case, heard a crash and came to see what happened. You," she said to the killer, "on the floor, hands behind your head. Dr. Oswald?"

"Yes."

"Nice to see you. Are you hurt?"

"No.

"While I watch our friend here, please dial 911, detective requesting backup, suspect armed and dangerous."

The killer did as he was told. Zeke grabbed the man's cell phone from the island. "I'll use his phone." But instead of 911, he called the last number called. A voicemail robot answered.

You have reached 831-1396. Please leave a message after the tone.

Zeke smiled. "Detective, make sure you call this number later and see who picks up."

"Already have it memorized."

Selinda had saved Zeke's life and prevented him from giving in to his addiction that night. Zeke had revealed enough information in his amateur investigation to lead her to the action and help solve two murders. And one attempted murder.

"Don't even think about moving," Selinda said before reading him his rights.

CHAPTER THIRTY-EIGHT

Patience grinned as she stepped out of the Nissan into the cold crisp air. Her boots crunched in the snow as she walked up the path to the church. It was December 15, her birthday, and she had a reason to be happy. She just received the results of her most recent blood test, six months after being stuck by the needle, and there was no evidence of HIV or hepatitis. This far away from the needle stick she suffered on that troubled summer night, there was almost no chance she was infected.

She was also happy that she would see Maddie later that day. They hadn't repeated what had happened at Ronnie's party but had developed a friendship over the past few months. It started after Patience had called her about Maddie's grandmother a few weeks after the man was caught trying to kill Zeke. At the end of the call Maddie had invited her out for a drink. Even though Patience had explained her drink of choice had been switched to herbal tea, Maddie had still wanted to see her, and the two met at a cafe.

"I can't believe someone would try to hurt my grandma," Maddie had said angrily over two cups of chamomile. "I mean, she's okay now, but what happened in that hospital?"

"The trial won't be for a while, but so far it seems like your grandma was given an infection on purpose so they would have a reason to readmit her to the hospital and charge her insurance for a new stay. Some good people working in the hospital became suspicious and it looks like they were killed because of it."

"But who would do such a thing, and why would they pick my grandma?"

"Apparently the killer, his name is Bettie or something like that, is a hit man who was hired by one of the hospital's vice presidents Garret Quackenbush."

"Bettie? Cute name for a murderer."

"I know, right? They have Mr. Bettie on federal charges so he sings like a bird to avoid the death penalty, naming Quackenbush as the person who hired him. And Zeke—Dr. Oswald tricked Bettie into calling Quackenbush when he tried to kill him so they have his cell number on our cute killer's phone. Even though it was a throwaway phone, Oswald and the detective witnessed the call. And there's a rumor that the hospital president, Safford, is behind it all and that Quackenbush will testify against him.

"They used nursing home patients because most of them are weak and frail and have memory problems, making them good targets."

"Sick! Preying on sweet little old ladies…"

Patience and Maddie shared tea several times after that and recently had joined a gym so they could take exercise classes together. Patience found her new friend to be a sensitive, caring person and someone she could talk to and lean on. Someone she could be herself with. Just what she needed right now. *Just Maddie,* Patience would think and smile fondly.

Patience was going to meet Maddie at the gym later on that evening but there was something she had to do first. Following her breakdown with Zeke when she admitted her drinking had led to her needle accident, Zeke went from babysitter to mentor. Although she had keeping her promise to stay sober if she emerged from the accident healthy, Zeke had found a twelve step program in a church near Patience's apartment. Tonight was her first meeting.

A man opened the heavy wooden door to the church and walked out. Patience turned partially, thinking about doubling back, getting back into her car and driving away. But she heard soft music coming from the open door. The music had a soothing, familiar quality so she continued to approach the doorway. The door closed again but as she stood in front of it she could still hear the music coming from within the church. The tune playing was an instrumental version of Elton John's "Don't Let the Sun Go Down On Me." Patience would hear this song many times in the coming months as it was played before each meeting.

Patience took a deep breath and exhaled slowly, her breath freezing in the winter air. She grabbed the iron door handle, pulled open the church door and walked inside.

The End

ABOUT THE AUTHOR

James Vitarius is a cardiologist by day and a novelist by night. He is the author of The Nocturnist series of books which chronicle the life of Dr. Zeke Oswald, the doctor with the dark secret who only works the night shift. He lives in the northeastern United States.

Like The Nocturnist on Facebook and follow @TheBoneRoom on Twitter.

29348573R00187

Made in the USA
Charleston, SC
09 May 2014